I passed Monty the discarded panties. He sniffed them, then wrapped them around his cock, shutting his eyes in bliss as he rubbed himself. I knelt down.

'Hands behind your back,' Poppy ordered. 'Fetch a ribbon, would you, Gabby?'

'Not tied!' I protested. 'Why do I have to be tied?'

'Because it's more fun,' Poppy pointed out, 'for us, that is, and because that way we'll have less nonsense out of you.'

'Okay,' I sighed.

Why not visit Penny's website at
www.pennybirch.com

By the same author:

THE INDIGNITIES OF ISABELLE
(writing as Cruella)
PENNY IN HARNESS
A TASTE OF AMBER
BAD PENNY
BRAT
IN FOR A PENNY
PLAYTHING
TIGHT WHITE COTTON
TIE AND TEASE
PENNY PIECES
TEMPER TANTRUMS
REGIME
DIRTY LAUNDRY
UNIFORM DOLL
NURSE'S ORDERS
JODHPURS AND JEANS
PEACH

FIT TO BE TIED

Penny Birch

Nexus

This book is a work of fiction.
In real life, make sure you practise safe, sane and consensual sex.

First published in 2003 by
Nexus
Thames Wharf Studios
Rainville Road
London W6 9HA

www.nexus-books.co.uk

Typeset by TW Typesetting, Plymouth, Devon

Printed and bound by
Clays Ltd, St Ives PLC

ISBN 0 352 33825 3

All characters in this publication are fictitious and any resemblance to real persons, living or dead, is purely coincidental.

Dedicated to Duncan and Ben,
the original dobbers,
who bear no physical
resemblance whatever
to Monty and Jeff

One

I stuck out my bottom, my cheeks came open and my finger touched the little wrinkly star between: hot, sensitive, and sticky.

I was sticky because before putting my finger on my bumhole I had stuck it in a large jar of honey – Colston and Harwell's Lincolnshire Clover, as it happens.

Masturbation is such a joy, one of life's greatest and most simple pleasures. Not that the way I was doing it was particularly simple. I'd decided how that morning, and it had brought me a delightful, teasing sense of anticipation for the entire day, popping into my head at every blank moment, between lectures, in the queue for lunch, while waiting for a student to arrive for her tutorial. She'd been late, and I had nearly given in and slipped a hand down the front of my panties to satisfy what by then had become an urgent need. I hadn't, fortunately, as she would undoubtedly have walked in at the exact moment I was coming.

It was a rude and silly game. On getting back to my flat, I locked the door, stripped from the waist down and put my socks and boots back on. I went about my usual tasks like that, my legs bare, my bottom cheeks just peeping out from beneath the tails of my blouse, my pussy showing in front. It was better than being naked, not the simple, natural pleasure of nudity, but a delight in my own deliberate exposure.

I managed to hold back, the desire to touch myself rising as I made myself a coffee, ironed, cooked, ate and washed up, all with my bottom bare. For the cooking I allowed myself a pinny, which made the feeling stronger still. I was covered at the front for one thing, and I had the string tight around my waist to lift my tails and show that little bit more flesh, with the ends dangling down to tickle my cheeks. I ate slowly too, sat bare-bottomed on a hard chair to keep myself conscious of how I was. Half a bottle of Italian red made it all that much easier and that much more urgent.

By the time I'd finished the washing up I was biting my lip with need and making little treading motions on the floor. I wanted to pee too, but I hadn't let myself go, and the knowledge of what that might mean was making my feelings stronger still. I could run to the loo at any moment, but I didn't want to. I wanted to let myself grow ever more flustered, even as I grew more aroused. When I could bear it no more I would run, and the relief would leave me weak and trembling. Or I might hold off too long, and do it on the kitchen floor, in a rude squat, or even standing, to fill my boots and leave myself in a big puddle. I'd have to mop up, crawling on my hands and knees with my bottom bare behind me, perhaps with some suitable object pushed up my bumhole to punish me for what I'd done.

I wouldn't go anyway, not until I'd done what I'd been thinking of all day, and I wouldn't do that until I'd finished washing up. So I made myself do that, drying every item of crockery and cutlery, every utensil, and putting each away, all the while with the urgency in my pussy and the pressure in my bladder growing. When I bent down to put the last saucepan away I very nearly wet myself, and as I stood a voice in my head was screaming at me to run to the loo. I ignored it.

The main cupboard was right in front of me as I stood. In it were basics, sauces, spreads, emergency supplies. I was going to close my eyes, open the door and reach out. The contents of whatever I touched first went up my bottom. I knew it was silly, the sort of lewd behaviour that would make respectable, sensible people look down at me in disgust, if only they knew. That made it all the more appealing.

It was silly. It was also scary. There was a bottle of chilli sauce which was going to hurt so much I would be in tears. I'd still do it. There were baked beans, canned button mushrooms, a tin of ravioli, all of which would be disgustingly messy. There was a huge jar of pickled gherkins, untouched, which I'd have to push up, one by one, until I felt I would burst. If I got the tea bags it was enema time.

I shut my eyes, squirming my thighs together in my desperation to pee. My hand reached out. I found the door, pulled it wide, once more extended my hand, touched smooth, cool glass. For one awful moment I thought it was the gherkins, but when I opened my eyes I found I was touching the honey jar. I smiled.

Honey was good. It was thick set, hard, and could be pushed up in lumps to melt in the heat of my rectum. I took it down and twisted the lid off with trembling fingers. The smell of honey filled the air. I leaned on the work surface and stuck out my bottom. My finger went into the jar, to scoop out a thick wad of golden honey, and back, between my bum cheeks.

I was purring as I found my rude little hole and pushed. My ring opened to the pressure of the honey, and up it went. I stood, revelling in the sticky feeling between my cheeks. I waited, wriggling my toes against the pressure in my bladder. Only when I was sure the big blob I had pushed up would have melted did I stick my bum out again.

So there I was, teasing my sticky bottom hole and struggling to delay the moment my fingers went to my pussy. Once I was frigging it was not going to take long at all, just seconds. My ring was already beginning to twitch, and to send delicious shivers of pleasure right over my pussy each time. I had to do it, soon, but I couldn't, not with my bladder a tense ball in my lower belly.

I just let go. My pee spurted backwards, to patter on the kitchen floor. I sighed in relief, the sensation too good, my need too strong, to even think of stopping. It was nice anyway, just to pee where I stood, to let it all flow out, onto the floor and down my thighs. It was going into my boots as well as on the floor, but I was just too far gone to care. I let it come, all of it, until the last few drops were hanging from my pussy lips and I had finished naturally. By then molten honey had begun to run down from my distended bumhole and into my pussy.

My finger went back into the jar, to pull out a bigger lump. It went up my bum, forced in as my ring spread, and well up, with my finger pushed to the hilt in my sticky, open hole. For a long moment I just enjoyed the sensation, feeling the honey melt slowly as I slid my finger in and out. My eyes were closed, my mouth wide, in utter bliss.

It would have been so easy to slip my free hand down between my legs and let that bliss become ecstasy. My muscles were twitching, my nipples aching to be touched, my head swimming with dirty thoughts. I followed one, not one that led directly to orgasm. There was kitchen towel on the work surface, a big roll of it. I pulled my finger out of my bumhole and stuck it in my mouth, feeling thoroughly dirty as I sucked it clean. Then it was down on my knees, to mop up the pool of my own piddle, crawling, near nude, my bum sticking out, bare behind, with the honey oozing from my well-fingered bumhole and down over my pussy.

I did it without touching myself, revelling in my humiliating task and rude position, wishing there was someone to watch me. I wanted to be beaten while I did it, with a long wooden kitchen spoon smacking down on my naked bottom as I worked. I wanted to be made to clean it all up, until the floor was immaculate, then to be pissed on so I had to start all over again. I wanted to be fucked, mounted from the rear and told to keep scrubbing even as my pussy was used. I wanted to be buggered, a fat cock jammed well up into my honey-filled rectum, pushed in and out until the last moment, then stuck in my mouth.

That was what broke my will, the thought of having a big, hard cock worked up my sticky bumhole, then pushed into my mouth at the last moment. I'd get the same thick, sweet taste I'd had on my finger, until he came and my mouth was filled with salty, slimy spunk as well.

My hands went back, one slapped to my pussy, to rub on the tight bead of flesh where my lips came together. Two fingers went up my bottom, stretching my sticky ring wide. My face went down, right onto the soggy ball of used kitchen roll I'd been mopping the pee up with. I took it in my mouth, chewing on it and shaking my head in wanton, ecstatic humiliation as I started to come.

I wanted more, even then, cocks in every hole, my bottom whipped, my hair pulled, a stream of pee in my face, the gherkins stuffed up my bottom. At the last possible moment I whipped my fingers out of my bumhole and stuck them in my mouth along with the fat ball of soggy kitchen roll. My peak hit me, blinding, ecstatic, hard enough to make liquid honey spurt from my bottom as my anus and vagina went into violent contractions. With that I hit a second peak and held it, my whole being focused on my sex until at last I could no longer bear it and found myself slipping slowly down into my pee puddle.

Eventually I remembered to spit the kitchen roll out.

I make no excuse for my obsession with my bottom; nor any apology. I adore my bottom. Just to reach back and hold my cheeks, to feel the shape and weight is bliss. As for letting my fingers slip between, to that secret, ticklish and, above all, rude, little rosebud, just the thought is enough to send a shiver right through me.

Physically, it's all very simple. The bulbocavernosus muscle runs from the base of my clitoris, round the mouth of my vagina and down to the central tendon of the perineum, which is in turn attached to the anal sphincter. The ischiocavernosus muscle comes down from the front of the genitals to the perineum. The perineal branch of the pudendal nerve serves the lot, and my ectoderm is liberally supplied with nerve endings. There are no free nerve endings within the lining of the rectum, any more than there are in the vaginal tube. There are stretch receptors, and they can be fun, but you can't actually feel with the rectum. That doesn't matter. I don't have to feel something up my bum, I just have to know it's there. It's all linked anyway, so it's not surprising that a finger up my bum feels nice. It's not even unnatural, which is a pity.

I'd like it to be. That way it's naughty, and naughty is nice. That's the mental side of it. The two are inseparable, but for me the mental is stronger. It's all those wonderful old-fashioned taboos – a bottom is rude, dirty, something to be ashamed of, something to be hidden. I love to break those taboos. It feels so deliciously naughty. Just to have my bottom showing is nice. To stick it out to make my cheeks spread, or to roll up my legs so that my pussy and bumhole are stretched wide to an imaginary audience, or a real one for that matter, is exquisite. To have it done for me is better still. That brings erotic shame and, if naughty is nice, then shame is superb.

So I'm obsessed with my bottom. To cure my obsession? That would be idiocy, like destroying my sense of taste so that I don't need to worry about fine food and wine. So I enjoy it, and everything that comes with it, exposure, spanking, buggery, enemas, every sort of penetration.

In an ideal world I would be able to get on happily with my life, and be spanked, buggered, given an enema or whatever at my convenience, with no consequences to my actions. Unfortunately, the world is far from ideal. There are consequences. There are always consequences, and with consequences come problems.

There were five problems, all the result of my obsession with my bottom. Once I'd cleaned up the mess in the kitchen, washed and put on a bathrobe, I poured myself a large glass of wine and sat down to decide what to do. Setting it all out clearly was an obvious first step, so I ran up my word processor and made a list of the five areas I needed to attend to –

Jade – my girlfriend.
Melody Rathwell – who is going to shave my head.
Razorback Paintball – who are going to get me arrested for flashing.

Aunt Elaine – who expects to spank me regularly on Tuesday nights.
Marjorie Burgess – who thinks I'm a pervert.

Having made the list out I printed a copy and considered each as I sipped my wine.

It did not look good.

Jade was the hardest to deal with. She was pretty and sweet and bubbly and full of life, great fun to be with and great fun to play with. If she was as submissive as I, that was no real problem. We were both happy to take turns. She had a lovely body too, voluptuous and feminine and soft, all boobs and bum and little round tummy. Unfortunately, her idea of fun was to be bullied by butch lesbians, preferably in gangs. I like a good spanking, I can take the cane, I'm even prepared to have my face slapped, so long as it doesn't bruise. I still need to be able to say when it stops, to retain final control. She preferred to have even that last piece of control taken away, as long as the people were right. Nights out with her were often more than I could take. She liked clubs. She liked to be bullied by her butch friends. They seemed to think that, as her equally submissive girlfriend, I was also a fair target. The cruelties they liked to inflict turned me on, as fantasy. In reality I was simply not in a position to go around with my face slapped until both cheeks were bruised, or with 'sit here' painted across my forehead. I'd seen Jade get both, and it was only a matter of time before something similar happened to me. It was very difficult to know what to do. I wanted to be with her. I was even beginning to fall in love with her. So I was not prepared to simply dump her. Nor did I want to try and impose restrictions on her, which is a sure-fire way to bring a relationship to an end. Yet every time I saw her I was running a risk.

Equally bad, but less emotional, was the situation with Melody Rathwell. Both she and her husband Morris had decided they were entitled to exact revenge on me for having her served up at a dinner, not actually roasted, but stuffed and trussed with a big red apple in her mouth. Not that she'd minded that so very much. It was having her head shaved first which had really got to her. Now they were determined to give me a dose of my own medicine. I could hardly deny it was fair, while Melody – black, built like an Amazon and extremely tough – was not somebody who took 'no' for an answer. I'd tried to bargain, attending six of Morris's paid spanking parties and being put over the knee by so many dirty old men I'd lost count. Afterwards he had said I was forgiven. She had told me I was going to get it anyway. They ran some of London's biggest and best fetish nights, which I'd been avoiding for months, but I knew they would catch up with me. The fact that she's a housewife and club organiser and I'm a university lecturer simply didn't matter to her. All I could think of was submitting to my fate on the first day of the Christmas break. That way I wouldn't have to walk into a lecture theatre full of students as bald as an egg. I'd still have to face my colleagues, my straight friends, my mother.

Marginally less bad were the boys from Razorback Paintball, who wouldn't do anything horrible to me without asking first, but were far too cocksure and took all sorts of risks. They liked to play macho games, pretending to be soldiers, hunters and so forth, with girls as their victims. It was fun, I had to admit, even running a two-mile paintball gauntlet of wannabe soldier boys with the seat cut out of my jeans, or running through the woods in nothing but a rubber snout and tail to make me look like a pig while they hunted me with nets and switches. Eventually something was going to go wrong. The land we played on was private, but it was also open, and there was always a risk. Some nosy prude would see us and report us, and there I'd be, probably stark naked, in the middle of Hertfordshire with the police chasing me instead of Razorback. It would take a bit of explaining. They were the easiest to deal with. I could hand in my honorary membership, or 'prey membership' as their organiser, the slimy Gavin Bulmer, called it, and that would be that. They might whine a bit, but they were not the sort to do anything really nasty. I would miss their exotic sex games and elaborate humiliations, but I would cope.

The situation with my aunt was the most emotional of all and, if the mildest, by no means easy to deal with. I would go to her house every Tuesday, a weekly ritual. We'd have dinner, talk for a while and then she would take my panties down and spank me. It was barely acknowledged as pleasurable by either of us, hideously embarrassing for me, yet fulfilling a deep need. She knew that, and in theory that was why she spanked me because, if I had to have it, it was better she do it than anyone else. If she hadn't been my aunt it would have been fine. It wasn't. It was far, far too close to home. Because nothing was ever actually said, I didn't really know how it affected her, but I knew she was not prepared to discuss it. It was clear that spanking me gave her immense satisfaction, and it was hard to imagine her actually telling my mother. If I stopped it, I had no idea what her reaction would be, and getting caught was a constant worry.

Last, least pleasurable by far, and most exasperating, was Marjorie Burgess. She had spanked me, in front of her husband and others, following an argument with her idiot nephew Graeme at a dinner party.

I had assumed it was a piece of carefully contrived sex play. Unfortunately it wasn't. My response, masturbating on their kitchen floor, had not gone down well. She felt I needed help, and was determined to assist. That was at least an improvement on telling everybody at the university where we both worked that I was a raving pervert, which was what I had expected her to do. It was still a constant worry, but I could at least do something about it. Marjorie was concerned for me, and felt I should visit a therapist to cure my 'sex-addiction'. I could do that. I knew Gabrielle Salinger, inventor of Whole Being Therapy, a fashionable Rogersian with a reputation by which Marjorie would hopefully be awed. As Gabrielle's idea of a sexy good time was to be put in nappies and suckled, I could guarantee a clean bill of mental health. I could then tell Marjorie I was 'cured', thank her for her help and go my way.

Had I been a lady of leisure the situation would have been part frightening, but in a not altogether unpleasant way, and part embarrassing. As it was, it was threatening to mix my sex life with my working life, which I have always kept rigorously separate. Worse still, my mother might find out what a pervert her only daughter was. She would not be amused.

As it was she found my failure to hitch up with some suitable man and get married exasperating, and the more so because her sister Elaine, my spanking aunt, already had grandchildren. The pressure had increased bit by bit over the years, and now it was getting serious. I couldn't even bear to explain that I am bisexual and generally prefer other women, never mind admit to the spanking, pony-girl play, anal sex, peeing games . . .

Any one of the five situations might result in my exposure, and I had to deal with them, fast.

Two

The first thing to do was to make an appointment with Gabrielle. She turned out to be booked solid, but as her receptionist and girlfriend, Poppy, was a playmate of mine I got an invitation anyway. Gabrielle was in Victoria, and after my 'therapy' session I could go up to Jade's flat in north London for a rude but otherwise relaxed evening.

I'd agreed to give a tutorial on the Saturday morning, to a first-year so dim I was amazed he'd got past his GCSEs, never mind into university. After a patient hour trying to explain to him the idea of conceptual thought, I left for London. Another hour and I was at the door of Gabrielle's block of flats. She buzzed me up, and an enormously fat, pasty-faced young man in an orange and blue anorak let me in, turning to have a good leer at my bum as I passed. That was hardly abnormal, but I was surprised by the intensity of his gaze, especially as I was wearing a coat, a thick woollen skirt, tights and winter panties, hardly revealing stuff. He looked, though, and when I met his eye gave me a dirty grin instead of the normal guilty turn of the head.

By the time I'd climbed up to the flat I had put the incident from my mind. Poppy opened the door to me. She was wearing a pink baby-doll, which made her look about the lewdest little slut one could ever hope to meet. Her fat little boobs were pushing out the front and her bottom wiggling in the see-through panties as she walked, barefoot. She was also sucking a dummy.

Evidently it had been her night to be the baby. Sure enough, Gabrielle was fully dressed, and looking severe with her hair up and her little steel-rimmed glasses balanced on her nose as she made the coffee. I'd met Gabrielle only briefly, and seen them together only once. They made quite a contrast, Poppy small, soft and curvaceous with short, curly black hair and a snub nose; Gabrielle tall, slender and elegant, pert at bottom and breast. Even when normally dressed Poppy managed to convey a cheeky sexuality, Gabrielle looked as if she'd disapprove of kissing in the street.

'Coffee?' Poppy offered.

I could already smell it, rich and tempting after the cold, clammy air outside. Gabrielle was grinding beans, and I accepted with a nod and made myself comfortable in one of her big leather armchairs.

'So what's this?' Poppy went on. 'You got spanked but you don't want some woman to know you're into it? Why not?'

'Because it was for real. I . . .'

'For real? You got a genuine punishment spanking? You lucky bitch!'

'Hardly. Well, okay, it would have been nice if I'd known it was genuine. I thought it was play and . . . and frigged off in front of her afterwards.'

'You didn't! Oh, my! Did you hear that, Gabby?'

'Yes,' Gabrielle answered as she came out from the kitchen. 'She was much older, this woman?'

'Marjorie Burgess? Yes, over fifty anyway, and very old fashioned.'

'She'd need to be!' Poppy squeaked in delight. 'Was it on the bare? Did she pull your knickers down for you?'

'Yes,' I answered. 'That's why I thought it was in play, mainly. She was furious with me, for getting into an argument with her idiotic nephew and wrecking a dinner party.'

'Are you certain she is not merely repressing her need?' Gabrielle asked.

'Very likely,' I admitted, 'but she would never admit it, even to herself. Certainly my reaction to it was completely unexpected.'

'Masturbating?'

'Yes, with a couple of parsnips.'

'Dirty slut!' Poppy broke in. 'One up your bum, any money . . .'

'Poppy!' Gabrielle snapped. 'Make yourself useful, go and finish the coffee.'

Poppy stuck her tongue out but she went, deliberately wiggling her bottom as she made for the kitchen. Always vivacious, she was in a particularly good mood, a naughty one too. I could smell baby powder and skin cream, making me wonder what they'd been up to.

'So she feels you are sexually obsessive?' Gabrielle asked.

'What she said at the time was "filthy, dirty, perverted little nymphomaniac tart",' I admitted. 'She changed that to "sex-addicted" once she'd calmed down.'

'Sex-addicted?' she answered. 'That is a heavily used term among anti-pornography groups, at present, especially on the Internet. I imagine she is involved with something of the sort?'

'Yes, but I think only after the incident. She seems to have picked up a fair bit of psychobabble anyway, which she never used to use. Apparently I'm a "compulsive/obsessive with an unacknowledged addiction to sex and a pornographically induced linkage between sexual behaviour and non-sexual behaviour leading to an inability to discriminate between sexual and non-sexual signals and therefore a tendency to interpret non-sexual clues as sexual". That's a quote, pretty well. I think she means I'm living in a fantasy world. Apparently it's caused by low self-esteem, childhood trauma and the pressure exerted by the pornography industry to accept rare and deviant sexual behaviour as normal etc etc . . . I'm sure you've heard it all before.'

'Bollocks,' Poppy put in from the kitchen. 'So you're supposed to get your panties dropped and spanked on the bare and not think it's sexual?'

'That was my argument,' I sighed.

'You attempted to explain it to her?' Gabrielle asked.

'Sort of, not clearly. I was a bit flustered.'

'Hardly surprising.'

'She was very angry at the time, but I do think she regards it as purely disciplinary.'

'I see. Can I take it that you are in fact at ease with your sexuality.'

'Absolutely, one hundred per cent. The trouble comes from being too open about it. If I kept it all bottled up I wouldn't have the difficulties I do . . .'

'You say difficulties? The problem with Marjorie Burgess is not your only difficulty?'

It all came tumbling out, the entire story, from start to finish, even the details of my first ever spanking across my Aunt Elaine's knee at the age of sixteen. Other people knew, but I'd never told it all at once, not even to Jade. They listened sympathetically as the three of us sipped coffee and the weak

November sunlight coming it at the windows moved slowly around the room. When I finally finished it was Gabrielle who spoke.

'Yes, it is the reaction of society that is the problem, as it so often is. You are bolder than I am, I must say. As you know, I work on the theory that the most important thing is to be at ease with oneself, regardless of how that fits with the expectations of society, but subject to boundaries set . . .'

'I know, I've read Rogers' work, also some of yours. In terms of creating a personal philosophy it's saying much the same as the sadomasochist's dictum, "Safe, Sane and Consensual". Being happy with oneself is one thing, getting other people to accept that as the truth is another. Even if I were to explain it to Marjorie Burgess she'd just say I was "in denial". She's one of these people who assume that their viewpoint represents some form of absolute truth.'

'Then we must cater to her viewpoint,' Gabrielle answered. 'I will write you a report, as if it were a letter to you, but couched in her preferred terms and catering to her prejudices.'

'Perfect, but I think she'd be suspicious of a miracle cure. Let's take it slowly, over a few months, with weekly sessions. I'll pay, naturally.'

'Not at all . . .'

'No, really, I insist. It's bound to take up a lot of your time, even if you just write the letters, and I think it would be better if I actually came to see you. For all I know, the wretched woman might have me followed or something.'

She gave a thoughtful nod. I felt wonderfully relaxed after telling her everything, and it wasn't just a case of getting it off my chest. Both Gabrielle and Poppy were the same as me. They understood how I felt, in a way that no ordinary therapist could even have begun to approach.

If I had stayed, it would certainly have led to sex. Poppy was in the mood, and her near-nudity was getting to me. Unfortunately Gabrielle had work to do and I wanted to buy a few things before going to see Jade. So I left, thoroughly pleased with myself and thinking about what Jade and I would get up to at her flat. Both being submissive by nature, we would usually play some sort of game when we stayed in together, to determine who was going to be on the receiving end. For all that I wanted to lose, deep down, it always gave me a delicious sense of dread, and we would both play as well as we could. The last time it had been cribbage, with a stroke of the cane for every point of the losing margin. I'd taken thirteen, touching my toes, and had ended up masturbating with the rounded tip of the cane I'd been beaten with pushed up my bottom hole.

It was cold outside, but fresher than when I'd arrived, with the sky clear blue and the leaves of the plane trees fluttering in a gentle breeze and stirring where they'd collected into piles on the pavement. I started toward the station, lost in my own private world, and almost jumped out of my skin when somebody tapped me on the shoulder. It was the fat man I'd seen coming out of Gabrielle's flats, and he was now wearing a shifty grin.

'Hi,' he greeted me. 'You're Penny Birch, aren't you? Sorry if I startled you.'

'That's all right. Sorry, do I know you?'

'I'm Monty.'

He stuck out one podgy hand and his equally podgy face lit up into a big, and very dirty, grin. I shook his hand, somewhat tentatively. I knew who he was, Monty Hartle, a friend of Gabrielle and also

Natasha Linnet, although 'friend' was perhaps the wrong word. Natasha had described him as 'de Sade in a Billy Bunter suit', and she hadn't just been referring to his bulging figure and reputation for enjoying cruelty. Apparently he approached sex with a boyish innocence, greed, an enthusiasm for the perverse, very few moral scruples and a deep delight in the humiliation of women. He'd worn out both Gabrielle and Natasha. Now it looked like my turn, only I could not possibly add him to my already overcomplicated sex life. I would have to make a polite but firm refusal to the date he was clearly about to propose as he waited for an elderly man with a Labrador to pass. What he actually wanted caught me completely off guard.

'Can I have your panties?' he demanded in a hoarse whisper.

'My panties?'

I was so taken aback I said it aloud, causing the man with the dog to turn sharply. A cabby leaning on his car about twenty feet away glanced up from his copy of the *Sun*. My face turned abruptly scarlet.

'Yeah,' Monty answered me.

'No!' I hissed.

'Why not?'

He was whining, petulant, but it was a genuine question. For a moment I just stared at him, mouth open, before I managed to find an answer.

'Why not? Well . . . obviously not! I mean, do you really think you can just walk up to a woman in the street and ask for her panties?'

'Not any woman, no, but you're into all that stuff, aren't you? Tasha says you like it up the bum, and a good spanking, and . . .'

'She does, does she?'

'Yeah. Don't be shy, I'm not judging you or anything . . .'

'You . . . you are not judging me?'

'No. Come on, nip into a doorway and slip them off. It won't take a second.'

'Look, Monty, I am not giving you my panties. I've got tights on, for one thing, so it's not just a question of slipping them off . . .'

'You don't mind doing it, then?'

'Yes, I do!'

'But you said you'd do it if you could get them off easily?'

'No, I did not! I said I couldn't get them off easily because I'm wearing tights, that's . . .'

'Yeah, but that sort of implies you're willing. I mean, if it's just a technical problem.'

'A technical problem? Monty, it is not a technical problem. It is completely unreasonable to expect me to take my panties off, for technical reasons or otherwise!'

'Why? Seriously, why? I mean, what's the big deal? I'll pay if you want, or take you in M&S and get you a three-pack . . .'

'Stop. Monty, seriously, do you not realise that there is something wrong in asking a woman you've never met before to give you her panties, and in the street as well?'

'Yeah, sure, but you're not just any woman, are you? Anyway, it's just bollocks, isn't it? I mean, when you really think about it, it's harmless. If girls weren't taught to get all stuck-up about it, then it'd be no big deal, yeah?'

Natasha was right. He was oblivious to shame, beyond all normal standards of decency. He was about to go on with his explanation, but I raised a hand to stop him.

'I understand all that,' I assured him, 'but in practice it is a completely unreasonable thing to do.

And in any case, as you say yourself, it's not practical.'

'No. There's no problem there. If you can't do it quick, come in the station. I'll buy you a new pair in one of those little kiosks, nice kinky ones, or whatever takes your fancy. You nip into the loos, change and give me the ones you've got on. D'you wear fancy silk ones like Tasha?'

'No, not usually. I prefer . . . Look, what am I doing, telling you about my panties? Look, it's not going to happen. Just go away, please.'

'Aw, come on, Penny, be a sport. Please?'

He looked so pathetic, and what he was suggesting was beginning to get to my dirty side. I was determined not to give in, though. I started walking. He followed, whining.

'Come on, Penny, please? I didn't think you were like that. I thought you were honest with your feelings and all that . . .'

'I am! That does not mean I have to strip off for the first pervert who accosts me in the street!'

I said it in a hiss. People were watching us. They obviously thought Monty was my boyfriend, that we were having an argument. That was hideously embarrassing in itself. I walked faster. Monty kept up, speaking in a low, gruff whisper all the time.

'I bet I know what sort they are. You've been to see Gabby and Poppy, so they'll be girlie. I'm right, aren't I?'

'No! Shut up, Monty!'

'Frilly pink see-throughs, like Poppy was wearing with her baby-doll, or big white ones with . . .'

'Poppy let you see her like that? The way she was?'

'Yeah. She doesn't care. She's cool, Poppy. She gave me a pair, see-throughs like she was wearing, only baby-blue. Took them off in front of me, she did. That was some fucking sight!'

I could imagine, but I couldn't imagine why.

'Are you collecting them or something?'

'Yeah. I had a collection, but it . . . but it got ruined. Tasha and Gabby and Poppy did it, so I made them all give me a pair. Tasha's are black and silky. Gabby gave me a pair of those big ones she likes, with little yellow ducks all over. She let me take them off her.'

'And you want mine to make a fourth pair?'

'No. Yours'll make seven. You'll do it, then? Great!'

'No!'

'Aw, come on, Penny! At least tell me what sort you've got on, yeah?'

'No, I . . .'

I stopped, thinking of Marjorie Burgess and her self-satisfied airs and superior little looks. She would have been so pleased to hear me putting Monty off. Afterwards she would have smiled and told me I'd done very well, so smug, so certain of herself . . .

'Okay, okay. They're big. Thick cotton. A bit like the ones Gabrielle gave you, I expect.'

'What colour?'

'White.'

'With a pattern?'

'Yes.'

'A baby-girl pattern. Ducks? Teddy bears? Rattles?'

'No! Just roses.'

'What colour?'

'Pink.'

'Oh, that is so cute! I'd like to wank in them, right now.'

'Monty!'

'So what did you get up to with Gabby and Poppy? Kinky stuff, yeah? Did they put you in a nappy?'

'No! I . . .'

'They spanked you, didn't they? That's your favourite, isn't it? It was OTK, I bet, and they peeled those big, white panties down off your bum, ever so . . .'

'Monty! For goodness' sake, people will hear! I didn't go for sex. I . . . it was just a casual visit, that's all.'

'Yeah, sure.'

'It was!'

His response was a snort of disbelief. We'd reached a doorway leading into the station. A group of people were coming out, and we were separated for a moment. He caught up with me inside, just metres away from a glass-sided kiosk selling underwear, rank upon rank of knickers facing us, cotton, silk, satin, lace, in every colour and a dozen designs.

'Any one,' he said. 'You choose.'

'And I have to give you mine?'

'Yeah.'

I stopped. He'd got to, me, made me feel rude. I could just imagine the look on the face of the girl in the kiosk. She'd see me choose. Monty would pay. She'd be sniggering behind her hand the moment my back was turned, imagining me bent over with the fancy knickers pulled aside as Monty fucked me from behind, my bottom pressed to the quivering bulk of his belly, his fat fingers sunk into the flesh of my hips, his cock embedded deep in my pussy . . .

I shook my head.

'No, thank you.'

'Aw, Penny!'

I walked on, fast, heading for the safety of the crowds around the tube stairs. What he'd said was playing over in my mind, round and round. Natasha had given him a pair of black silk panties. Poppy had taken hers off in front of him. Gabrielle had actually let him pull hers down. Now he wanted mine.

I walked straight past the stairs. It wasn't much to ask, not really, and it would leave me in a fine state for Jade. Men scared her, the same way I feel about the cane or birch, a horrid fascination. When I turned up pantiless and told her how I'd lost them she would be fascinated, and very, very aroused. There was the risk too, of finding somewhere quiet enough to pop off my shoes and tights, to slip my panties down and off . . .

'Come on,' I sighed, and beckoned to Monty.

He followed, grinning. My heart was hammering as I hurried though the throng and across the insane system of crossings. It was broad daylight, crowded and my panties had to come off. Now I'd decided to do it I was trembling with anticipation. I didn't want to do it in the loos. I didn't want to swap what I had on for a new pair. I wanted to do it the way Monty had first suggested, in a doorway, scarlet with embarrassment as I struggled it all down under my skirt and coat. With them off I'd be left pantiless; bare as I went my way, bare because I'd let my knickers down for a pervert . . .

I cut south from Victoria Street, Monty puffing and blowing as he struggled to keep up. We passed a drinking school and I caught a remark and a laugh, clearly directed at us. Dirtier thoughts filled my head as we pushed in among smaller streets, fantasies; of being seen, caught, spanked in the street for being a slut, by some irate passer-by. I imagined being cornered in an alley by the drinking school, made to suck their dirty cocks, bent over and fucked, a cock in each end, used, as Monty watched. No, he wouldn't watch. He'd join in. He'd wank in my hair, make me suck his balls, bugger me and stick his filthy cock in my mouth . . .

'Here,' he said suddenly. 'Here's good.'

He was well behind me, and it took me a moment to realise what he was talking about. He was right though. The brick wall of some large building rose beside a fence, the two coming together at a narrow angle. The fence bordered a small gardens, with a laurel and the trunk of a massive plane sheltering the apex of the space. A delivery van blocked the view from across the street.

It was still painfully exposed. Anybody walking down the street was bound to see. Nobody was, though, the crowds left behind with the shops and offices of the main roads. I was in before common sense could get the better of me. My coat came up, my hands trembling so hard I could hardly grip my skirt. I managed, though, and it was up. My thumbs went into the waistband of my tights, high up around my tummy, leaving my skirt rucked up not far under my boobs. I struggled the tights down, urgently, apprehension and embarrassment burning in my head. My panties came with them, all the way, to my ankles, and suddenly my bare bum was showing, pressed to the cold bars of the fence. I hastily covered myself with my coat.

Monty was standing in the mouth of my little hideaway, grinning. His hands were in the pockets of his anorak, one pushed deep. It was quite obvious what he was doing, playing with his cock. I called him a dirty bastard. I wanted to suck it.

Squatting down, I made quick work of my shoes, unlacing one, then the other. I pushed one off, almost overbalancing as I wrenched my tights and panties off my foot and stuck my toes back in. One leg was out. I put my shoe back on, my tights still right down, the air cool against my pussy in my lewd squat. My second shoe came off, my foot came free, tights, then panties. For one awful moment I was in a tangle, then I had them off.

Monty bent down immediately, to snatch up my discarded panties and stuff them in his pocket. I was already forcing my foot back into the tights. A toenail caught, the tights laddered, but I had done it, and an instant later I was wriggling my now bare bum into the seat of the spoiled tights. A few quick adjustments and I was decent. Monty was still grinning.

'Okay?' I panted. 'Have you got what you wanted?'

'Yeah, thanks. I love cotton.'

His hand was still in his pocket, the one in which he'd stuffed my panties. I realised, suddenly, that he hadn't just been stroking his cock. He actually had his cock in his pocket, pushed through a hole. He was wanking, with my panties, and nobody who passed could possibly fail to realise.

'Monty! Stop that, we'll get caught! It shows, you know.'

'You do it, then,' he moaned. 'Open your coat. Pretend we're snogging. Come on, Penny. You've turned me on.'

'You've turned yourself on! Monty, I don't . . .'

He had pushed forward, squashing me into the narrow angle between wall and fence.

'No . . . Monty . . .'

His hands were fumbling for the buttons of my coat. One came undone.

'Monty, no, this is not a good idea!'

He ignored me, popping my second button.

'Monty! Will you . . .'

My third button came undone. His hands found my tits, squeezing gently.

'Monty!'

He let go of my boobs, and for a moment I thought caution or even decency had got the better of his lust.

No such luck. He tugged his anorak wide, I saw the thick shaft of his cock pull free of the hole in the lining. He was fully erect, and big, with bits of lint from his pocket and my new panties stuck around his helmet. One hand squashing in his huge belly, he offered me my knickers.

'Go on, quick.'

'Monty! What makes you think I even want to touch your dirty cock? I . . .'

He had pushed against me, enfolding me in his anorak. His cock was hidden from sight, but I could feel it, poking against my tummy, and smell it. I took the panties and folded them around the thick shaft.

'Fucking gorgeous,' he drawled. 'I love a good panty wank. Kiss me, it looks better.'

It did, but I still had to force myself to respond as his great, blubbery mouth was pushed to mine. I was already jerking at his cock as our tongues met. He tasted of fried breakfast, and he was clumsy, his tongue pushing down my throat. One fat arm came around me, to clutch at my bottom, through my skirt, then up it, kneading my cheek through my tights. I pulled faster and harder, terrified we'd get caught, desperate to make him come. His fingers pushed my tights into my bottom crease. I moaned as he began to tickle my anus.

I was scared stiff of being caught, but that didn't stop me from revelling over what I was doing. I had no panties on, and they were wrapped around a man's cock as I masturbated him, outdoors. It was such a sleazy thing to do, but I wanted more, my mouth used, my pussy fucked, my bumhole invaded and spunked up . . .

He went tense. I jerked hard. His cock head popped from the leg hole of my panties. Spunk erupted up my arm, over my jumper and skirt. Our mouths broke apart. I cried out in shock and disgust, but I was still wanking him and the second spurt arched high between us, catching in the soft blue wool of my jumper. Monty was puffing as he leaned quickly back to check the street, but he was already grinning as he turned back to me.

'You look like you've blown your nose down your jumper!'

'Thank you for that, Monty. Now put yourself away.'

He already had his anorak closed, but complied, returning his still half-erect cock to his trousers with one, obviously well-practised motion. I used my panties to mop up my jumper and skirt as best I could, then handed them back to him.

'I hope you're satisfied?' I demanded, trying to sound cross.

'Yeah, great,' he answered. 'You're a good little wanker.'

'You have a way with words, Monty.'

'Yeah, Tasha says that, too. Fancy a coffee?'

Three

Most men buy you a coffee first, then make a pass. Monty preferred the opposite technique, which must at least have cut down on his bill for coffees. I accepted, as I felt it was the least I deserved. An orgasm would have been nicer, and he'd put me in a fine state, but if he was prepared to risk arrest in order to get his kicks, I wasn't. I wasn't going back to his house either, or to a hotel.

I'd done it, and I'd enjoyed it, but I was not getting involved with Monty Hartle. Our encounter had been good, but horribly risky, while some of the things he'd done with Natasha and Gabrielle made it look very tame indeed. Even then I might have had a shot at it, but I was determined not to take on any more baggage until I'd sorted out three of my problems at minimum.

With Gabrielle's agreement to help me, I had at least started on one. It looked like being three or four months before I was done, but I had made a positive start. The next one to apply myself to was clearly Jade's unbridled desire for extreme submission. I thought about it on the tube after I'd left Monty, wondering what I could do without putting a strain on our relationship.

The real problem was where we went. Everybody knew her, and most of them knew her reputation.

London isn't exactly overflowing with bars exclusively for lesbian sadomasochists, and Jade was regarded as a reliable floorshow in every one. Her favourite, Whispers in Soho, gave her free admission on the grounds that her presence guaranteed a line of butch dykes stretching back to Centre Point in the hope of admission to their notorious back room.

When I'd first started going out with her the others had been a bit wary. I'd made the mistake of admitting to being bisexual – which Jade never does, despite having taken the very occasional cock. Many of them didn't feel at ease with bisexuality, or even felt it was an impossibility. I am bisexual, and always have been, so I argued my case, but it only provoked antagonism and in some cases a determination to make me see the error of my ways.

It was pointless trying to pretend to be butch, or dominant, or diesel, or anything of the sort. That just isn't me. So, after a couple of times watching Jade, once having her enormous breasts roped up and her nipples clamped, another time being stripped to her panties and tickled until she wet herself laughing, I began to wonder if I couldn't get a little attention myself.

I got it, in spades. I wanted a spanking, with plenty of people watching, and chose a pretty but tough looking girl called Naomi. Her deliberately rough, retro-punk look appealed to my memories of being scared by the appearance of Sid Vicious as a little girl, but I'll bet he'd a have been a lamb next to her. I went to ask for my spanking, casually, the way I would at a naughty party.

Her response had been to take me by the ear and drag me into the middle of the floor. She'd sat down on a short bar stool and hauled me across her lap. Before I realised what she was doing, she'd slit the waistband of my jeans with a knife and torn the seam wide. My panties were also slit at the back, even as I screamed out my protest. I was ignored, my ruined clothes hauled open and down and my bare bottom given one of the longest, hardest spankings I have ever taken. Fortunately it was only by hand, but it left me gasping in shock and pain, blubbering too.

That wasn't the end. I was passed around, to Naomi's friend AJ, then a girl called Sam, then the barmaid, then some huge, brawny woman I'd never seen in my life, and so on and so on. When they finally let me go, my poor bottom was a swollen, throbbing ball of purple flesh and my face a mess of tears. I'd been stripped too, and gagged with my own ruined panties to shut me up when I'd started to howl. They'd just laughed.

I'd come in the toilets, masturbating myself to an exquisite trio of climaxes as I stood with my legs cocked wide and my bottom showing in a mirror. Some of them had watched. Afterwards I'd been made to lick AJ, on my knees on the floor as she sat on a loo. It had been good. In fact it had been wonderful, but the fact remained that from the moment I'd asked Naomi to spank me to when AJ came in my face, I'd had no say whatever in what was done to me.

Jade said it was the best way. That was all very well, but my bum had been so badly bruised I'd been unable to sit down without wincing for over a week. I hadn't been able to do anything that risked showing too much flesh either, which meant no bikini, as even the most modest left two good slices of plum-coloured bum cheek sticking out around the leg holes.

Then there had been the face-slapping incident, a little military cabaret with Jade being interrogated and tortured. She loved it, and it put her on a sexual high for the whole weekend. Two weeks later they had tied her spread-eagled on the floor and used her face as a stool, with 'sit here' painted across her forehead. She had to go back on the tube like that, and even after we'd got the paint off the letters could be made out in reddened skin. Both times she'd had to cancel her work on the Monday because of the state of her face. She was a temp, and seemed to think it was worthwhile. I simply could not risk it.

Parts of it were great. They called her Dumplings because of the size of her breasts, and me Little Miss Muffet for my hairy pussy, which had been given a good airing during my spanking. That was nice, and it was exciting being the focus of so much sexual attention. Unfortunately they believed a submissive's choice extended to deciding to be submissive in the first place, and not a lot further. They weren't going to do anything really awful, like have our faces tattooed or our pussies sewn up, but they seemed to have a pretty loose definition of 'trifling and transient'.

It was very hard indeed to see a way of avoiding my fate. The only thing I could think of was to introduce Jade to heterosexual clubs and parties and hope that her ambiguous mix of fascination and revulsion for men would keep her interest. Unfortunately the phrase 'out of the frying pan and into the fire' could have been invented for the situation. Heterosexual clubs meant Morris and Melody Rathwell. Morris and Melody Rathwell meant getting my head shaved, probably as the main turn in one of his cabarets.

I was none the wiser by the time I reached Turnpike Lane. Jade lived in an upstairs flat, smaller than mine and a great deal more messy. Not that I minded. Being with her was a bit like being a student again, carefree and simple. She threw the keys down to me when I rang the bell, as bubbly as ever, and already trying to explain something to me as I opened her front door. She kept trying when I got upstairs, in between kisses, but I finally managed to get my mouth open on hers and shut her up.

She was still in a robe, and I slipped it off her shoulders as we snogged, to take her soft, naked body into my arms. I could feel her breasts against mine, and the smell of hair and the taste of her mouth was bringing back the feelings I'd been building up all morning, very rapidly. When I moved down to suckle her she started to babble again, and I realised that just for once I was going to have to take charge.

'Be quiet, Jade.'

I stood and she squeaked in delight as I twisted my hand into her hair. There was a chair near me, and I sank down, taking her with me. She knelt obediently, shaking slightly as I quickly rearranged my clothes, coat open, skirt up and tights down, leaving my pussy bare.

'No panties? Hmm . . .'

'Lick, now.'

She immediately buried her face in my sex. I took her by the hair again, just to make sure she stuck to her task and let my thoughts drift. She was serving me, and I felt I ought to come over that, but there was too much going on in my head. The only fair thing to do was to involve her. I knew how too. I began to talk.

'The reason I've got no panties on is that they were taken off, by a man. He's called Monty, Monty Hartle. He's big and fat, and pasty and he has a huge, ugly cock . . . No, Jade, not yet, not my clit.'

I'd gasped in pleasure as she had begun to flick her tongue onto my clitty, but I wasn't ready, not quite.

She moved lower, to stick her tongue firmly up my pussy. I rolled my legs up, slipping deeper into the chair and went on.

'He's a dirty bastard, too. He collects girls' panties. He made me take mine off in the street, where somebody might have seen. And when I'd got them off, do you know what he did, Jade? He made me masturbate him, with my panties wrapped round his big, ugly cock. A panty wank, he called it. Isn't that crude? Isn't that dirty? He came in my hand, Jade. He squirted spunk all over me . . . Kiss my bumhole, Jade, you little slut, then do my clitty . . . now!'

An instant later her puckered lips touched my bottom hole, a gentle kiss, right on my ring, right on my dirty little hole, an exquisite gesture of submission. Then she was licking my pussy properly, full on my clit and I was gasping and moaning. She was masturbating too, her body jiggling as she rubbed herself, and as her finger began to tickle my bumhole I was babbling.

'He did it, Jade, he made me take off my panties in the street. I wish he'd done it properly . . . in the open . . . so everyone could see. There were a load of drunks. He'd have made me do it in front of them. I'd have had to stand there, right out in the street, in front of them. I'd have had to pull up my skirt, show everyone as I took down my tights . . . stick out my bare bum as I pulled it all down. They'd have come around, asking to have me. He'd have let them . . . made me suck them . . . their dirty cocks hard in my mouth, one by one . . . They'd have fucked me, Jade . . . bent over . . . up my pussy . . . my cunt . . . up my cunt and up my bum too, right up . . . big, fat cocks in the dirty little hole you've just kissed, you darling, dirty . . . filthy . . . little slut! Ah, Jade!'

I came, right in her face, my pussy and bumhole contracting on the fingers she'd pushed up at the last moment, my clitty a burning point of fire under her eager tongue. She kept licking, until I could take it no more and pulled her head back. Her eyes were glazed with pleasure, her body shaking to the movements of her own masturbation. I let go. Her head went straight back between my legs. Her tongue found my bottom hole and begun to burrow in. She was going to come, and soon. I caught my breath and went on.

'They'd have had you, too, Jade, if you'd been there. They don't care if you're lesbian or not, not that sort, not Monty, that's for sure. He'd have fucked you, and buggered you, with his gross cock stuck so deep up your bum his balls were slapping on your pussy. And he'd have come up you, right in your . . . in your dirt box, and when he pulled it out he'd have stuck that big, fat cock right in your pretty little mouth, all covered in your own . . .'

She screamed, a strangled, desperate sound, as she was still trying to lick out my bumhole. I held on, smothering her face in my bottom as her body jerked and trembled in orgasm, making sure she could barely breathe for her mouthful of bumhole, until at last she had subsided. She rocked back on her heels, gasping for breath, her lipstick smeared across half her face, along with my pussy cream and her own spittle.

'Nice?' I asked.

'You are a dirty bitch, Penny Birch. You know I don't like men!'

I just laughed.

'And what you said! Yuck!'

'But you liked it, didn't you?'

'Yes,' she answered, quietly, and with the sweetest, sulkiest pout on her face.

It was worth tormenting her just for her reaction, never mind the superb orgasms it gave her, and she gave me. That was one reason we worked so well together. We understood each other. She just made it a little too real sometimes.

'Now,' I asked. 'What was it you were trying to tell me before?'

'We're going out,' she said, 'to Sugar Babe's.'

My heart had jumped at her first words, but I relaxed at the mention of Sugar Babe's. Sugar Babe's was not really a lesbian bar, and her hard-nosed friends were unlikely to be there. It had apparently started as the place to relax for pole-dancers, revue artists and so on, and become popular through its bad-girl reputation. Now most of the people who went there were mainly those aiming for a bit of urban chic without actually having to get their hands dirty – or, more accurately, without having to get their boobs and bums out. It was an odd mix of gay, bi-curious and simply curious, but was not the sort of place girls got public spankings.

'What's happening?' I asked, trying to keep the mixture of relief and instinctive disappointment out of my voice.

'They're under new management . . . new ownership, I think. It's free to get in, drinks half price, and they're having this big striptease competition. Zoe's in it.'

That perked me up. I'd met Zoe, too briefly. She was nineteen, out of school that summer and so cute it made me melt. She was also what Jade called a 'baby dyke', a young girl experimenting with lesbianism and getting there. The thought of watching her strip was delicious, the possibilities it offered better still. I was sold.

What to wear was a different matter. I was dressed for the weather, not for a club. Jade is my height but has a lot more bottom and boob, something I adore but enjoy teasing her about. Her tops or trousers would be ridiculously baggy on me, although with her waist just an inch or so more than mine, a skirt was a possibility.

That made sense, and we decided to go in school uniform, which is always popular. She has a bit of a thing for uniforms, and even used to collect them, so there was no difficulty in finding matching skirts, pleated and in red Stuart tartan. She had ties too, and a few careful folds and a safety pin worked on one of her blouses. The problem was panties, as Monty had mine and hers would barely stay up on me. She wanted me to go without, and nearly made me do it, but in the end I lost my nerve. After all, it was not really a sex club, and my bum showed under the hem of the skirt if I bent more than a few degrees. Flashing my panties is one thing, but a bare bum was likely to get me thrown out, strippers on stage or not. So I borrowed a pair from Jade, using a safety pin to keep the waistband tight.

It felt good, pleasantly naughty, with the uniform on under my coat as we went in on the tube. There was a good-sized queue outside Sugar Babe's. When we did get in I was disappointed to find that the 'striptease artists' were only allowed to go down to their bras and panties, which was a bit too much tease and not enough strip for my liking. It was also noisy and crowded, with many more straight men than when I'd been before and a laddish atmosphere that was not me at all.

I stuck with it, and watched Zoe strip, which was at least worthwhile. She was dressed in an oriental style, with a figure-hugging dress and her long dark hair held up in bunches with huge flowers. Both dress and flowers were red silk, patterned with gold, and she looked good enough to eat. The audience was less impressed, apparently because she didn't have enormous fake boobs and dyed blonde hair, which seemed to be what they were after. She danced well, delightfully naughty, wiggling her bottom at us and sticking it right out. Once she was down to her thong she lay on her back and rolled her legs up, so that the little star-shaped lines around her bumhole and the sides of her shaved pussy lips both showed. That got plenty of cheering and whistles, but when she jumped up she flashed her tits; it got more, and earned her a disqualification.

She came straight to us when she was changed, now in low-slung jeans and a crop top, leaving her pierced tummy button showing. The music was so loud we had to shout in each other's ears, and I greeted her with a grin and got a kiss in return. My arm was already around Jade, and Zoe took the other side. My thoughts immediately turned to the prospect of the three of us in bed together. She'd had sex with Jade. She and I got on well. It had to be possible, but she still lived with her parents, and if it was going to happen we would have to get back to Jade's flat in plenty of time.

I shouted to Jade, suggesting we go. She shouted to Zoe in turn, who nodded. It was going to happen. We made for the cloakroom, and in minutes we were out in the cool night air. Wardour Street was crowded, Soho's usual night-time mix, faces showing but glad rags hidden beneath coats. My ears were still singing from the music, and my head from alcohol and also arousal. I held out my hands. Jade took one, Zoe the other. It really was going to happen.

'Home?' I asked.

'Already?' Jade queried. 'Let's go to Whispers.'

'Yes, let's,' Zoe agreed.

I was going to speak, to make a straight suggestion, but stopped, uncertain how Zoe would react. Yes, she had been to bed with Jade, and more had been hinted at, but I wasn't certain. She was young, inexperienced, and the last thing I wanted to do was scare her away. We had time, too, for a quick visit to Whispers, maybe a spanking for me, which would let her make her own choice. I just had to hope none of the really rough girls were there.

They weren't. In fact very few people indeed were there, just a handful of girls even Jade didn't know, and the bar staff. There wasn't even any music on. The back room was empty, but Jade chose it anyway, from force of habit. Gina, the barmaid who had spanked me, was there, reading a paper.

'Where is everybody?' Jade demanded.

'Concert,' Gina answered, barely glancing up from her paper.

'Oh. May we have some drinks?'

'Sure.'

She turned to pull beers from the fridge without even bothering to ask if it was what we wanted. I didn't complain, thinking of how firmly she had taken me across her knee. I'd been made to go behind the bar, and had it done with her hand twisted in my hair and my face pushed down almost to the floor. The idea of getting the same treatment appealed, and this time I wouldn't get passed around, while Zoe would be there to watch.

'Shame,' I remarked. 'I was hoping I might get a spanking.'

Gina was putting the money in the till, and didn't react. Someone else did.

'I'll do it,' Zoe chirped up, as casually as if she was suggested buying the next round.

I turned to her. It was totally unexpected, and far, far too good an offer to turn down. It was just so shameful. To be spanked by a nineteen-year-old, a girl no older than my students, younger than most. I was going to be put across her knee. She would turn my school skirt up and take down my panties. She would spank my bare bottom. There was even a small and select audience to witness my humiliation. I nodded, struck silent at the sheer emotion of the situation.

She took her beer and went to a chair, so cool, so casual as she patted her lap for me to get over. I took a quick swallow of beer and went down, lying across her knees with my bottom well up and one hand on the floor. My hair had fallen down around my face, and I glanced through the curtain of fine black strands, to find Gina now leaning on the bar, Jade beside her, watching. They had a prime view of my rear end, and would see everything, a thought I held as Zoe's hand found the hem of my ridiculously short school skirt.

It wasn't hiding much anyway, the curve of my cheeks and a good slice of my panties already on show. Zoe made a big deal of lifting it anyway, using both hands as if she was unveiling something. She was, my bottom, or at least my baggy panty seat, and I knew that wouldn't be left for long. It wasn't. With my skirt turned up onto my back, her fingers found my waistband. I shut my eyes, in rapture as the big white school panties were eased slowly down over my bum.

I came bare, always the best moment for me, when my panties come down and that last scrap of modesty is taken away from me. She took them well down too, all the way to my knees, maybe just for convenience, maybe to make sure the others got an unobstructed view of my pussy. I could just imagine myself, my bottom looking big and fleshy because it was stuck in the air, my cheeks just open enough to hint at my puckered, brown bottom hole in her nest of hair, my pussy lips on plain show, pouting out, plump and hairy, with the fleshy pink folds of my inner lips between.

Just thinking about it had me shaking, as it always does. No matter how many times I get punished, the exquisite humiliation of being stripped for it never fades. It is just such a gross indignity for a woman, to have her panties pulled down for spanking. Nor does the pain ever lessen, but Zoe was a sweetie, not some mad butch dyke out to prove how hard she could slap. I was purring as she set to work on me, with my bottom stuck high and my eyes closed in pure bliss. It was gentle, just pats really, enough to make my cheeks quiver and bring the blood up, no more.

I was moaning in no time, and eager for her fingers where they would do the most good, curled under my tummy to frig me off as I was spanked. My legs came open, stretching the dropped panties taut between my knees and offering my sex. I could smell my pussy, and I knew she could see, but the gesture was ignored, her smacks merely growing a little harder and a little faster.

'Slut,' Jade remarked.

'Put some effort into it,' Gina suggested. 'I've got a paddle back here, if you want?'

'Does she like it hard?' Zoe asked.

'Who cares?' Gina responded.

'She deserves it hard,' Jade put in. 'Do you know what she was doing earlier today? She was wanking men off in her panties. That's why she's wearing mine.'

'A man!' I protested.

'Slut,' Gina stated. 'Go on, Zoe, give her what she deserves.'

I glanced out through the curtain of my hair in sudden alarm. Gina had taken the paddle from behind the bar, a thing like a ping-pong bat, only black leather.

'No, please!' I managed. 'I was enjoying that. I like it by hand!'

'It's not what you like that matters,' Zoe said, stretching out to take the bat.

I was pouting as she pressed it to my bottom cheeks. Of course a spanking is supposed to hurt, but gentle ones are so nice, and now I was going to get it properly. I didn't try and stop it though, but hung my head down. My cheeks clenched as the bat lifted, I heard my own whimper, and suddenly my bottom exploded in pain. I screamed, my legs kicked out and I was being spanked for real, properly, a good, hard punishment, and really what I deserved.

It hurt so much, smack after smack landing full across my cheeks, to leave me kicking and wriggling and yelling blue murder. Zoe had to take me around my waist to keep me on her lap, and I could feel my bottom flesh squashing out with every impact. My control went in seconds, and if I was making a thoroughly lewd show of my pussy and bumhole, I had no say in the matter at all. I knew they were showing though, and even in my pain the knowledge filled me with humiliation.

That was just part of my humiliation. Most of it came from knowing that the girl holding me down across her lap and giving me a well-earned brat spanking was only nineteen. Older spanks younger, normally. Jade was younger, and that was nice. Now I had my bum cheeks bouncing to a girl not even out of her teens.

She knew how to spank too, ignoring my screams and pleas for mercy. Even when my tears started she kept on, with me snivelling pathetically and trying to swallow the snot running out of my nose in the vain hope they wouldn't notice. It didn't work, spraying everywhere when the next smack landed on my bottom and sending Jade and Gina into gales of laughter.

It stopped, suddenly, leaving me breathless and limp across Zoe's lap, my bottom throbbing and hot. I gasped out my thanks as the pain slowly began to fade to pleasure. Zoe didn't answer, and as I felt the hem of my skirt tucked up into the waistband I knew it wasn't over after all. Resigned to a thorough whacking, I stayed down, even pushing myself up to let her get at the buttons of my blouse. They were opened, the front pulled wide, my bra jerked up and my tits were out, hanging under my chest in plain view as the blouse was tucked up high.

Zoe went back to spanking me, hard methodical swats delivered full across my cheeks. My bum was hot, my pussy ready, the burning shame of being punished by her running high in my head. I wanted it, but that didn't stop my tears coming again, or kicking my legs and yelping as the pain grew once more. It got harder too, until she had me writhing, my legs pumping in my lowered panties, my boobs quivering and bouncing under my chest. Her grip tightened. She laid in harder still, and I was screaming and babbling pathetic entreaties, although I knew full well I wanted more, needed more . . .

'You'll wake the straights up, Zoe,' Gina remarked.

It stopped. Zoe let go of me and I fell on the floor, landing hard on my aching bum.

'Sorry,' she said.

It wasn't addressed to me. It was addressed to Gina. I managed to get to my knees, and turned my tear-streaked, snotty face to Zoe. She beckoned, crooking a single finger. I crawled forward, between her knees, and cuddled into her, purring as I rubbed my face against the soft flesh of her midriff, completely submissive to her. Her hand settled on my head, to stroke my hair for just a moment before taking a firm grip to pull my head back.

'Now you lick cunt.'

I nodded, accepting her right to make me do it, the crudeness of her words adding a fresh depth to my burning humiliation. I was on my knees, crawling, tear-stained, red-bottomed, and the girl who had punished me was going to make me say thank you, make me lick her sex in front of the others.

'In the loos,' Gina remarked. 'You know the rules.'

'Please, Gina?' I managed. 'There's no one here, after all.'

She merely jerked her thumb in the direction of the ladies. I hate lavatory sex, but a lot of people seem to take it for granted. Zoe was obviously one of them. She took hold of my tie as she stood, to pull me after her. I went, bare red bum on show to Jade and Gina as I was led into the loos. Jade followed. Zoe went straight into a cubicle, pushing her jeans down over her hips before she sat down, thighs open to show off the crotch of her panties. They were little more than a string, a tiny triangle of material covering her pussy but doing very little to conceal the shape of her sex. My eyes fixed to it as Jade pushed me down to my knees.

I went, crawling on the cold, hard floor, into the cubicle. Zoe pulled her panty crotch aside, exposing a trim little pussy, pink and moist and ready for my tongue. Her bumhole showed too, a shadowed wrinkle between her cheeks, and as I came to her I was wondering if she'd let me lick it clean. She was looking down on me, stern and cool for all her angelic face and bunches. I realised I'd misjudged her, badly. As our eyes met I opened my mouth in submission, ready to lick. She spoke.

'Tie her hands, Jade. I don't want her being rude with herself while she does it. I want her to concentrate on me.'

It was an order, as certain and dominant as any I'd heard. I nodded as I put my wrists behind my back, crossed and ready. Jade giggled at my ready acquiescence. I heard her pull her school tie free, and then she had squatted down behind me. I felt the tie, and her fingers, as she twisted it around and between my wrists, locking them together. It was tight, and left me helpless, adding to the haze of submissive ecstasy in my head.

My skirt had fallen, but Jade tucked it up again, once more exposing my bare bum. The door was open too. Anyone who came in was going to see me in my abject submission, on my knees, my wrists tied, my bottom smacked, licking a nineteen-year-old girl's pussy. I look up again, waiting for the order, or to have my head dragged in between her thighs.

'She's a complete dirt pig,' Jade said. 'She'll lick anywhere you like.'

I nodded eagerly. Zoe chuckled and her thighs came a little further apart. She reached out, to take me by the hair and I was being drawn in. A little pink bottom hole had appeared between her cheeks as she moved, a tight knot of baby pink flesh, perfectly regular, with a spray of thin pink lines disappearing into the firmly closed hole, so pretty, so kissable. I had to.

As she drew me in I puckered up, to plant a firm kiss right on her darling little bumhole as my face met her flesh. She moaned and I was licking, tasting her, cleaning the little ring as it twitched in response.

'You dirty bitch,' she sighed, and her grip tightened in my hair.

I burrowed my tongue into her bumhole. She was loose, unresisting, and my tongue tip slid up into the muscular little ring. My face was pressed to her pussy, nose to clitty, and I began to rub, hoping she'd use my face to masturbate on. She got the message, her hand twisting so tight it hurt as she began to manipulate my head. Behind me, Jade was masturbating, moaning and making wet noises as she worked her hand down her panties.

They were going to come, both of them. I couldn't, my hands were tied behind my back, leaving me helpless, to be used as they pleased. All I could do was pray they'd take mercy on me afterwards and see to it that I gave Zoe's bumhole a proper tonguing.

She was getting urgent, her sighs deep and even as she worked my face on her pussy. Her ring began to pulse, tightening on my tongue, loosening again to let me get deeper, and tightening once more. Behind me, Jade gave a cry of ecstasy and I knew she'd got there first. Then Zoe was coming too, her pussy and bumhole pulsing, my face crushed to her sex as she forced her clit to my nose. She cried out, her fingers locked hard in my scalp and she was there, coming full in my face.

Even when the last of her contractions had died away I kept licking, praying they would take mercy on me and Jade would rub me off while I still had my tongue up Zoe's bottom. It was denied. I was pulled back and could only squat there, waiting in my agonising frustration as the two of them came slowly down from their climaxes. I didn't want to ask, I wanted them to just do it to me, but when Zoe finally let go of her panties I broke.

'May I come too, please?'

She didn't answer, but blew her breath out slowly. Her face and neck were flushed pink, her eyes closed. She was leaning back against the cistern, her knees braced on the walls.

'Please?'

She sighed.

'I'm not sure she deserves it,' Jade remarked.

'I do! Please!'

'Oh, all right,' Zoe said. 'Give her a rub, Jade. I'm going to bogwash her.'

'No! I didn't mean that! I meant . . . I don't know . . . untie me, let me frig . . .'

'Shut up. Your head's going in.'

'No . . . Zoe . . .'

'Yes, it is, Penny, right down on the bowl.'

'No, Zoe . . . come on . . . not that . . .'

'I said shut up, Penny.'

I shut up, not because I wanted to, but because Jade had pulled my panties off my ankles and stuffed them in my mouth. She held them there, ignoring my muffled protests completely as Zoe stood up, to straddle the toilet bowl. I managed one last, imploring look and then she had taken me by the hair again and I was being dragged down.

There was nothing I could do, not with my hands tied and my head held. Jade tipped my legs up, Zoe pushed down on my head, and over I went, face first into the lavatory bowl with my bum wiggling in the air as I struggled for freedom.

'Hold her,' Zoe ordered, and Jade's grip tightened.

It wasn't necessary. I could do nothing. Zoe moved forward, her legs pressing to my shoulders. I thought she was just making sure I couldn't get up, until I heard Jade's lewd giggle and felt the warm wetness of Zoe's pee as she began to urinate down the back of my neck and over my head. Jade found my sex, her fingers pushing to my clit, and I stopped even trying to struggle.

Even as Zoe's piddle began to drip from the hair hanging down around my face I knew I was going to come in an instant. It hurt, a lot. My arms ached, my chest was pressed hard to the porcelain of the lavatory bowl. That didn't matter. I was being rubbed off, rubbed off with pee running down my back and into my hair, and I was about to be bogwashed, to have my head flushed in a used lavatory by the girl I'd just licked to ecstasy, the girl who'd just spanked my bare bottom in front of an audience . . .

My mouth came wide as I started to come. The now soggy panties fell out, into the water beneath my face. I began to shake my head in the overwhelming emotion of what was being done to me. The motion dislodged the trickle of Zoe's pee, and suddenly it was running from the tip of my nose. My sex twitched in orgasm, my hot bottom clenched tight, and I heard Jade's voice.

'Now, Zoe, flush her!'

There was a roar. Water exploded around my head even as I screamed in ecstasy. My mouth filled immediately, the taste of Zoe's pee strong in my head. I couldn't see. I couldn't breathe. I was still coming, and still they held my head firmly down the lavatory. My body began to jerk, my muscles going into spasm. Fresh pee squirted over my back, my aching pussy gave one final, violent contraction and I lost all control, thrashing in their grip as they held me under, unable to stop myself, unable to do anything.

I really thought I was going to pass out when they finally let go. I came up, my hair flicking back to spray dirty water over Jade and down my back. She gave a squeak of shock and disgust, moving hastily away as I rocked back on my heels. I lost my balance, slumping against the wall, then slowly down on the toilet floor. I lay gasping, lavatory water dripping from my nose and mouth, one boob squashed out on the floor in a slowly expanding puddle.

Four

It had been a close thing, very close. I'd let myself get carried away, and I'd nearly come badly unstuck.

I had only just finished cleaning up when Naomi, AJ, Sam and a good twenty others all came back to the bar. Five minutes earlier and they'd have caught us in the toilets. They might have had us, they might not. Twenty minutes earlier and they'd have caught me with my head down the lavatory, and I would have been in real trouble.

I knew them. They'd have taken turns with me. It would have got harder too, each one trying to outdo the others. If I'd come I'd have been able to stop it, with a lot of determined effort. If I hadn't come, I wouldn't have wanted to. I would have ended up in a serious mess, more than likely with my face slapped. They liked that.

As it was I'd bruised my chest, across my collar bone and the top of my boobs where they been pressed to the lavatory bowl. My bum was fairly well smacked too, covered in colourful bruises and extremely tender. That was fine. Within reason I like a bruised bum as it keeps me in mind of the spanking. My upper chest was not fine, and I had to wear a polo neck sweater for the next week, even in the labs where it was baking hot most of the time.

In future I was going to have to be more careful. For one thing I'd completely misjudged Zoe. Just because she was young did not make her sweet and innocent, especially innocent. She looked it, but it was far from the truth. As Jade explained the morning after, she had been involved with the London lesbian scene since the age of seventeen, and had never been short on attitude. At her age I'd been mousy, quiet, the shyest girl in my year, with three partners to my name. Of those, one had only ever buggered me and another had been my cousin Kate. There had been spankings too, and the odd dirty encounter, such as posing for the local weirdo to spunk all over my bottom . . .

Okay, a complete pervert, but still shy and innocent, relatively.

Zoe had picked up her outlook from Jade, Naomi, AJ and others, so it was hardly surprising that she assumed my submission gave her *carte blanche* with my body. I knew she wouldn't have done anything really dangerous, and in ways I wished I could make that level of sacrifice. I didn't want to upset her, or make her feel she had done the wrong thing, as underneath she was still just nineteen, and desperately keen to do the right thing.

I found that out on the way back, with her asking tentative questions to make sure I was okay. Not wanting to put her off, I gave her a hug and told her she'd been perfect, but I did tell her about the bruising. She smiled, thanked me and promised to remember. I knew what Naomi's response would have been, as I'd heard her give it to another submissive girl, the old line – 'if you can't stand the heat, stay out of the kitchen'.

Heat was about right too. My bottom was still hot the next morning, and I made Jade rub cream in, which not surprisingly led to sex. We'd put Zoe in a cab from Turnpike Lane, and we were alone, allowing us to spend a lazy Sunday, just padding about the flat in tops and knickers between bouts of sex. I left late, by which time it was raining, my euphoria dissolving quickly in the cold and damp, until by the time I got home I was feeling distinctly lonely.

I'd also begun to mull over my situation again. It was so easy to be with Jade, and to let things take their own course. She made me feel happy, and naughty, and allowed me to express my sexuality without restraint. Given that, I could hardly put restrictions on her, and I certainly didn't want to lose her. So that was stuck, but I had at least made some progress with Marjorie Burgess.

Not that I was looking forward to speaking to her. Just the thought of it was enough to have me blushing with embarrassment. If it had been in an erotic context, that would have been fine, but there are different types of embarrassment. There's the 'oh, no, I'm about to have my panties pulled down and everyone's watching' embarrassment, which I adore. Then there's the sort of embarrassment that comes from having to discuss the most intimate details of my sex life with some condescending, disapproving, self-righteous old mother hen, which I hate.

It had to be done, though, and delaying it would only make things worse. My only excuse was that I needed Gabrielle's letter, which arrived on Tuesday morning. I could have kicked her.

Marjorie worked as a manager in the admin block, a job that suited her penchant for running other people's lives. She was actually very useful, as an essential cog in the hideously complicated process of research grants and funding in general. That was another reason I didn't want to alienate her but, even when I was 'cured', I knew I would need to keep her at arm's length. She had a nasty habit of matchmaking, which was how I'd become involved with her ghastly nephew, Graeme, in the first place. That was not going to be easy, as she seemed to have decided I was in need of special attention, but I could hope that as a reformed sex-addict she would consider me beyond the pale.

She finished work promptly at five. My last lecture was at three and by four I was sitting in my room, staring blankly at my enormous model of the *Ariolimax columbianus* genome and trying to decide what to say. It was going to take a lot of pride-swallowing, but I'm good at that after a lifetime of practice.

I left the department at ten to five, hoping she would be working late, or have left early, or have fallen down the stairs and broken her leg. Inevitably she hadn't, but was as punctual as ever, emerging from the admin block even as I approached it. She saw me immediately, and her mouth set into the condescending little smirk I had come to dread. I returned a smile, or at least attempted to, my mouth working into a little knot as she approached.

'Ah, Penny, dear,' she greeted me. 'I hope you have some good news for me?'

'Yes,' I answered her. 'I . . . er . . . I took your advice. I went to see a therapist, in London. Gabrielle Salinger.'

'Ah, good, I am glad you're being sensible at last. I don't know of Miss Salinger, but . . .'

'She's very good. She . . .'

I'd been going to say that Gabrielle had a reputation for making people feel at ease with themselves, but it wasn't what Marjorie wanted to hear. I was struggling for the right remark when I realised somebody was standing to one side. It was one of my graduate students, Mark Petrie, a young man so painfully thin he looked on the edge of starvation. Obviously he wanted to talk to me. He was not the sort to butt in, and I was about to address him when Marjorie got in first.

'Young man, this is a private conversation, a very private conversation.'

The blood went straight to my face. He was bound to wonder why I would be holding intimate conversations with one of the admin staff, and I could only hope he thought it was something to do with exams. He stepped away with a mumbled apology, but not too far. My cheeks were burning as I turned back to Marjorie.

'Gabrielle is one of the best respected specialists in her field,' I managed, desperate to keep my remarks neutral and as far as possible from anything to do with sex, let alone spanking.

'Miss Salinger, I think you should say, Penny,' Marjorie responded. 'I think you will find it easier if you show more respect to those who are trying to help you. In fact, I feel you should address me as Mrs Burgess, for the time being.'

I had never heard anything more self-righteous, pompous or condescending in my entire life, and it took a strong effort not to give her the answer she deserved. I managed, and dropped my gaze to the ground as I replied in a muffled undertone.

'Yes, Mrs Burgess.'

'Good,' she went on. 'You have a letter or something from Miss Salinger, I trust?'

It was an outrageous thing to ask. She not only obviously thought I was liar, but stupid as well.

'Yes,' I answered.

'May I see it, please?'

I passed the letter over. My cheeks were flaming. Petrie was just metres away, and I was sure he could hear. There were plenty of other people around too, many of whom I knew at least by sight. I'd imagined the conversation in her house, or at least somewhere quiet, and had never once thought she could be so insensitive. I realised I was twisting my fingers together in my lap and treading from one foot to another. I stopped. Marjorie was reading the letter with a serious expression. Either she was a painfully slow reader, didn't understand it, or read it over three times, because it took an age before she finished. When she did, she gave a complacent nod.

'Yes, Gabrielle clearly understands her subject, and your problem. It is curious that I haven't heard of her.'

So Gabrielle was Miss Salinger to me and Gabrielle to her, although they'd never met. Presumably that was because they were grown-up, responsible women and I was a worthless little pervert who needed help from my betters. It was enough to make me scream.

'I will keep this,' she went on, folding the letter, 'and assist where I can, of course. Now, you do understand that with Miss Salinger you must be completely truthful, don't you?'

'Yes . . . I will be.'

'I do hope so, Penny, but I will tell Gabrielle what happened. I have to, and I hope you will realise that it is in your best interest?'

It was monstrous, so arrogant it left me speechless. I gave a miserable nod, my head hung low.

'Good,' she replied. 'Now, as you know, I have been studying your problem. Have you been surfing on the Internet for pornography?'

'No!'

'Penny, you must be truthful.'

'Yes . . . I have . . . I'm sorry.'

I hadn't, but it was what she wanted to hear, and I didn't dare continue to deny it with Mark still in earshot. Obviously she had been looking at websites about sex-addiction and boning up on the 'symptoms'. So had I. They were absolute drivel, written by a collection of mad Christians, outright bigots and people terrified of their own sexuality.

'And have you masturbated?'

If I'd thought my face was hot before I hadn't understood the meaning of blushing. My cheeks flamed to incandescent heat as my mouth came open in horror. I couldn't speak. No words would come. There were none to express the sheer enormity of what she was doing.

'You have, Penny, haven't you?' she went on. 'I can see it in your eyes.'

'I . . . I . . .'

'You must stop, Penny. When you are tempted, just say a little prayer. Jesus will come to you.'

All I managed was a vague croak. I wanted to tell her that I had masturbated, frequently, that I'd done it kneeling in a pool of pee with a finger stuck well up my honey-coated bumhole. I wanted to make a crude joke about Jesus coming to me while I was doing it. I didn't. I didn't dare. She smiled at me.

'You will overcome this, Penny. Believe me, you will. I must hurry, but remember, a little prayer . . . oh, and I'll come over to install what are called "blocks" on your computer at home. Thursday night, shall we say?'

'Yes.'

It was all I could say. No other words would come. She walked away, whistling what I think was a hymn. I stayed where I was. Mark Petrie came towards me.

'Dr Birch? Are you okay?'

'No . . . yes . . . What is it, Mark?'

'I was just wondering if there was any demonstrating work for me? I'm a bit hard up, and . . .'

'Yes, take . . . take basic stats tomorrow, and Friday's *Euphorbia* thingy . . . practical . . . anything.'

I was going to cry, and I couldn't let him see me. Already there was a catch in my voice and I could feel the sting of tears in my eyes.

'I'm not really very up on Botany, I was . . .'

'Then bloody well learn it!'

I turned away, already crying, and with bubbles coming from my nose. He had to have seen them, and my tears, and my blushes. It was worse than when Marjorie Burgess had given me my spanking. At least I'd been drunk.

She was an utter bitch. She had to know what she was doing to me. I simply could not accept that all the bollocks about sex-addiction was anything but calculated sadism. I know enough people who get off on mental torment of others to realise what a powerful drug it can be, and she had spanked me, bare. Surely, if one woman is prepared to punish another in such an intimate and humiliating way, there must be something sexual in it?

I'd read the sex-addiction sites. I knew other people did think like her. Okay, so none I'd visited so far actually recommended spanking as a solution to sex-addiction. One or two suggested some truly agonising self-immolation, such as openly proclaiming one's 'sex-sin' in Church. It might not hurt as much physically, but that was really the only difference between that and taking a public spanking.

There was no question that she took pleasure in my suffering, either way. So even if she was genuine in her beliefs she was still a sadist, albeit in denial of her true nature. That made me feel a little better. I knew my true self, and accepted it. She didn't.

I was still snivelling by the time I got to my car, walking around behind the admin block so that nobody would see my tears. Once there I got in to wipe my eyes, blow my nose and generally tidy myself up. Before long I had managed a weak smile. I'd done what I had set out to do, after all, and with a little more effort I'd be home and dry.

Slowly my misery began to turn to anger and defiance. I began to think of doing things she would disapprove of, like masturbating then and there, or finding some complete stranger to suck off and doing it in front of him with his spunk smeared all over my pussy. Unfortunately I had a nasty suspicion that it would only serve to make her even more self-righteous.

I had no time anyway, not for anything elaborate. It was Tuesday, and Tuesday meant dinner with Aunt Elaine, and my weekly bare-bottom punishment. After Marjorie Burgess it was going to be harder to handle than ever. I was sure to end in tears, but that was okay. I usually did.

When I finally decided it was safe to drive I set off, east and into the pretty hills along the Pang Valley. It was impossible not to think of how Marjorie Burgess would have reacted to what I was doing. I had a sneaking suspicion she would have approved, maybe even openly.

After all, she had spanked me, and it was what I was going to get. Aunt Elaine knew that it was a cathartic experience for me, something I needed, and reasoned that it was better I take it from her than seek other outlets. That kept it in the family, an embarrassing and shameful secret, like having a mad uncle or a jailbird cousin, something that had to be dealt with but was never discussed.

When Marjorie had done me it had been because she had lost her temper and punished me in the most effective and satisfying manner she could. I didn't believe either of them, and it made a lot more sense to accept them both as closet lesbians and sadists. Having said that, Marjorie hadn't done it again. Elaine had, many times.

She was going to do it yet again and, for all the Tuesday nights before, my heart was still fluttering as I drew up outside the house. It was full of memories, including my first ever session across her knee, at Kate's wedding, so long before. Just being there made me feel weak, pliable, a young girl once more, too unsure of herself to even think of resisting as she was hauled squealing across her aunt's knee. There was a huge lump in my throat, as there always was, every time.

It had become a routine, with little variation, yet it had never lost its strength. Always we would have dinner first, and never once mention what we both knew was going to happen afterwards. Usually there would be a bottle of wine, which made it so much easier for me. If I was staying over, there would be sherry or port, sipped slowly over conversation about the family, my work, her garden, the weather. Then I would be spanked.

The first time I had taken it standing, my clothes lifted to make my bottom available. She'd taken my panties down herself. The second time I had gone across her knee, jeans down. Again she had dealt with my panties. Since then it had usually been across her knee, on the big, comfortable sofa in her drawing room. Sometimes I had worn a skirt or dress, more often jeans. It made no difference. My bottom always ended up bare, save on those few occasions I had been on my period.

She liked to take my panties down herself, either that, or she felt that it was necessary but too much to ask me to do myself. I wasn't sure which, any more than I really understood her motives. Possibly she was completely genuine, and really did feel she was fulfilling a need in me that it would be improper to express outside the family. Possibly she was a complete hypocrite and took the same cruel delight in my submission, pain and humiliation as did Zoe, or Naomi or Gina.

I cried more often than not, and this time I knew I would. I already felt fragile, deeply insecure, and desperately in need of the catharsis of what was to be done to me.

Dinner was a rich stew, washed down with a strong, Spanish red and followed by home-made apple pie. It was delicious, and left my tummy a hard little ball beneath the waistband of my skirt. I had to get back home eventually, but she let me digest, sitting in her drawing room and talking quietly as my apprehension rose and rose.

She always seemed to know the right moment, when I was just about to break and ask for it. I had, once or twice, and she didn't like it. It embarrassed her, and she was always harder on me. She felt nothing should be said. So I waited, my emotions growing stronger and stronger, until at last, at a lull in the conversation she put down her sherry glass, adjusted her skirt and patted her lap.

I stood, feeling numb, the tears already welling in my eyes. She responded with the faint, slightly sad smile she always gave to the sight of my tears. I forced myself to smile back, then looked away, unable to meet her eyes as I began to bunch up my skirt. It was thick, wool, and wouldn't stay, adding to my embarrassment as I tried to tuck it up. She waited, patiently, as I fidgeted with myself. Finally I got the skirt up, only to find my tights came up so high that it fell down again as I tugged them down from my waist. She sighed.

'Oh, do take it off, Penny.'

I nodded, biting my lips. My inability to get myself ready was making me flustered, and my fingers were shaking so hard I had real difficulty undoing the button at the back of my skirt. By the time it came open I had big, slow tears rolling down my face and a choking lump in my throat. I did the zip more easily, pushed the skirt down over my hips and stepped clear of it. Knowing her feelings on untidiness, I folded the skirt on a chair, only then realising that I had nothing to tuck the tails of my blouse up into.

That didn't matter. She could lift them as easily as she could pull down my panties. I did my tights, though, pushing them down around my thighs in the vain hope that they would keep my legs together and stop me from making quite such a rude show of my pussy and bumhole when I started to kick. I knew I would kick. I always do.

Ready for punishment, I stepped forward, to lay myself across her lap on the sofa, my legs up to stop my shoes from touching the furniture, a cushion clutched to my chest. Her fingers found the hem of my blouse and the tail was lifted, right up, leaving my lower back bare. Only my panties hid my bottom, the cotton taut across my cheeks, my sole concession to modesty, and shortly to be taken away. I could feel myself trembling and hugged the cushion tighter, then her fingers were in the waistband of my precious panties and they were coming down, peeled slowly off my bottom, exposing my cheeks, leaving me bare behind. Again she spoke.

'Oh, you haven't. Penny!'

She'd seen my bruises. She knew I'd let somebody else at me. There was disappointment in her voice.

'Sorry,' I managed.

She sighed and adjusted my panties, leaving them just far enough down to let her get at the full swell of my cheeks, no further. It was always that way, thoroughly practical, my bottom bare because that was how girls got spanked, no other reason. I was still crying softly, feeling more vulnerable than ever, but wanted, comforted.

Her arm came around my waist, gently, just firm enough to hold me in place, and she began to spank me. It was firm, regular, steady, each slap delivered to the meat of my bottom, no teasing, no silly games. The smacks stung, especially on my bruises, but it wasn't hard, not at first.

It made my tears come, though, more and more, an outpouring of sheer emotion, until I was absolutely blubbering. She didn't say a word, but kept spanking, harder, and harder still. I broke down, my feelings pouring out in a flood of tears. I began to kick and wriggle, my legs pumping up and down and my bottom jiggling to my own movements as much as the smacks.

'Do keep still, Penny!' Aunt Elaine chided. 'Must you always wriggle so?'

I didn't answer, or stop. The spanking hurt, and my emotions were coming out in a helpless, unbridled display, pathetic maybe, but completely honest and such a release. She began to smack harder still, taking her own feelings out on my poor bouncing bottom. For one moment I was really thrashing, and squealing too, a pig-like incontinence as my self-control vanished completely.

Then I was over the hump. My bum was starting to warm, the stinging slaps had become welcome, and I was there, in the ecstasy that only comes with a well-smacked bottom. I heard my own sigh, and I was sticking my bottom up, eager now, my cheeks open to make my sex available, my bumhole twitching to each slap.

'There's no need to be rude, Penny,' Elaine said softly. 'Just a few more.'

She'd got me where I had to be, and she knew it. The last few were for her, a series of a dozen ferocious slaps, right under the tuck of my cheek, to set my whole bottom wobbling behind me and send twelve jolts straight to my sex. I cried out at every one, droplets bursting from my lips and my tear-stained face, a long piece of mucus hanging from the tip of my nose waving wildly in the air. It stopped. I slumped down over my Aunt's lap. She patted my now burning bottom.

'There we are, now run upstairs, and do wipe your nose.'

I nodded, sniffing to try and stop myself crying. There was a box of tissues on a table near my head and I reached for one, to wipe my snotty nose even as I clambered off her lap. My bottom hurt, sore and hot, my skin tender and rough to the touch as my hand went back to feel myself.

She'd told me to go upstairs, and that was where I was going. I had never once acknowledged my arousal to her, but she knew. Generally I'd run, half-off panties clutched in one hand, to throw myself down on the bed in a tantrum that would become masturbation within minutes. This time I felt more aroused still, and would have done it in front of her if I'd dared. I didn't, and I shuffled away, holding my well-smacked bottom.

I always went to her bedroom, another of those secret gestures of submission. She knew, and she knew what I did. I was sure. I went bum up, one hand back to stroke my cheeks as I let the full-blown erotic power of the spanking build in my head. It was wonderful, like no other, a real punishment delivered because I needed punishment, the consequences something rude, something secretive.

Usually I come over the sheer emotion of having it done to me, the knowledge that I've just been across my own aunt's lap, that she's had me bare behind, as she always says, that she's seen my pussy and bumhole, that she's smacked my little fleshy bum to a glowing ball. Now was no exception.

My fingers went down between my cheeks. My bumhole was wet, relaxed. I stuck one finger up, splaying the others out across my hot flesh. I was full. My mouth came open in bliss as I began to finger myself, working in and out of the sloppy little hole. I pushed my hips up, to slide my other hand under my tummy. My pussy was sopping, as she always was after being done by Elaine. I spread my legs, stretching my lowered tights and panties taut between my thighs, and I began to masturbate.

It was so easy, so inevitable. I began to rub at my clitty and wiggle my finger about in the squashy mess in my rectum. Two fingers went up my pussy. I felt hot, urgent, already close to orgasm. My surrender was absolute, my body spread, my smacked bottom turned up, my holes penetrated. I'd been spanked, by my own aunt, made to show myself, had my panties taken down and spanked, bare behind, spanked and spanked and spanked . . .

I came, my whole body tense in a long, wonderful orgasm, my mind burning with images of what had been done to me, on and on, until I could hold it no more. As I went slowly limp on the bed it was to find myself free of all stress, all tension, everything bad.

Five

That was the problem. It felt so good. It was still a really silly thing to be doing, logically, but it was very hard to focus on logic. Emotionally it was something I needed very badly indeed. That was ironic, as I'd hated it at first. I still did, in a sense, but now I wasn't prepared to do without it.

Even if Elaine kept the secret, it was still risky. I'd been getting it for over a year, once a week, with only two brief breaks while I was away. In all that time we'd never come close to being caught, but that didn't mean it couldn't happen.

For one thing, it wasn't unknown for my mother to turn up at the house uninvited, even after dinner. True, she would have to knock on the door and I'd have time to get covered up and wipe my tears away, even if I was in the middle of my spanking. Then again, she might simply look in at the drawing room window. All it needed was a chink in the curtains, and there I'd be, her daughter, bare-bottomed and howling across her younger sister's lap. It didn't bear thinking about. I do howl, too, I can't help it, and I was sure I could be heard outside the house.

If it wasn't my mother it might be neighbours, in which case it would only be a matter of time before it did get to my mother. Some of them had known her for years. The house opposite had recently changed hands, and Elaine didn't know the new occupants all that well, while fortunately the hedge had grown up and their windows no longer looked directly into the drawing room.

That was only so much consolation. The house was big, and rambling, the garden a maze of walls and hedges, usually pretty overgrown. Neighbours tended to take the attitude that just because Elaine didn't answer the door, it didn't mean she wasn't there. A few times during the summer we'd eaten outside and I'd been given my spankings *al fresco.* It was always in the walled kitchen garden, one of the most tranquil and special places on earth for me. It was where I'd first had sex with Kate. Dangerous or not, in my fragile emotional state it had been more than I could resist to be taken down across Elaine's knee there, with the cool air on my bare bum as it warmed. Each time I'd been terrified afterwards that somebody might have seen us, or heard my squeals and the slap of flesh on flesh. It was at least less likely to happen during the winter months.

The solution struck me as I drove back afterwards with my bum warm in my panties and full of that wonderful post-spanking glow. I often think best then, after a good meal and a good spanking, with a minimum of distracting needs. There was nothing to be gained by worrying about Elaine breaking our secrecy. I got spanked, and even if I stopped it would still have happened, so whether it was still happening or not made no difference. The risk was in being caught. So it was simple, laughably simple. I would make her take me upstairs, and have one of the empty rooms redecorated.

It would be my special spanking room, just for me, and it didn't even need to look out of the ordinary. I was amazed I hadn't thought of it before, but then I'd always let her lead, simply because that was what it was all about. Now I needed to be assertive, briefly, but it made sense and I couldn't see her disagreeing.

I was in an excellent mood when I got back, so much better than when I'd left. It was nearly midnight, but I treated myself to another frig, this time squatting nude on my bed as I fed vibrators in and out of my holes. I even left the one in my bum up when I'd finished, which gave me delightfully rude dreams, about being buggered on a beach with several hundred people watching.

Wednesday was the basic statistics practical, which took up most of the day. I apologised to Mark Petrie for being rude and made up some story about being upset over a failed grant application. He seemed to accept it, presumably putting me down as an over-emotional female, and that was that.

Thursday night was when Marjorie Burgess was coming round to put a parental control system on my PC. I'd seen something on more than one of the sex-addiction sites about 'cleaning up your life', and made sure my flat was not only porn free, but pristine. That wasn't hard, as the way my sexuality works I don't really need accessories. I'm not really bothered with rubber or leather, my faithful long-handled hairbrush takes care of my bum as well as any paddle, and I have very little use for dirty magazines or videos.

I was still feeling distinctly resentful as I hid my vibrators, my school cane and the handful of spanking magazines and books I'd picked up over the years. What she was doing was seriously intrusive, but the answer was not antagonism but duplicity. Stand up to her and I could really get myself in trouble. Fool her into thinking she'd got her way and I'd be fine.

My PC was pretty well clean, except for the picture from Melody Rathwell's 'Black Goddess' femdom group, which I had as an optional wallpaper. It showed her standing tall, in a black leather catsuit that left her breasts showing and holding a whip. It was cute, but I'd only saved it after reading a comment that claimed no woman could look dominant with her breasts bare. They obviously hadn't met Melody. I put it in the recycle bin, and after a moment's hesitation deleted it.

Marjorie was going to be suspicious if I was too good, and as she was convinced I spent my time surfing for porn I found a couple of sites, bookmarked them and hid the evidence with deliberate clumsiness. I then printed out a list from one of the sex-addiction sites, entitled 'Making your Home fit for God's eyes', and left it on the coffee table in my living room. As with the porn sites, it was meant to make her feel I was trying to seem better than I was. That way she could feel superior to me and was less likely to do anything really destructive.

I actually read the thing, just in case I could pick anything up from it. It started by suggesting I throw out anything vaguely pornographic, including clothing catalogues, which was beyond me until I realised that the author thought of sex-addiction as a purely male problem, women being pious, passionless creatures incapable of 'sex-sin'. Presumably the poor sap couldn't even handle pictures of women modelling underwear without giving in to temptation.

There were other things to be thrown out too, including pop music and ordinary videos with anything even vaguely sexual in them, but I wasn't prepared to go that far. Then there was confessing my sex-sin to close Christian friends, but I didn't have any. There was prayer, which Marjorie had already suggested, but posting key Bible verses on my PC seemed like a good idea. The last ones were not to make any rude remarks, which seemed a bit irrelevant, and to 'walk with the Lord', but I wasn't sure what that actually involved.

I had a bit of trouble choosing my Bible quotes, as it was almost impossibly tempting not to put up something bizarre from among the ones turning up on my search engine. In the end I forced myself to choose something sanitised from the maddest of the sex-addiction sites.

By the time she turned up I was ready, outwardly the perfect little reformed sinner, with a layer of easily discovered imperfection to keep her happy, a second level of sorrowful repentance, and the real me carefully hidden beneath.

She fell for it completely, although she nearly missed the bookmarks, and I had to accidentally click on History to get myself caught out. I got a long and sanctimonious lecture for my behaviour, which she enjoyed giving immensely. I took it remorsefully, biting my lip as I stared at the carpet, and mumbled apologies until she was done. Before she'd had me in tears. Now I was trying to stop myself giggling, partly because there was nobody to witness my humiliation, but mainly because I'd made it a game.

I even thought she might spank me again, something I felt highly ambivalent about. She didn't, but contented herself with installing three separate anti-porn filters and making me go into the kitchen while she set the passwords. She then took a brief look around my flat, peering suspiciously at the Journal of Genetics as if she expected to find dirty magazines bound into the covers.

Satisfied, she gave me a final little lecture, told me she would want to know if I masturbated and left. I'd neglected to tell her about my laptop, and spent the rest of the evening surfing for spanking pictures and rubbing my pussy over the sight of girls getting their bums warmed in a hundred awkward and humiliating situations. I was actually laughing as I came.

On Friday evening I decided to deal with Razorback Paintball. I was determined to be strong willed about it, and not let them talk me into one final meeting, which they were sure to try and do. It was equally sure to be the one where something went horribly wrong and we were all arrested, probably with me done up as a piggy-girl in snout and tail, or something equally embarrassing.

Using the telephone or email was just asking for trouble. Gavin would argue back, and he could be highly persuasive. A letter was a better idea, explaining the situation honestly and in detail, which basically meant pointing out that it was simply too risky for me to be playing his crazy games once a month. I sent it off on the Saturday morning, assuming it would arrive Monday or Tuesday, and that he would be too busy with work and preparing for the following weekend's event to worry about me backing out.

The weekend was quiet. I had my session with Gabrielle, which involved me moaning about Marjorie Burgess' behaviour for an hour while she listened patiently, but Poppy was out and she was on her period, so once again nothing happened between us. I knew it might, but I didn't feel the need to push. Jade had been out on the Friday, to a dom she liked to visit, Andrea, who stood six foot tall and worked out. They liked to act out uniform scenarios, most of which involved Jade being slapped around while Andrea played an authority figure of some sort. I was not going near it.

They had been playing Wardress and Prisoner, a favourite. Jade had slap marks on her face and boobs, and her bottom was a mess. So we stayed in, just doing ordinary things and cuddling in bed. I told her I wouldn't be going to the Razorback event, and she said she wouldn't either, as she needed me to feel secure with so many laddish men around. I left late on Sunday, after a leisurely sixty-nine with her on top to spare her badly smacked bum.

The week was uneventful. I took my Tuesday night across Elaine's lap in the kitchen, and afterwards suggested making one of the upstairs rooms up. As always she didn't want to discuss it, and said I should do whatever made me feel comfortable. I picked a room before I left.

I managed to avoid Marjorie Burgess all week, and I didn't hear from Gavin Bulmer, so by the Friday evening I was feeling I had achieved something. That was until I came home to find Gavin's Jeep parked right outside my flat. It was unmistakable, painted in camouflage colours with 'Razorback Paintball' on the side in brilliant scarlet, orange and yellow letters. There was a picture too, of a huge razorbacked boar pig, standing on his hind legs, his body criss-crossed with ammunition belts and a gun in his hands or, rather, his trotters.

The pig was wearing shades, and so was Gavin Bulmer, who was leaning on the bonnet. He was also wearing an army greatcoat, open at the front, a khaki shirt, camouflage trousers and highly polished black boots. It was supposed to make him look like some sort of mercenary, or at least, the Hollywood concept of a mercenary.

I like my neighbours to think I'm quiet, shy and respectable. The combination of Gavin and the Jeep looked anything but quiet, and it didn't exactly suggest shyness or respectability either. I walked quickly over to him.

‘Gavin?’

‘Hi, Penny. We’ve been waiting for you. What’s this about you not coming this weekend?’

‘I explained, didn’t I? Look, come inside. Who’s with you?’

‘Fat Jeff,’ he answered. ‘He’s gone to get a Chinky and some beers.’

So they’d invited themselves to dinner. That wasn’t too bad, as long as my mother didn’t decide to turn up, or Marjorie Burgess. Even then they were only an embarrassment, not actual proof of depravity. I pushed the key into the lock, hurriedly, as Gavin spoke again.

‘You working tomorrow, then?’

‘No. I explained why I couldn’t come in my letter.’

‘Yeah, right.’

I’d opened the door, and he went in, only for Fat Jeff Bellbird to appear at the corner of the street, lumbering along with a brown paper bag in one hand and two packs of beer in the other. Like Gavin he was dressed in pseudo-military gear, only on him it looked even more ridiculous because he was nearly as fat as Monty Hartle. He was just about as lecherous too, with little piggy eyes in a heavily bearded face that always seemed to be focused on my tits. I waited and ushered him upstairs as quickly as he would go.

Gavin had taken my keys and had already let himself in. Jeff followed, going straight to the kitchen without bothering to ask. I let him get on with it, hanging up my coat and freshening up before joining them. Jeff already had the food out, three plates, each with a thick layer of mushroom chow mein topped with beef and pineapple, sweet and sour pork balls, king prawn with spring onion and some sort of chicken dish. There was another plate in the centre of the table, containing pancakes, spring onion, hoi-sin sauce and an entire roast duck.

'Tuck in,' Jeff insisted, pushing a beer towards my place.

They'd left me the sofa, and I sat down, looking doubtfully at what was more food than I'd have eaten in three days. Both of them were busy stuffing their faces, and neither spoke until Jeff was licking the gravy from his plate. I'd barely started.

'That's gross, Jeff,' Gavin stated.

Jeff put his plate down and belched.

'So what's this crap about not coming tomorrow?' he demanded.

'Yeah,' Gavin put in. 'We need you, Penny, you're the best.'

'You've got plenty of other girls,' I pointed out.

'Well, yeah, but not like you. We need the dirty bitches to get things going.'

'Thanks, Gavin.'

'You know what I mean. A lot of the girls don't want to be the first to get naked or . . .'

'Or have a tail plug stuck up their bums?' I finished for him. 'That's true, sometimes, but you'll have Sophie Cherwell, won't you, and Natasha?'

'Not Tasha. She wrote her bloke's car off. She gets twelve of the cane every weekend. Out of commission.'

'I heard. My cousin Susan?'

'Nah, she's not up for it. She's with some weird bloke from a band.'

'Well, Sophie, at least. She's better than me.'

'Not much,' Jeff said as he set to work on the duck.

'Not at all,' Gavin put in quickly. 'She's dirty, sure, but . . . I don't know, you seem to get them going better. We need four girls anyway, and your Jade's cute and all . . . those tits, fuck me!'

'Fuck them, more like it,' Jeff added. 'I love little fat birds, so long as they're in proportion. Plenty of arse, plenty of tit, that's fine. I hate it when it's all on their hips and gut.'

I looked at him in astonishment. He was concentrating on rolling a shredded duck pancake, clearly oblivious to the irony of his remark.

'Sophie will have to do,' I said firmly. 'And I'm sure you can find three others. As I said, there's just too much on my plate right now ... literally, as it happens. Do you want this, Jeff?'

'Sure.'

I pushed my half-finished plate over to him. My tummy was already feeling stretched and I knew I couldn't manage another mouthful. Gavin pushed the duck towards me.

'The thing is,' I went on, 'you've been taking too many risks lately. I know it's private land, but there's still a chance of being seen, especially with so many people turning up. It's only a small village, you know. People talk. It's getting cold too.'

'Not a problem, either way,' Gavin answered. 'We've got this great new place for the winter. It's an industrial estate, right. It's being done up, but we get to use it at weekends.'

'One of Rathwell's properties?'

'Yeah.'

'Then that's doubly impractical. If Mel catches me she's going to shave my head.'

'Oh, yeah, we heard about that. What a laugh!'

'Not for me! I have to work, Gavin. I have to give lectures, go to symposia, make presentations for funding. How am I going to look with a bald head?'

'Tell 'em you lost a bet, or you got that disease, what's it called?'

'Alopecia,' Jeff added through a mouthful of food.

'No,' I said firmly. 'I'm sorry, but you're just going

to have to do without me. I'm sure you'll have a great time anyway.'

'Yeah,' Gavin protested, 'but we've got something really special this time . . .'

'No.'

'It's called "Night of the Clowns",' Jeff added. 'It's a well freaky idea. It . . .'

'No.'

'Come on, Penny! You'll love it!'

'No.'

'It's your thing, it really is . . .'

'No!'

He made a face but didn't answer. I'd done it. I adore shredded duck in hoi-sin sauce, and I needed something to do with my hands, so I made myself a pancake, stuffing it in despite the swollen feeling in my belly. I'd already drunk one beer, and opened another as I sat back.

My tummy was so taut my jeans were hurting me, so I undid the button, reasoning that as they'd seen me nude and worse it hardly mattered in front of them. Gavin gave me a suggestive wink anyway, and Jeff's eyes swivelled to the little bit of tummy flesh showing between the buttons of my blouse. I ignored them, stretching out to take the strain off my stomach and sipping my beer as they finished the food.

They ate every mouthful, Jeff even sucking the duck bones, which seemed extraordinary, even for a man of his size. He finished last, and cracked what I think was his sixth beer. I'd won, but I was wondering what was going to happen, especially whether they'd demand their cocks sucked, and if they did, whether I could cope or would end up being sick in somebody's crotch. It was the question I expected when Jeff gave another monumental belch, and I was ready to tell them that if they wanted their cocks sucked they could deal with each other, and not in front of me.

'So,' he said. 'No show?'

'We really can't persuade you?' Gavin added.

'No,' I confirmed. 'Sorry, boys.'

I relaxed. Clearly even they had had their fill, and I really had won.

'Shame,' Jeff said. 'Bag, Gavin?'

'Bag, Jeff.'

'You two, no . . .' I began, absolutely certain that whatever was going on it was not to my advantage.

I was right. Gavin had stuck his hand in his pocket, and what he pulled out was something I recognised immediately, a red sphere the size of a big plum or a satsuma, on a leather thong, a ball gag. That wasn't all. He had a roll of sticky tape, a big one.

'No!' I said. 'Not that, not now, boys . . . I'm too full.'

Gavin was grinning as he stood up. I was trapped, the wall behind me, one of them to either side. The table was in front of me. I jumped it.

'No,' I insisted. 'I said no, and I meant no. Later maybe, not now . . . Stop it boys! Red, red, red!'

Red was the stop word we all used, simple and effective. They took no notice, advancing on me around the table. Jeff was blocking the route to the front door. I began to back towards the kitchen, still talking.

'No, boys, this is not funny. I'm just not up for it, especially in bondage. I'll be sick . . . Look, I'll suck you both, but later, okay?'

'Thanks, Penny,' Gavin said. 'Nice offer, but it's not what we're after.'

'No?'

'No.'

I realised what they were after immediately. Jeff had pulled something out from under his jacket, a sack. I knew full well what was going in it, me. The kitchen door was open. I made a dash for it, slamming it behind me.

It was a big mistake. I just ended up trapped, and Gavin got to the door before I could jam it. He was too strong for me, and when Jeff put his shoulder to the door I had to jump back quickly. They had me cornered, and all I could do was back away with my hands stuck out, babbling denials and reasons they shouldn't put me in the sack.

My face betrayed me. I was serious, genuinely, but I couldn't stop myself from grinning like an idiot. It didn't matter what I said. They didn't believe me. I still kept backing away, until I was up against the work surface. The drawer with the knives in it was right next to me, but that was just silly.

I was caught. Jeff grabbed my arms, pinning them to my sides. Gavin pushed the ball gag at my mouth, forcing it against my lips. It hurt, and I gaped, taking it in, and my last chance of talking my way out of it was gone. Jeff held me as Gavin fixed the gag in my mouth, then turned my body and pulled my arms tight behind my back. I went limp, knowing that struggling would only make it worse. My wrists were crossed behind my back and taped together, quite hard, so that I could feel the buttons on my blouse cuffs pressing into my flesh. Still Jeff held on, as Gavin ducked down to pull off my boots and wind tape around my ankles.

They didn't even molest me, much, just a quick grope of my boobs and bum through my clothes before the sack was pulled down over my head. It was big, reaching right down to my knees, but they put me on the floor and pushed my legs up into it anyway, taping the mouth closed to leave me helpless. It was hemp, so I had no trouble breathing, but I was still in immediate distress. The rough material tickled my face and hands. I could see only the spots of light and the brown interior of the sack. I could only breathe through my nose and make muffled gurgling noises. I was upside down, too, as they hefted the sack between them and carried it into the main room. Gavin spoke as I was dumped on the sofa.

'Better wait a bit before we take her to the car. Wouldn't want to be seen.'

'Dead right,' Jeff agreed. 'Fritters?'

'Sure. What did you get?'

'Mix. Pineapple, banana and apple.'

'Great.'

A chair wheezed as Jeff lowered his weight into it. Gavin had obviously gone back into the kitchen. A moment later his voice sounded once more.

'Shit, they're pretty mean on the honey. Got any honey, Penny?'

I managed a grunt in a vain effort to tell him where he could stick the honey, only to remember that I'd done exactly that only a couple of weeks earlier. All I had was my pot of Colston and Harwell's Lincolnshire Clover, undoubtedly still with my finger marks in it. Sure enough, an instant after I heard the pop of the lid being twisted open Gavin's voice came again.

'What . . . here, Jeff, Penny eats honey with her fingers, looks like.'

'Slut, ain't she?' Jeff answered. 'Probably make that Jade lick it off her cunt.'

'Her arsehole, more like,' Gavin answered. 'You know what she's like. Dirty bitch.'

I found myself blushing at how close he was to the truth. Jeff gave me a prod with the end of his boot, where the sacking was stretched taut across my bum. There was a pop as he opened another beer, footsteps, the sounds of crockery and cutlery being handed out, then of eating.

'Nice,' Gavin remarked after a while. 'Pineapple's best.'

'Nah, banana.'

'Too soggy.'

'There's this place in Lewisham where they do pear, and mango. That's good.'

'Yeah?'

'Yeah. Pricey, though.'

I tried to speak. My discomfort was growing by the minute, and if they were going to drive me back to London in the back of the Jeep I was going to be in the bag for hours. I was prepared to submit if they let me out, even if they bagged me up again when it was time to go. All I could manage were muffled grunts and gurgles, and to wriggle pathetically about, which they ignored.

They ate the fritters. Jeff finished the beers while Gavin made himself a coffee. They talked about paintball, and the stock market, curry, beer, football, even the best way to get onto the M4. All I could do was wait and squirm in my bonds to keep the circulation going.

I'd soon lost all track of time, with only my growing discomfort and their inane chatter to judge by. It had to be getting late though, and while I was dreading the moment when they would carry me out to the car, another part of me was praying for it. I'd drunk two large cans of beer, a litre in all, and the strain was beginning to tell on my bladder. They both lived in London, and it couldn't take more than two hours to get to either flat. I could hold it, just, as long as they hurried up.

When they finally decided to go, they just left, not even bothering to stick the take-away cartons in the bin. Jeff hoisted me onto his shoulder, as if I was a sack of potatoes, and carried me down the stairs like that, which was terrifying. That wasn't all I was worried about as I desperately tried to make myself understood. I was in a blouse and jeans, that and my undies. I had no coat, no jumper, no bag, no money. The only thing they took were my keys.

I was ignored, as always. Jeff reached the hall without dropping me. Gavin checked outside. I heard his okay and the click of his car door. Jeff ran forward and I was dumped unceremoniously into the back of the Jeep. Something heavy was pulled over the sack and I was in utter darkness.

It smelt of mud, and stale sweat, and paintball dye, a revolting combination so strong in my nostrils I was scared I would start gagging. My bladder was getting bad too, and when Jeff dropped me I'd very nearly wet my panties. I was going to anyway, before long, but I was sure I could hold on if I really tried.

The car started, drew away and turned the corner at the end of my street, fast, rolling me against a box which seemed to be all corners. I could hear them, just, their voices muffled. Fortunately Gavin had restricted himself to a single beer, but he drove like a lunatic anyway, taking corners as if he was in a rally, and every time sending a painful jolt through my bladder. We crossed some speed bumps at one point, and I think if there had been just one more I'd have given in and done it in my clothes.

He found a main road after that, then the motorway. That was easier, and I clung on, trying to fight down the growing pain both in my muscles and in my bladder. It seemed to take for ever, but finally he slowed, the driving changed and I knew we were in London. That didn't mean we were there, not by a long way. I was going to make it though. It hurt like anything, but I could hold it. They'd have to let me out in the flat . . .

Only I knew they wouldn't, not if they thought I was going to wet myself. They'd make me do it, maybe even tell me they wouldn't release me until I had. It was essential they didn't realise how desperate I was. So I stayed quiet, breathing deeply through my nose and trying to think about anything but the stretched feeling in my stomach and the pain in my bladder. Finally I heard Jeff's voice again.

'Lewisham . . . pull in when you can . . . yeah, over there.'

Lewishham was where the Chinese take-away that did the pear and mango fritters was. It had to be near his flat. We had to be near his flat. A great wave of relief swept over me. I was in agony, but I was going to make it. Five, maybe ten minutes more and I would be able to get to the loo. I heard a door open. Gavin spoke.

'Get us a portion of spare ribs too, yeah? Here's a fiver.'

'They'll get cold, mate.'

'So we'll eat 'em in the car.'

They were going to eat Chinese in the Jeep. I just gave in, with a broken sob. Urine exploded into my panties, bubbling out of me and up over my pussy, between my bum cheeks too. I burst into tears, shaking with reaction as I did it, the warm piddle soaking through my knicks and into my jeans, spreading, warm and wet, across my seat and down my legs. I didn't even try and stop it, but just lay there snivelling faintly as it all came out, more than I'd have thought I could possibly hold. Soon the sacking under my hip was wet, and even my tummy where it had soaked up into my blouse. I was soiled, utterly, and unmistakably, my pee-sodden jeans clear evidence of what I'd done in them even if it hadn't been for the smell. They would find out as soon as they opened the boot.

Gavin noticed anyway.

'You all right, Penny?'

All I could managed was a muffled sob, barely louder than the noise my pee had made when it first came out.

'You've pissed your panties, haven't you?' he demanded.

I nodded, even though I knew he couldn't see me. He chuckled.

'Never mind. We're going back to Jeff's now, once we've had some grub.'

They did it too, ate spare ribs in savoury sauce and mixed fritters as I lay there bound, gagged and wet with my own piddle in the back of their car. By the time they'd finished, my pee was cold, and starting to get sticky where my panties were tight over my pussy and down between my bum cheeks.

The final insult came when I found out that Jeff's flat was only another ten minutes or so away. I could have made it, if I'd really tried. They did let me out of the bag at least, and untied me, leaving me in Jeff's bathroom to sort out the mess I was in. Everything was wet. My pee had even soaked into my socks, and my panties were absolutely sodden. It was no surprise to find that Fat Jeff didn't have a washing machine, so I rinsed everything and put the lot in a bucket of cold water.

His idea of décor was seriously strange, creepy even, running to leaping clown mannequins in the hallway, fantasy art posters and endless militaria. There was even a blow-up doll in the bedroom, also in a clown outfit, only a rude one, the breasts, bottom and genitals sticking out through holes in the pink and green harlequinade. I'd known, and I was too tired to be really freaked out anyway. I was fed up too, but inevitably what they'd done to me had brought out my submissive feelings. I was not going to give them the benefit, and that was that.

Stark naked under the huge bathrobe I'd found on the back of the door, I could hardly leave, and I knew I wouldn't be able to persuade them to drive me home. I wasn't prepared to do anything drastic either, or even pinch Fat Jeff's bed and leave him to the sofa. He would just get the wrong idea, taking it as an invitation, and I'd probably have woken to the feel of his cock nudging between my bum cheeks about half a second before it was jammed up my pussy.

They were in the kitchen, so I went to the living room. There was a sofa, piled high with military magazines and general junk, so I pushed the lot on the floor and lay down. Exhaustion flooded over me, and I must have been asleep in under a minute.

The next thing I knew was an odd rubbery sensation against my lips. I moved away, by instinct, not really sure what was happening or even where I was. A big hand took the back of my head, the rubbery thing was pushed to my lips once more and my eyes came open. It was dim, the only light coming from across the hall, and most of that blocked out by the bulky shadow towering over me – Fat Jeff. He saw I was awake, and spoke.

'Give us a suck, Penny.'

'Go away!'

'Oh, go on. I won't fuck you or anything, promise.'

'Go away, Jeff. I was asleep!'

'Go on, babe. I'll be quick.'

'Oh, for goodness' sake!'

I opened my mouth. His cock went in and I was sucking. He was pretty big, and hairy, with his pubes tickling my face as he fucked it, holding himself by the balls and pushing his erection in and out between my lips. I was still half-asleep, and just about able to make a slide of my mouth. It didn't seem to bother him, and he kept his word, spunking down my throat after maybe a minute. I let him milk himself into my mouth and swallowed dutifully, then pulled back. He thanked me and left, and that was that, or it should have been.

It was impossible to get back to sleep. For one thing he'd left the door open and one of his hideous clowns was visible outside, the white and rich pink of the face grotesque in the dim light, and staring, as if peeping in on me. Jeff was snoring too, about two minutes after coming in my mouth, which was not doing much for my taste either.

Finally I got up, to wash my mouth out and down a glass of orange juice. Jeff didn't stir, and there was no sign of Gavin, who had presumably gone home. I went back into the living room and closed the door on the clown. The displays on his bank of equipment showed three twenty-seven. I lay down again, staring up into the darkness.

They had abused me, with a vengeance. In fact they'd gone a lot further than they should have done, ignoring my stop word and every other protest. Wetting myself had been their fault too, because if a girl is in bondage, she needs constant attention. They'd treated me like a sack of spuds or a bag of old clothes.

Okay, so if I hadn't known them, or they not known what I'm like, it would have been a very different story. That didn't excuse it, but I hadn't even had a go at them. Far from it, I'd sucked Jeff's cock with no more than the most token resistance. I sighed. I was hopeless. In the morning I would tell him what I thought of him. For now, I was going to masturbate.

To think was to act. I pulled the robe open and made myself comfortable, one leg up, the other on the floor, my pussy spread to the cool night air. I began to stroke myself, just on fur, and took hold of one little boob, caressing my nipple as I let my thoughts drift.

They had handled me so easily, gagging me, binding my wrists and ankles, stuffing me in a bag. I'd been utterly helpless, and if they'd wanted to, they could have done anything. It would have been the works of moments to pull down my jeans and knickers, stripping my bum for their amusement. They would have fucked me, and buggered me, Jeff using the honey to open my bumhole after Gavin had left my pussy sloppy with spunk. If I hadn't had the stupid ball gag in my mouth he could have stuck his cock in after he'd had me, maybe spunked in my mouth, the way he had, only after being up my honey-smeared bumhole.

No, the ball gag had been good. It had stopped me from calling out, from making them untie me when I needed to pee. Without it, I wouldn't have wet my panties. I wouldn't have suffered the pain and tension of trying to hold it in. I wouldn't have had the awful frustration of knowing there was absolutely nothing I could do but hold on. I wouldn't have known that final, dreadful moment of utter despair when they said they were going to eat in the car and I'd just let it go, pissing in my panties, wetting my jeans, soaking myself in hot, wet urine . . .

As I started to come I was wishing it had been everything, not just pee, but the full works, right in my panties, bulging in the pouch of my jeans, squashing up my bum crease and over my sex . . . my cunt, as they always called it. I'd have lain there, thoroughly soiled, the fat bulge of my own dung squashing in my panties as I moved, tears of pure humiliation streaming down my cheeks. They'd have caught me like that, pulled down my soggy jeans, stripped my bum out of my filthy panties, laughed to see what I'd done in them, buggered me in it, fucked me, and spunked up in my dirty holes, or done it in my mouth, after . . .

I cried out as I came, my whole mind fixed on my disgusting fantasy as I rubbed hard on my clitty. My back was arched, the muscles of my thighs and bottom locked tight, my teeth gritted, perfect ecstasy, which broke in a welter of shame the instant my peak was past.

Six

The first thing that came into my head in the morning was that I'd sucked Fat Jeff's cock, and swallowed, then frigged off. I am nothing if not self-aware, and I knew it had been inevitable, later if not then. I was still feeling pretty resentful as I pulled myself up and wrapped his robe around my body.

I was thinking of what I'd frigged off over as I padded to the bathroom, and I managed a wry grin for my own filthy mind. It had been pretty dirty, but I knew it wouldn't have happened, not really. Gavin and Jeff just weren't that depraved, and if they had been they certainly wouldn't have done me outside a Chinese take-away in Lewisham High Street.

Jeff was still asleep. Some of my friends would have given him what he deserved, perhaps peed all over him and then run off in whatever clothes they could snatch. Unfortunately it would have meant wandering around London looking even more ridiculous than one of his clowns. That was out, I had no money, and I was sure they wouldn't have made it that easy. They hadn't kidnapped me to let me wander off again.

Sure enough, the front door was on the mortice lock, and even if Jeff hadn't purposefully hidden the key it might have been anywhere. It wasn't in his pockets anyway, which I checked, with some vague thoughts of taking it as a bargaining counter. So I was stuck.

I wasn't even entirely sure what I wanted. It seemed a bit pathetic to throw a hissy fit and storm off home, besides which I needed to be at Gabrielle's later on, then go on to Jade's. If I wanted my clothes back I was going to have to persuade Jeff to take them to the laundrette. With luck I could have them dry in time for me to get to Gabrielle's and all would be well. To achieve that I had to make Jeff do as I wanted, which meant being nice, but firm.

So I made him coffee, a fairly revolting process in itself, and went to wake him up. He was well under his duvet, a huge lump with only a tangle of red-brown hair sticking out at the top and one huge foot at the bottom. I tickled the foot and the lump went into a convulsion like a minor earthquake. Jeff's head appeared, his little eyes half closed under a mat of hair.

'Coffee?'

'Oh . . . yeah, right . . . thanks.'

He sat up, took the mug and sipped at the coffee. It had three sugars, which was evidently a good guess. His blow-up doll was on the only chair, so I pushed it off with my foot. It toppled over, slowly, ending up on the floor as if on all fours, with the 'realistic' vagina and anus showing through the hole in its absurd clown costume. I gave it another kick and it fell on its side.

'That was a laugh, eh?' Jeff said as I sat down.

'Very funny,' I answered him.

'You should have seen the look on your face!' he chortled.

I shook my head in despair. There was no sensible reply. To him, and to Gavin Bulmer, it was clearly just a game, a laugh. I wondered if he even began to understand the depth of emotion it had involved for me, let alone the pain. I took a swallow of coffee. He had sat up in bed, exposing the great hairy breadth of his chest, more bear-like than ever. I wondered if he was nude beneath his duvet, then remembered that he'd had a pair of underpants on when he'd made me suck his cock. I pulled the robe tighter around me.

'I need to get going soon, Jeff,' I told him.

'Get going?'

'Yes, Jeff. A joke's a joke, but I need to be in Victoria by midday, and my girlfriend's expecting me later on.'

'Oh . . . right. But you're coming to Night of the Clowns, yeah?'

'No! Did I say I would?'

'Yeah, but I thought . . .'

'What, that because you'd kidnapped me I had to go?'

He didn't answer.

'I'm sorry,' I went on. 'I'm all right about last night, okay? But I still need to be in Victoria, and my clothes are still in to soak. Could you do me a favour and get them washed and dried for me? We should just about have time.'

'Well, yeah, but you've got to come tonight.'

'Why? What's so special about me? You've got Sophie, and others. Who's coming?'

'Sophie, and a girl called Emmeline. We were counting on you, Penny, and on you bringing Jade. She won't come without you.'

'Well, no, but why so few? You had what . . . eight girls, last time?'

He shrugged. A thought occurred to me.

'So Mel won't be there?'

'No.'

'Morris?'

'No.'

'Oh.'

That put a different complexion on things. Presumably Morris had something else on, which probably accounted for why they had so few girls. Generally they relied on contacts from Morris' club, Sophie included. Obviously she'd decided the 'Night of the Clowns' thing would be more fun. I hadn't seen her in a while, and if Mel wasn't going to be there . . .

'All right,' I told him. 'I'll come, and I'll bring Jade, but only if you help me out this morning. Okay?'

'Yeah, fine.'

He took another sip of coffee. His eyes flicked to where my bare feet stuck out at the bottom of the robe, then moved up. The duvet moved.

'Jeff, please? We need to hurry.'

'Right, yeah . . . shame, I've got one serious boner for you.'

As he spoke he pulled his duvet away, exposing the bulk of his gut and legs, with his huge cock sticking out from the Y of his underpants, balls and all. He was fully erect.

'Put it away, Jeff,' I sighed.

'Go on, Penny, give us a wank, just a quick one.'

'No! I'm in a hurry, Jeff.'

'Oh, go on.'

'No! I . . . later, if you really insist, but not now! Please hurry up, Jeff?'

'Oh, all right,' he answered, covering himself, 'but we're not going to make it. It's twenty minutes to my Mum's, and . . .'

'Your Mum's? What's she got to do with it?'

'That's where I take my washing.'

I let out a long sigh. He went on.

'Why don't I just drive you to Victoria anyway?'

'Yes, Jeff, fine, but what am I supposed to wear? Look, there must be a laundrette . . .'

'No, that's cool, I've got some girlie stuff.'

The thought of Fat Jeff as a transvestite was too hideous to contemplate, and he'd have taken a size thirty in dresses anyway, so I assumed he meant he actually had some ordinary female clothes. For all I knew he even had a girlfriend, in which case she might not be best pleased, but that was not my problem.

'Great,' I answered him. 'My size, I hope?'

'Yeah, more or less.'

More or less was a lot better than stark naked, especially when I intended to stay firmly in the car. Poppy was my size, and I could borrow something from her.

'Okay, fine,' I agreed.

'Cool. How about that wank then? We've got time now.'

He had twitched the covers back again, exposing himself. Sometimes it's best to just get on with it. I shook my head in mute resignation as I turned on the chair, to kneel down, my bum stuck out towards him. I twitched the robe up at the back and settled my arms on the chair.

'That is not an invitation, Jeff, but you can wank over my bum . . . I mean, I'll show off my bum while you wank.'

'Fucking nice!'

He began to tug on his cock, his eyes glued to my bare bum. It wasn't going to take long, not the way he was going at it, or so I thought, until he stopped pulling at the shaft and began to stroke his helmet with his fingertips.

'Nice cunt,' he said. 'Hairy, aren't you?'

'Yes. Get on with it.'

'Stick it out a bit more then, show us your brown eye.'

I pulled my back in, making my cheeks spread wide to show off my anus. He licked his lips.

'Fucking nice!' he repeated. 'You have one gorgeous arse.'

I could just imagine the view. My furry pussy lips would be peeping out from between my thighs with the wet, pink crease showing in the middle. My bum would be looking big and broad because of the rude pose I was in. My anus would be on plain show, puckered tight in her nest of hair. It seemed to be my bumhole he wanted to see, what he wanted to come over.

What he wanted to come over, eventually. He was in no hurry, stroking himself as he feasted his eyes on my rear view. He'd seen me bare before, at Razorback events, but never so close, never one to one. It was getting to me, because it was such a rude thing to do, to pose my naked bottom for a man to wank over. Suddenly he went on, hoarse now as he began to tug at himself once more.

'I love a dirty girl. I love a girl who'll show her bare arse for kicks. You are fucking great . . . cunt and all, and I love your little starfish. One day I'll fuck it for you, maybe, yeah?'

'No . . . yes, maybe . . . some time. Just come, Jeff . . . you're humiliating me . . .'

'Sorry.'

'Don't be . . . go on. I'm going to frig too, while you talk, but don't fuck me.'

He laughed. I slid a hand back under my tummy, pushing the folds of his robe aside to get at my pussy. I wasn't ready to be fucked, not by him, not after what they'd done, but the tension was still there, the same as when I'd come the night before, brought back by his dirty behaviour. As I began to masturbate, he started to talk once more.

'You like it up the arse, don't you? Like plugs and stuff, and when that Morris fucked your arsehole for you . . . You are a dirty bitch, aren't you, Penny? And you sucked his cock, didn't you? You sucked it after it had been up your arse, you filthy fucking dirtbag bitch . . .'

It came back to me, Morris Rathwell buggering me and putting it in my mouth. Jeff had been watching. So had other people, watching me get my bumhole used, then my mouth, the same filthy, dirty piece of deliberate degradation I'd come over the night before. The memory left me weak with humiliation. My leg started to shake, my knee hammering briefly on the chair before I got control of myself. I was going to lose myself, my self-control slipping to the obscene memory, breaking and I was begging.

'Do it, Jeff . . . pop it in . . . up my bum. Please?'

He didn't need asking twice. In an instant he had rolled out of bed, snatching at a thick blue tube among the mess on his floor. I saw the words on it as his hand closed, 'Lube-Up'. He got behind me. There was a rude farting noise and cold jelly squirted over my bumhole and pussy. I realised it had to be the lubricant he used for his blow-up doll even as his helmet pushed to my anal ring. I opened easily, my slippery bumhole welcoming his cock as I pushed out to let him in, imagining myself in place of the revolting doll, my anus used, the same way it was.

I felt the fat cock head go up into my bum and sighed in ecstasy. Now penetrated, I was clutching the chair as he forced himself deeper up, his thick cock easing up my slimy bumhole bit by bit. I was full, and I felt myself stretching inside as it went up, adding a fresh pang of humiliation at the knowledge that he could feel what was in me. I heard my own sob as his fat belly squashed to my bottom. His balls met my empty pussy and I was in heaven, his cock wedged in my rectum to the hilt. I felt utterly bloated, well and truly buggered, so full, and so dirty.

As he began to pump into me I started to rub myself once more. I could have come just over being sodomised, but there was more. I'd begged for it, acting the wanton little slut just because he'd shown me his cock. I should have been disgusted. I should have done what the modern woman is supposed to do when confronted with the grosser side of male sexuality, put him down, stuck my nose in the air . . .

It wasn't my nose I'd stuck in the air, it was my bum, and his cock was up it. What had he called me? A dirtbag bitch. He was about right, and I'd got what I deserved, what a slut is sure to get for showing off to men, especially showing her bumhole. I'd got it, and now he was going to use me thoroughly, maybe even do what I'd fantasised about, for real, bugger me well and then stuff his dirty cock in my mouth for his orgasm. I'd do it, too, I knew I would, utterly disgrace myself, and come while I did it, frigging my sopping pussy as I sucked on the fat cock now wedged deep up my bumhole . . .

'You're a snerd! Nurgle, nurgle!'

I'd been on the edge, so close to what should have been the most glorious orgasm. It broke, completely, at his words. My bumhole had even started to contract on his cock, which he was now wiggling about up my bottom instead of pumping into me.

'What are you doing?' I wailed. 'I was coming!'

'Sorry, I . . .'

'Just fuck me, Jeff, and if you want to . . . if you . . . ah!'

He'd begun to bugger me again, hard, knocking the breath from my lungs. I'd been going to tell him he could stick it in my mouth, but the next instant he had began to grunt. Then he was pounding into me so hard it left me gasping and shaking my head in reaction, totally unable to speak. Then it stopped, and I knew he'd come up my bottom.

I hadn't come, my fantasy broken by his idiotic comment at the worst possible moment. I didn't even feel like it any more, and I was feeling resentful to say the least as he pulled his cock slowly out of my bumhole.

'Nice,' he remarked. 'Er . . . you're a bit messy.'

He made for the bathroom and I followed. I used the loo, then got in the bath to wash, with my bum stuck out under the cold tap. Jeff seemed to think I looked hilarious, and watched me as he washed his cock at the sink. I was in an odd state, still aroused, but not really at ease. Part of me wanted to be rude, which was why I'd let him watch me on the loo and washing my bum. Part of me wanted to be as far away as I possibly could. The best thing to do was wait until I was with Jade, and even when he had left to fetch my clothes I didn't frig off. There was no powder, and only one rather grubby bath towel. I did the best I could, and put the robe back on to cover myself. Jeff was in the bedroom, dressed.

'Did you get the clothes out for me?' I asked.

'Sure,' he answered, and gestured to something hanging over the chair I had so recently been buggered over.

It was pink, a sort of body suit, and in the most bizarre cut, tight at the body but baggy at the thighs, like a pear. Three large, bright red pom-poms decorated the front. It was a clown outfit.

'You are joking,' I managed.

'It's the get-up for this evening,' he explained.

'Yes, Jeff, fine . . . no, not fine, but never mind that. I have to go to Victoria, then to Turnpike Lane. I can't go around London dressed in that thing!'

'Why not?'

'Because . . . because it's a clown outfit, for goodness' sake, and a pretty stupid-looking one at that!'

'I thought you liked that sort of stuff? Humiliation and that? Look . . .'

He turned it over, revealing the back. There was a fourth pom-pom, positioned so it would go just above the girl's bum, like a ludicrous rabbit's tail. Beneath it was a buttoned slit, a drop seat, so the wearer could bare her bum, or more likely have her bum bared by other people. I tried to explain.

'Yes, Jeff, I am into humiliation, erotic humiliation. I cannot walk around London in your ridiculous clown costume. Have you got no sense at all? And what is it with you and clowns, anyway?'

'I thought . . .'

'And what about undies anyway, and shoes, for goodness' sake?'

He just shrugged. He looked genuinely hurt. I really am too soft.

'Okay, dress me up in it this evening. Do whatever you have to do. Spank me, fine, even fuck me, if you like. I suppose you may as well after what you just did.'

He brightened up immediately as I went on.

'But I am not wearing that in the street!'

'Yeah, but I haven't got anything else.'

'Nothing?'

'No. Well, you can borrow some of my stuff if . . .'

'Don't be silly. I'd look like a clown anyway, in a pair of your trousers. One of those ones who get the whitewash poured . . .'

'Hey! Neat idea!'

'Oh, shut up, Jeff. All right, I'll put on the clown suit and one of your coats, but you're to drop me right outside the door. Okay?'

'Sure.'

I picked the horrible thing up. It was at least easy to get into, with a row of poppers down the front. Jeff watched me put it on, obviously enjoying himself. It felt very odd indeed, especially when I was nude underneath. I had never seen such an absurd garment, let alone worn one. Even the pink and green harlequin suit on his blow-up doll had more style, although it was a good deal less decent. In it, I felt utterly ridiculous and comprehensively humiliated, feelings only slightly reduced once I'd put the largest of his coats over the top. I still looked silly, barefoot with the pink trouser legs and collar showing, but a great deal better than before.

There were one or two odd looks as we made for Jeff's car, and I was extremely glad I didn't live anywhere near. Once in the car I felt a little better, and he even managed to get me to Gabrielle's a few minutes early. I knew Poppy would laugh at me, and I was seriously considering taking my feelings out on her bare bum when she did. What I hadn't expected was Monty Hartle, who was sprawled on Gabrielle's couch. I kept the coat on.

'Out, Monty, go and get lunch or something,' Gabrielle ordered immediately, calling from the kitchen. 'Hi, Penny.'

Monty went, like a lamb, which impressed me, considering how much difficulty I'd had in getting him to even discuss anything other than the removal of my panties.

'Thanks,' I said as the door shut behind him. 'Look, Gabrielle, is Poppy around? I need to borrow some of her clothes.'

'In here,' Poppy's voice sounded from beyond a closed door.

She was in the special bedroom, Gabrielle's playroom.

'What's the matter?' Poppy asked as I opened the bedroom door to a blaze of pink. 'Monty been at you?'

'No,' I answered, and shrugged the coat off. 'I just . . .'

She burst out laughing.

'Stop it,' I told her, 'or you go over my knee right now!'

'Make me!' she taunted, and stuck her tongue out.

'I will,' I promised, 'just as soon as I'm out of this idiotic costume. Anyway, you're one to talk!'

It was true. She was in her blue baby-doll, only in place of the panties she had a big towelling nappy wrapped around her hips and fastened in place with an enormous pin. She gave me a twirl, showing off the seat of her nappy as I slipped out of the clown suit.

'What have you been up to?' she demanded.

'What have you been up to?' I countered. 'Dressed like that with Monty Hartle in the flat?'

'He has a half-hour before you,' she explained. 'Gabby's supposed to be curing him of his perverted ways.'

'And this involves you being in a baby-doll nightie and nappies? How about some clothes?'

'Sure. The thing with Monty is, he used to be a panty thief . . . Whoops! Shit! Gabby'll kill me if she knows I told you!'

'Don't worry. What do you mean, used to? He still is!'

'No, he used to nick them off washing lines and stuff.'

'And now he asks girls he accosts in the street to take them off?'

'Only if he knows them.'

She had ducked down beside a chest of drawers as she spoke. It was pink, like just about everything else in the room, and had several large, cuddly toys on top, mostly pink as well. So was the pair of panties she tossed over her shoulder. I grabbed them and struggled quickly into them.

'Gabby's bras will fit you better,' she stated. 'In the other drawers.'

'So why the nappy?' I demanded as I crossed the room.

'To give Monty a little show,' she admitted. 'If he's getting kinky stuff from us, he doesn't feel socially inadequate, so he doesn't need to pinch stuff or go peeping.'

'He's a Peeping Tom too?'

'Reformed. These jeans will fit you. Top, jumper . . . socks. Boots, yeah?'

'Please. I must say, Gabrielle's methods are pretty unorthodox.'

'They work.'

I nodded my agreement. Gabrielle was nothing if not practical, as I was finding out. Her bra was slightly loose around the back and left even my little boobs bulging slightly from around the cups, but it was acceptable. The top and jumper were fine, and at least Jade was going to approve of the jeans. They barely covered my bottom at the back, so that the waistband of my panties showed.

'Not really winter wear,' I remarked, and pulled the side of a curtain back to peer out into the grey November day.

'Better than going around in a clown suit,' Poppy replied. 'So what did happen?'

I didn't answer. Down in the street I could see Jeff's car. He was standing by it, talking to Monty, grinning through his beard, then laughing. There was only one conclusion. They knew each other. Somehow it didn't surprise me.

'Bother!'

'What's the matter?' Poppy asked, pushing in beside me at the window.

'The guy down there,' I pointed out, 'the one talking to Monty, is Jeff Bellbird, Fat Jeff. You know about the paintball thing?'

'Yes, Tasha told us. That's Fat Jeff, then. How does he know Monty?'

'I hate to think. He's the one with the obsession about clowns.'

I began to explain as we turned away from the window. She giggled her way through the story, and made me repeat the details of how I'd wet myself for Gabrielle. I was feeling very glad to be dressed sensibly again, and to have some female company, making it easy to relax and talk to them. Most of the hour was spent discussing my feelings about what had happened, and I even told them about my less than perfect anal sex session with Jeff.

'So what's a snerd?' Poppy asked.

'I have no idea.'

The buzzer went, and Poppy got up to answer it. It was Monty.

'Let him up,' I offered. 'I'm over time anyway.'

Poppy buzzed him up. He quickly appeared. Sure enough, he knew Fat Jeff, who had apparently gone off to some specialist cheese shop. Both were into fantasy role play, not the sexual sort, but pretending to be heroes and wizards and so forth. Trolls seemed more appropriate to me, or the sort of giant that goes around saying fee-fi-fo-fum, but I kept my opinions to myself. We carried on talking, although less easily than before, and on more neutral subjects, that was until Poppy chirped up during a lull in the conversation.

'Monty'll know. Monty, what's a snerd?'

'A snerd?' Monty answered. 'That's when a girl turns out to have logs up her chute when you give her one in the dirt box.'

'And nurgle?'

'That's when you bum her anyway, your cock goes in it, and you sort of wiggle it around. Why?'

I'd gone absolutely scarlet, and put a hand up to stop Poppy saying anything more. Unfortunately Monty was far from stupid.

'Penny got it, did she? From Jeff?'

I nodded dumbly.

'Neat.'

'Where do you get these words?' Poppy asked.

'Off the net,' Monty told her. 'Some are old slang. Most of them just get made up, but if you pass them around in chatrooms and on discussion boards, people soon start using them. It's great, being able to make your own words up. I did one, dobbing, now loads of people use it.'

'Dobbing?'

'Yeah. It's when you feed a girl stuff off your cock.'

'What? Not . . .'

'No, that's a Hot Carl, or a Corn Fed Chicken, 'cause gay guys say a Hot Carl's when you –'

'I'm not sure I want to know!' I managed.

'Suit yourself, anyway, dobbing's with peanut butter, or jam, shit like that.'

The buzzer went again. Monty answered it, letting Jeff up, briefly, before we left. It didn't surprise me at all to learn that Monty was coming with us. I ended up in the back of the car as we drove north, the two of them talking in a more or less continuous stream, most of which was meaningless to me. I sat back, watching the scenery and trying to ignore the smell of the cheeses Jeff had bought. There were several, but the really bad one was a Vacherin, as he had explained to Monty. It smelt like a year's worth of old socks.

My bottom was still sore and I still had the faint background need for sex. Unfortunately I couldn't see how I could find a moment to play with Jade with Monty and Jeff around. Not that she was completely averse to sex with men, but when it did happen she was generally very drunk, or had to find herself a pretty good excuse. What she would do was watch if I let them have me.

It would fill her with a sort of horrified delight, much the same response some people give to watching a scary movie. I knew what would be going on in her head, with my humiliation a substitute for her own. Meanwhile, I would get as big a kick from having her see what was done to me, as having it done. In that sense, Monty and Jeff were perfect, just about as inappropriate as they could be. It was only a shame they weren't both in their sixties and our uncles.

By the time we got to Jade's I was determined on it, and on what I wanted done to me. I'd been thinking about Monty's bizarre invention of a word, dobbing, and the more I thought about it, the more I wanted it done to me. I knew what with too.

I just took charge, knowing Jade would let me have my way if I was bossy with her. Monty and Jeff were a little surprised to be invited up, and Jade a little surprised to see them. She went into an immediate panic, trying to tidy up the mess in her flat. They failed to notice, taking the two most comfortable chairs and asking her if there was a coffee going. She went into the kitchen and I decided to act.

'Right, you two,' I ordered. 'It's time to finish what Jeff started this morning.'

'What?' he demanded.

'Me,' I told him. 'You're going to dob me, both of you, in front of Jade.'

'Shit!'

'No, Vacherin cheese. Go and get it.'

'But we just came . . .'

'Go and get it, I said. Monty, get your cock out.'

'What, you really want a dobbing?'

'Yes. I'm going to give you a nice suck, then you can feed me the Vacherin, okay?'

'Fucking right!'

Never one to turn down a good offer, he immediately began to struggle with his trousers, which meant lying back in the seat to get his gut out of the way. His cock came out as the door slammed behind Jeff, thick and ugly, the red tip emerging from his foreskin as he peeled it back. I went down to my knees, to take it in my mouth, even as I heard Jade's voice from behind me.

'Penny? What's . . . Penny!'

I ignored her, sucking hard at Monty's cock and swallowing down the thick male taste. He spoke.

'Search me.'

She said nothing, but she stayed. They'd met just minutes before, and now she was watching me, her girlfriend, suck on his cock. I could just imagine her feelings, and her concern for herself. I pulled up.

'They're going to punish me,' I told her. 'Watch, please?'

Her response was a nod. She was staring, her eyes fixed on Monty's fat, wet penis as it lay in his lap, waiting to be taken back in my mouth. I did it, settling myself into position with my bum stuck out to make a round ball in my jeans for his pleasure. Jade was still watching, in just the sort of appalled fascination I had anticipated.

As Monty's cock stiffened I took his shaft in hand, wanking him into my mouth. Before long he was rock hard, and getting urgent too. I stopped, determined not to let him come and leave me frustrated once more. If I was going to be dobbed, it was sure to get messy, so I began to strip, hurrying out of my clothes, or rather Poppy's clothes, until I was nude.

It felt good, bare, to be used by two men in front of my girlfriend. I put my hands behind my head and stretched, showing off, then walked into the bathroom, beckoning them to follow. The door sounded again as I got down on the floor. Jeff appeared, holding the Vacherin.

'What . . . what are you going to do with that?' Jade demanded.

'You'll see,' he answered, and threw Monty a slightly embarrassed grin.

Sometimes men just can't do it in front of each other. Not Monty and Jeff, they simply didn't care. Monty was wanking at an impressive erection, and Jeff lost no time in pulling his own cock free. He pushed it at my face and I took it in, sucking him as I played with my boobs. Monty took the Vacherin and went to sit on the loo, his huge thighs wide, his cock and now his balls sticking out in blatant, obscene display.

Jade was in the doorway, her eyes wide, her mouth a little open. She had a T-shirt with some slogan blazoned across her chest, so taut over her boobs the letters were distorted. Her nipples were hard too, poking up under the cotton to make two tempting little humps. I gave her a wink as I let Jeff's now hard penis free of my mouth.

Monty was ready, the Vacherin box open in one hand, his cock in the other. I crawled close, sticking out my tongue as he touched his cock to the surface of the cheese. He pushed down, his helmet pressing to the thick orange crust, which split. Runny yellow cheese oozed out, around the bulbous tip, smearing his flesh and squashing out to either side. He pulled back a little, his cock leaving the cheese with a sucking noise, to pull up thick yellow strands. Again he pushed, right in this time, the whole of his cock head disappearing into the cheese, right up to his foreskin. When he took it out again he lifted, bringing up a thick blob, and pulling up yet more, so that as he lifted his erection, long, yellow streamers were hanging down from the head. I swallowed hard.

'Quick,' he said, 'or it'll fall off.'

My mouth came wide. I leaned forward, and in it went, the cheese-smeared penis filling my mouth, The smell was almost overwhelming, but the taste wasn't so bad. I began to feed, sucking the cheese off and swallowing. Monty groaned in pleasure. I pulled back. His cock went into the cheese again, and back into my mouth.

I was being dobbed, and it felt glorious. I would come, when I was ready, used and dirty on the floor, with two big erections to play with. Jeff was ready, and came to sit on the bath. Monty passed the Vacherin, Jeff stuck his cock in to pull out a thick, sticky blob, and in my mouth it went. Now I had both.

Soon I was getting really into it, proper cock worship, sucking and licking at their erections as they fed me the cheese. They shared me fairly, Jade watching all the time, as again and again their cocks were dipped into the Vacherin, now a pool of sticky yellow fluid within its crust and the surrounding ring of bark. Soon I was dizzy with it, and badly in need of my orgasm.

'Okay, boys,' I offered. 'I'm all yours, anything.'

'Nice,' Monty drawled, 'get your face back on my cock then.'

Jeff came around behind me, cock in hand, wanking himself as his eyes feasted on my naked body. I knew what he wanted, and sure enough.

'I'm going to bugger her,' he announced. 'I love her arsehole.'

I nodded and cocked my bottom up, offering my anus for entry.

'Pass the cheese.'

Monty held out the Vacherin box. Jeff dipped a finger in, scooping out a thick clot, which went straight between my spread cheeks, to sit, warm and sticky on my bumhole. He took more, smearing it over his cock even as he shuffled up close to me. His cock found my bum crease, then the hole. I felt the cheese squash out around my anal ring as he pushed, and tried to relax. It stung a little, from earlier, but I ignored the pain. I wanted him up my bumhole, and this time I wanted to come as I was buggered.

He pushed again, harder. I winced, but forced myself to let my hole push out. There was a thick, soft squelch as my ring gave way, and he was up me, my bumhole stretched around his cock head. I felt the cheese squash out around his shaft as he forced himself deep, my bumhole closing slightly on the neck of his cock.

'Suck,' Monty demanded, once more offering me his own cheese-smeared erection.

I took it in again, sucking eagerly as Jeff slowly forced my passage. He'd got me slippery with cheese, and soon his balls were pressed to my sex and his fat gut was resting on my bum, just as they had that morning. They began to row me, mouth and bumhole, keeping the pace even to make my body rock back and forth and set my tits swinging under my chest. I wanted to come like that, well filled with cock at both ends, my only regret that there wasn't a third man to fill up my pussy.

They had me, stuck on their cocks, well enough supported to let me frig. My hand went back, to find my pussy wet and puffy, my hole clogged with a piece of Vacherin that had squeezed down from my well-buggered anus. I touched Jeff's cock, feeling the thick shaft and the straining skin of my penetrated hole. I took his balls, rubbing the fat, hairy sack on my sex, to smear the cheese and juice over myself. He gave a grunt of complaint, but I ignored him, holding his balls to my pussy as Monty stuck his cheese-stained cock in my mouth just one more time.

I was nearly there, my clitty bumping about under the rough skin of Jeff's ball sack, his hair tickling, his cock bloating out my rectum. Monty took hold of my head, to fuck my mouth. I stuffed a ball up my empty pussy hole, feeling the entrance fill. Again Jeff protested, but I had to come, my fingers locked on his balls as I used his scrotum to rub myself. They'd used me so badly . . .

No, I'd used myself, demanding to be dobbed, making my girlfriend watch as I deliberately subjected myself to being fed cheese off two fat men's cocks, to being buggered in it as I sucked, a penis in each end, filthy with rich, smelly cheese, my body utterly soiled, and I'd done it to myself . . .

I came, my bumhole tightening on Jeff's cock, his fat balls squeezing out of my pussy as I contracted. He grunted in pain as my nails dug into the flesh of his scrotum, but my anus was in spasm on the cock shaft and he was not even trying to pull away. Instead he pushed in, once, hard, then in a sudden flurry, and right at the peak of my orgasm I knew he had spunked up in my bottom hole.

Perfection would have been for Monty to do it in my mouth at the same instant. He didn't, and he was still happily fucking my head as I came down. I kept sucking, for all my exhaustion. Jeff took my bum cheeks, spreading them with his thumbs as he eased his cock from my anus. I pulled close to Monty, squatting down, my buggered bottom stuck out behind, cheese and sperm oozing slowly from the hole.

Monty's hand closed in my hair. I looked up as I was pulled off his cock. His face was red, with beads of sweat running down over his forehead and the fat cheeks. He took his cock, wanking it as he held my head, and I realised I was to be given a sperm facial. Then he had let go of me and taken the cheese. He dug his fingers in, to scoop the remains of the Vacherin out of its box, a mess of orange crust and yellow slime. It went to his cock, folded around it and he was wanking again, now with cheese squeezing out between his fingers.

I gaped wide, willing for whatever fate he had in mind for me. He immediately squeezed the cheese forward, encasing his bulbous cock head, and stuck the lot in my mouth. I was gagging immediately, my throat blocked with cheese and cock, well past my tonsils. He groaned as my throat went into helpless, agonising spasm on his helmet, his cock head burst the cheese crust in my gullet, and suddenly I had received the full load of his come down my throat.

It was too much, far too much. My stomach contracted violently. I lurched back. His cock came out of my throat with a sticky noise and my mouth was filling with sick. I held it, somehow, clapping my hand to my mouth as I struggled to swallow the filthy mess in it once again. Monty snatched my hand away, pulled hard, and once again my mouth was full of cock. His hand twisted tight into my hair, the fucking motions began again and once more my stomach revolted.

He just held me, finishing himself off in my mouth, indifferent to the frantic hammering of my fists on his legs, or the filthy mess bubbling out of my nose and the corners of my mouth. I couldn't breathe at all, with my mouth and throat and nose clogged with the sticky mess of Vacherin and puke I'd brought up. He didn't care, he just held me tight, and only pulled out when he had finished completely. Even then he held my jaw to force me to clean off his cock as it came free.

Half the Vacherin crust was still in my mouth, and it was more than I could do to swallow it. It came out, falling to the floor at Monty's feet. I stayed down, gasping for breath, with sperm and saliva and mucus and cheese mess dripping from my mouth and nose. Jade spoke.

'Penny? Are you all right.'

I managed a feeble nod.

'Gagged on your cock did she, Monty?' Jeff asked.

'She was sick on it,' Monty said proudly. 'We've got to have a name for that one, maybe a Reverse Carl?'

Seven

I suppose I had got what I asked for, and both Natasha and Gabrielle had warned me that Monty had a nasty habit of getting girls into a submissive state and then going a lot further than they expected. So I tried not to be resentful, although that was not particularly easy when it was me who ended up cleaning the mess on the bathroom floor.

By the time I'd done that, still in the nude, washed and recovered myself, Monty and Jeff had managed to talk Jade into attending the Night of the Clowns. She'd been turned on by watching what had happened to me, and was in that state of mixed arousal and apprehension I knew so well.

Their games always following the same formula, with men and sometimes women hunting girls in some form of competition, where the prize for the winning hunter is also the punishment for the losing girl. Given Jeff's obsession with clowns, I was assuming that they would be in 'scary clown' outfits and make-up, hunting us with paintball guns. I knew the idea, that clowns are somehow supposed to be horrifying, but it had never affected me. Certainly, the idea of Jeff leaping out on me with a paintball gun was no more terrifying with him in a clown outfit than in his normal phoney battle gear. On the other hand, if it played to their childish sense of humour, that was fine by me. I could scream and run with the best of them and, if I lost, the punishment would be no less painful, humiliating and exquisite then usual.

I couldn't have been more wrong. As I should have realised after being put in a girl's clown outfit that morning, it wasn't the men who were going to be dressed as clowns. It was us.

We didn't find out until we reached the industrial estate. It was somewhere in north-east London, but after having Jade in the back with me and in such high spirits I wasn't sure exactly where. It was huge place, a great maze of brick and breeze block buildings, some old, some not yet finished. There was security, of sorts, a greasy-looking man seated in a hut at the gates. He obviously knew what was going on, as he greeted Jeff with a dirty leer and a thumbs-up signal. I managed a smile, faintly sure that by the end of the night either Sophie or I would have been made to thank him, probably by sucking his cock.

Sophie was already there, looking as if butter wouldn't melt in her mouth with her neat blonde hair and sweet, pretty face. She was in a jumper and jeans, as were Jade and I, all looking completely normal. We greeted her with nervous kisses and hugs, and it occurred to me that anyone passing the three of us in the street would never have suspected for an instant that our sex lives were anything but completely normal either.

Whatever the boys had planned for us was going to be anything but normal. We were in a big warehouse, empty but for one corner. I knew Fat Jeff had retrieved my clown outfit, but after all it was his. It was only when he threw it across a rail on top of three others that I realised I was going to have to wear the horrible thing again. That wasn't all either. Beneath the rail were four pairs of absurd boots, in the same bright primary colours as the body suits, pink, apple green, baby blue and banana yellow. Each toe was graced with a pom-pom in a darker shade of the same colour, matching the thick laces. They were calf-length, and looked quite a snug fit to the leg, but the actual boot parts were huge, maybe size fifty, with great rounded ends big enough to get a normal person's head into, never mind her foot.

So we were going to be the clowns, and it looked like we were going to get the full clown treatment. Not that clowns usually get shot in the bottom with paintball guns. They do get whitewash poured down their trousers and custard pies pushed in their faces, and both had been provided for. Gavin Bulmer was making the custard, along with a man I didn't know. Another man was mixing up buckets of whitewash.

They were three among seven. Gavin, Fat Jeff and the weasel-like Jeff Jones I knew. One of the others had been at another event but his name escaped me. The remaining three I'd never seen before. Then there was Monty, who was the only one not in combat gear.

A door on the far side of the warehouse opened and a girl emerged, presumably Emmeline. If the three of us didn't suit the conventional image of female sexuality, then she missed it by a mile. She was smaller than any of us, maybe less than five foot, and petite, pretty, but with mousy hair and glasses, making her look intensely vulnerable.

'Emmeline,' Sophie confirmed. 'Nice girl, a bit shy.'

'But she's up for this?' Jade queried.

'She's Andy's girlfriend,' Sophie explained. 'The tall bloke with the bald spot.'

She was coming towards us, her face set in a nervous smile. So was Gavin Bulmer. He was rubbing his hands.

'So babes, ready to get clowned up?'

'Soon,' Sophie answered. 'It's a bit cold.'

'You'll warm up quick enough,' he assured us.

'How does the game work?' I asked.

'Simple,' he said. 'There's going to be a circle in the middle of this room, with custard pies and buckets of whitewash inside it. That's neutral ground. Anywhere else you can get each other . . .'

'Each other?'

'Yeah. Custard pie in the face, whitewash down the pants. We . . .'

'What about you?'

'Let me explain, will you? You've got to get each other, and fetch balloons from around the estate to bring back here. The balloons are in four colours, to go with your suits; red, blue, yellow and green. You've got to get them back here, and we try to shoot them, or shoot you so you let them go. We have to stay in the buildings, and we're not allowed in this one.'

'We'll be in goggles, I hope?' Jade queried.

'Full protective head gear,' he promised. 'What do you think I am, some sort of psycho?'

'No comment,' she answered. 'So the one who gets most balloons back wins?'

'No. A balloon is worth a point. A custard pie in the face is five points off, whitewash down the pants, ten points off. There are twenty balloons each.'

'I see. When's it over, and what happens to the loser?'

'It's over when all the balloons are in here, burst or lost. The loser gets gang-banged, second worst gets to give the best two a bit of tongue action, third has to give old Dirty Dave on the gate a blow-job. There's a grand down for the winner.'

'Gang-banged? By everyone?'

'All the guys, yeah.'

'But it's normally just the winner.'

'Well, yeah, but there isn't really a winner this way, so we thought . . .'

'Gav,' one of the others broke in, 'you got the head gear?'

'In the Jeep,' he answered. 'It's locked. I'll sort it.'

He wandered off, leaving us to contemplate our fate. I know my luck. I was likely to get fucked by eight men or end up sucking Dirty Dave's cock. Then there were the paintballs, which hurt like hell, although when we play I always get an awful compulsion to tease with my bottom – and get shot there. It was heavier than I'd expected, and typically sadistic, enough to fill my stomach with butterflies. We had to gang up on each other to avoid defeat, which was going to mean alliances and betrayal, something I was sure the boys would love. It was tricky too. With the gear in the central circle we would be at our most vulnerable while coming to collect it. In order to get the balloons we were forced to go out into the night where the boys would be waiting, and possibly other girls. To win the game as it was designed was going to require a lot of tactical skill. That was not the right way to go about it.

I did not want to lose. I would have to be in a very submissive mood indeed to take on eight men, especially when four of them were complete strangers. After the game I might well be, but I'd been buggered twice, my bottom hole was painfully sore and my mouth and stomach still felt tender. It would be worse for Jade, who for all her earlier excitement was biting her lip and looking genuinely worried. Poor little Emmeline looked absolutely terrified, and I knew I couldn't bring myself to pick on her.

The only sensible thing to do was fix it for Sophie to get gang-banged, Jade to do the licking, and me to suck off Dirty Dave, maybe Emmeline. We could still put on a good show, and make it a close finish, so that the men wouldn't realise and do all four of us. I didn't feel right about taking the money, but the others could split it. I put an arm around Sophie, beckoned to Emmeline and we closed together.

'We're going to have to work this out in advance,' I whispered.

'So you're up to lose?' Sophie hissed.

'No, I thought you . . .'

'No way!'

'You've done worse, and we can split the money, or you three can share it. I'm really sore, Sophie!'

'So am I! I was at Morris' last night. I got it up the bum.'

'So did I, twice!'

'I . . . I'm not sure I could,' Emmeline put in, her voice little more than a squeak.

'I'm a lesbian!' Jade insisted. 'I can't!'

'Oh crap!' Sophie answered her. 'Don't give me that lesbian shit. I've seen you, Jade . . .'

'Look, sh!' I urged. 'We have to stick together!'

'Fine, you lose,' Sophie answered.

'Look, just ask them not to bum-shag you!' Jade hissed.

'Oh, yeah? If I say that, all eight will do it!'

'We could just refuse,' I pointed out. 'At least make them tone it down a bit.'

'If we refuse, we have to back out completely,' Sophie answered. 'Otherwise they just get carried away. I for one could do with the money.'

‘Me too,’ Jade agreed. ‘Go on, Penny, you can handle it. Look what you did earlier!’

‘Yes, and now I’m sore!’

‘What did she do?’ Sophie demanded.

‘She made Monty and Jeff feed her some stinky cheese off their cocks,’ Jade answered. ‘That’s made, M A D E, not gave in to, or was made to. She made them. It’s called dobbing.’

‘You slut!’ Sophie answered.

‘You’re one to talk, Sophie Cherwell!’

‘And Jeff had her up her bum,’ Jade added. ‘Come on, one of you has to take it. Look, how about this? The big loser gets five-hundred, the second three, the third two, the one who escapes just one?’

‘No way!’ Sophie snapped. ‘That means you get three hundred quid for licking two of us out! I’ll take it if whoever wins promises me the full grand.’

‘No way!’

‘Look . . . Sh, Gavin’s coming back.’

He was just feet away, and he was holding the most peculiar objects. They were head shields, but each had been fitted within a bulbous, plastic clown head, complete with pure white skin, thick red lips set in an idiot grin and a fat red nose. A cheap wig had been fitted to the scalp of each, in the four colours. All that would have been bizarre enough, but the eyes had been cut out to accommodate the goggles, producing a weird, insect-like effect.

‘No risk of getting hurt in these,’ Gavin explained. ‘Even your neck’s covered, and a pie in the face won’t knock them off. You all set?’

I exchanged a look with Jade. She nodded. I followed suit, as did Sophie.

‘Em?’ Gavin demanded as he set the clown heads on the ground.

‘I suppose so,’ she answered quietly.

'Good girls. Come on, then, strip down! Oh, and one other rule. Bums stay bare once you've been whitewashed.'

He gave Emmeline a resounding slap on her bottom as he turned away. She squeaked, but said nothing, and the next moment she had begun to unfasten her jeans, very hesitantly. It was impossible not to feel concerned for her, and to wonder if she'd been pushed into it. When the suggestion of backing out had come up she'd said nothing, but that didn't necessarily mean anything.

'Are you all right, Emmeline?' I asked.

She managed a weak smile and nodded. I shrugged. She was a grown woman, and she knew she could walk away. She had also giggled when Jade had mentioned my dobbing. That decided me. If me getting dobbed and buggered was funny, then she could handle whatever was coming to her, shy or not.

It was cold, and I peeled quickly, indifferent to the stares of the men. For all my aching bumhole, my sense of erotic humiliation was building. I'd still do my best, if only in the hope of leaving Sophie last. She deserved it, because she was being unfair. Morris has a pretty weedy cock. Jeff's was huge. I'd also had it twice, and she was a lot more used to rough treatment than I, and a bigger show off. It was time to think about tactics.

Gavin had implied we should go bare under our costumes, but we hadn't actually been told to. So I kept my panties in the vague hope of cushioning some of the impact of the paintballs that would undoubtedly be aimed at my bum once the flap had been opened. Gabrielle's bra was uncomfortable anyway, so I took that off, giving the boys a deliberate flash of my tits in the faint hope it might do me some good.

I'd been in pink before, so I chose the same outfit, extremely grateful that this time I didn't have to risk being seen in public in it. I was still going to get laughed at, humiliated in front of an audience and possibly fucked by eight men, but I knew in the end that would bring me to orgasm. With the full costume I still felt utterly ridiculous and extremely vulnerable. I could only walk in an idiotic, flat-footed waddle, with my shoes stuck out at right angles to each other. Running was out of the question.

Jade had chosen yellow, Sophie blue, leaving Emmeline in the green. All three of them looked pretty put upon, and obviously felt as foolish as I did, but Jade was in a class of her own. The costume simply could not accommodate her boobs, and they were bulging out the front of her clown suit like two squashy yellow water balloons. Sophie was better, but still looked rude, while Emmeline was pretty well swamped. Even with the ridiculous clown heads on it was going to be easy to tell who was who without remembering the colours.

The man who'd been mixing the whitewash had gone to paint a circle on the floor, while others were carrying equipment to it. There was a table for the pies, and a clothes rail to fix our balloons to. The buckets were on the floor, twelve of them, all huge and all full of whitewash. I saw Fat Jeff straining as he carried two of them over, and realised that I would probably need both hands to lift a single one. If I wanted to get Sophie I would need the other two to help.

I'd finished, and Emmeline was still doing up her boots. I crossed to Jade and drew Sophie in with us. A moment later we'd agreed to catch Emmeline, drag her in and give her the full treatment. As Sophie struggled to get her clown head on I had a brief word with Emmeline.

With my own head on I made my way to the centre circle, just as two of the boys pulled up the big roller door. Outside it was dark, the estate lit dull orange by the dim security lights. A trio of tower blocks could be seen, but they were too far away to matter. Otherwise there was darkness beyond a high wall topped with jagged glass. We were sealed in, safe, which was a great relief.

In the heads we looked more inane still, and less individual; comic girls, with all the emphasis on our tits and bums, sexual, yet absurd, and therefore completely unthreatening. So many men adore putting women in that sort of role, and I have to confess it gets to me. I could be fucked, anonymously, my flap unbuttoned and my bum exposed, my pussy made available, without the man even knowing who I was.

There was no referee, just Gavin, who stayed after the others had dispersed, long enough to give us a final dirty grin before he blew a whistle and stepped out into the night. Emmeline immediately tried to run, her huge green shoes slapping loud on the concrete floor. Jade and Sophie followed, as agreed, me lurching after them with one of the huge whitewash buckets.

They caught her before she made the outdoors. I heard male laughter as I staggered up to the others. Emmeline was struggling, trying to stop Sophie from undoing her flap. I put the bucket down, stepped forward, tweaked one button open. Emmeline screamed in indignation, my signal. I grabbed Sophie's arm, jerking her sideways. She came, off balance, and Jade was on her, the two of them tumbling down together. I snatched at Sophie's flap, taking her weight as she went down under Jade. It tore, and she had her bottom showing, plump and cheeky and bare.

Emmeline was supposed to help, but just ran. Sophie was howling with fury, and fighting, but Jade was heavier, and on top. I snatched for the whitewash, tipped, and Sophie got the lot, the full contents of the bucket down her trousers, soaking her bare bum and the costume too, not to mention my legs and Jade's own seat.

I was laughing as I jumped back, dropping the bucket. Sophie was cursing me, Jade and Emmeline, but she was done, her bottom filthy, her costume soaked. It would slow her down too, and she was sure to lose. I waddled away, leaving her and Jade grappling on the floor. One of the pink balloons was just metres away, tied to the handle of a wheelbarrow, but they were still fighting. I made for the circle, padding frantically across, to grab two pies. Both noticed, trying to rise but slipping in the pool of whitewash. I got Jade, full in her ridiculous clown face, then Sophie, and waddled off into the night.

They couldn't follow, not without ammunition, and I was around the corner and into an alley beside the warehouse before they got back. There was a pink balloon, fixed to the barbed wire on top of the wall. I reached up, tugging it loose, and jerked back as a splash of brilliant yellow paint exploded just inches from my fingers. The balloon drifted up into the sky.

I couldn't even see the hunter, but moved on, away from pursuit. The balloon didn't matter. Sophie was fifteen points down, an impossible amount to make up, so long as I stayed clean. I was determined to do exactly that, but as I rounded the back of the warehouse I realised I'd made a serious mistake.

There was no way out. A gate of iron mesh closed off the end of a car park. It was hung with balloons. I hesitated, then went back, sure I would run into Jade and Sophie coming the other way fully armed. I didn't, and as I reached the end of the alley I saw a green balloon rising into the sky, to disappear quickly into the darkness.

They'd caught Emmeline. She was struggling frantically in Jade's grip, but she could do nothing. They weren't even hurrying. Sophie had a bucket, but had put it down to undo poor Emmeline's bottom panel. I watched, pressed into the shadows as one button, a second, and a third were popped open with deliberate slowness. With each one Emmeline's kicking grew more desperate, her squeals louder. Her clown head fell off in her desperate attempts to break free, but still they held on. The fourth button went, the panel fell, and her pert little bottom was revealed within Emmeline's clown costume, quite bare.

Emmeline went crazy, thrashing in Jade's grip, her face set in rigid consternation. Sophie picked the bucket up, holding it to make sure Emmeline got a good view, and began to tip. Emmeline gave a wail of despair as whitewash splashed over her bare bottom and it then was too late. She went silent and stayed still as the entire bucket was emptied slowly down her clown trousers, with whitewash pouring out of the leg holes and soaking quickly into the material.

Jade let go. Emmeline staggered back, her face set in disgust and outrage. She was dripping, her whole lower body soiled, whitewash even soaking through around her pussy. Looking thoroughly fed up, she bent to retrieve her clown head. It was impossible not to laugh, but as I caught the sound of my own muffled giggle I realised that there was a hysterical edge to it. I was next.

If they caught me. They'd gone back for more stuff, leaving Emmeline standing in the middle of the yard, a bedraggled mess. I moved, into the shadow of a pile of breezeblocks. Ducked down, I waited, watching as

Jade and Sophie emerged from the warehouse and disappeared down the alley, flapping slowly along in their absurd clown shoes. Jade had a bucket, Sophie two pies.

There was a pink balloon just metres away, but I knew at least one of the men had the yard covered, maybe two. I had to try, and waddled quickly to it, praying their attention was still on Emmeline, who had gone into the warehouse. It wasn't. No sooner had I tweaked the balloon loose than a paintball hummed past me. I dashed for the warehouse, my feet cocked sideways to stop me tripping over my own shoes. A paintball burst on the ground, another on the pile of breezeblocks, their aim probably spoiled by their helpless laughter at my appearance.

I made the warehouse with a burst of elation and relief, quickly stifled as Emmeline's pie caught me full in the face. Suddenly I was blind, my goggles completely obscured by custard. I tripped, still clutching the balloon, and went down. I felt her fingers on my bum, groping for a button. I rolled, snatching at my clown head. One lens cleared to a yellow blur and I was crawling, with Emmeline clutching at the seat of my costume. It tore, my panties were showing. I lashed out in desperation. Emmeline went down, I was on my feet and a moment later fixing the balloon to the rail.

Emmeline hadn't even had a bucket, but she had torn three of the four buttons from my bum panel. So I had my panties showing, and a custard pie in the face, but I was still ahead. I paused to clean my goggles and get my breath back. The costume felt hot and sticky, despite the cool night. I was sweating, my legs aching from the sheer effort of moving in the ridiculous shoes.

I could hear the pops of the paintball guns from behind the warehouse. Jade and Sophie were braving the dead end, but it was a fools' game. All the balloons were on the gate at the end, and to get them back they had to run a gauntlet, which was going to be painful and probably futile. Yet I too would have to do it, with maybe five of my precious pink balloons fixed to the gate.

Only there was another way. Emmeline had fled, but I took a pie just in case, and set off, not into the yard, but through the buildings. All were open, and connected by passageways and doors. I made the main yard, which was empty, the balloons bobbing in the light breeze. The hut in which Dave the gateman was sitting was visible, and so was he, the light inside glinting off his greasy hair. I moved forward, ducked low, from one piece of cover to the next. Laughter, the pop of the guns and the occasional female shriek sounded faint behind me.

I reached Dave's shed, passed it in a crouch, and I was through, into the maze of warehouses, compounds, car parks and alleys outside the estate. It was empty, deserted, and I walked as casually as I could, silent save for the occasional plop as a bit of custard detached itself from my clown face. In maybe five minutes I was at the back gate to our estate. The dead end was now empty, but colourful with paintball splats and bit of yellow and blue balloon showing in the bright security lights. My pink ones were still there, all five. Getting them over the gate wasn't easy, but I managed, and was soon heading back the way I'd come.

The car came as a complete surprise, headlights illuminating a wall well ahead of me, then turning into my alley. There was nothing I could do. I was caught, blinded by the light, escape impossible in my cumbersome clown shoes. So I just stood there, holding the balloons and the pie, undoubtedly looking a complete idiot.

They drove straight past. What they thought a small and obviously female clown was doing on a deserted trading estate in the middle of the night I could only guess. The car was a black BMW, quite new, but going slowly, and as it passed I saw two figures within. They couldn't be joy riders, not at five mph, which meant a couple, maybe adulterous, maybe a kerb-crawler and a girl, maybe just courting. In any case there was nothing I could do but continue, as fast as I could, in the hope that they wouldn't decide to turn back and interfere with me.

They didn't, and I made the gate and sneaked past Dave's box without trouble. Back in the estate the game had dissolved into chaos. All three girls were in the main yard, desperately trying to get their balloons. It was hopeless. The boys had them at an impossible disadvantage, able to get off shot after shot. Emmeline had caught a pie across her chest at some point, leaving her tiny pointed tits sticking up under custard-plastered cotton. Jade had had her bum stripped but not whitewashed. She'd been hit, though, both buttocks spattered with paintball dye. Sophie and Emmeline were worse, their bottoms filthy with dye and whitewash, their costumes ruined, their clown heads a mess of colour.

All I had to do was get back to the circle and I was sure to win. It proved easy, the boys too busy with the others to notice me as I crept around the edge. I knew where the boys were too, using the empty window squares in the buildings to fire from. One was close, and as I entered the safety of a covered passage I found myself behind him. Peering through a door, I made out a bulky shadow against the dull orange light from outside. It had to be Monty or Fat Jeff, and it was too much to resist. I made for him, step by cautious step, close, closer still, and close enough to give him my custard pie full in the face from behind.

He nearly jumped through the roof, but I was already away, giggling as I made for the door. I needn't have worried about pursuit, having covered his goggles with custard and blocked his breathing holes, to leave him gasping and blowing and clawing at the mess on his face.

I was laughing so hard I could barely stand as I made for the original warehouse and the circle. It was empty, so I tied off my balloons and paused to take a drink of beer from the cases the boys had stacked up for afterwards. It was pretty horrible, but cold and refreshing, which was exactly what I needed. I had six balloons and, with one gone, that left thirteen. I might get none, I might get some, but it was hard to see how I could fail to win. Only three other balloons were on the rail, two yellow, one blue. That put Jade second and left her with the prospect of sucking Dave off, something I was going to thoroughly enjoy watching.

They came back as I was finishing the beer, Jade and Sophie, both dripping dye and limping from the battering their bare bums had taken. The moment they saw me they came at me, both screaming for the other to fetch the whitewash. I made for the corridor, Sophie chasing me in a sort of slow motion pantomime of pursuit as Jade went for a bucket.

There was no way they were going to catch me. Sure enough, I made the yard, my fear growing abruptly as I saw the splats of paint and bits of coloured rubber. It had to be done, and I went straight for the balloons. The instant I touched the first I was met with a hail of paintballs. My leg was hit, my back, my chest and I doubled up. Immediately one caught my bare flesh, right between my bum cheeks, to make me scream and go into a completely involuntary, flapping, waddling dance of pain.

Their laughter at my absurd antics saved me further hits, but my balloon was gone. It didn't matter. All I had to do was release them. It was going to hurt, a lot, and my fear and sense of humiliation was coming back with a vengeance as I padded frantically around the yard, trying pathetically to cover my bum with one hand. As I touched each balloon I was shot, repeatedly, leaving me jumping and squealing to the impacts and clutching at my bottom and boobs. Still I waddled from one to the next, snatching at each, dizzy with pain. Soon I'd lost all reason, save that tiny spark that kept me going for the balloons. My bottom was a mess of paint and throbbing with bruises, my boobs, tummy and back not much better with just the thin cotton of the clown outfit to cover me. A ball had burst across my goggles and I could only see with one eye, while my whole body was slick and slippery with sweat and vegetable dye.

I quickly lost count, again and again jumping to the pain of the paintballs as they smacked into my flesh, until it was all I could do to stand. The boys were laughing at me, the girls too, from under a light near Dave's box. The sound came high and mocking through the haze of my pain, mingled with the hum and splat of paintballs, each one bringing me a new jolt of fear and panic. All I could think off was that if I got more balloons it would stop, and at last, it did.

I collapsed, battered but victorious, my mouth curving slowly up into a delighted grin as I thought of watching Sophie gang-banged. It was immensely satisfying, but as I raised my head to look at her I realised I was wrong. The girls had a bucket of whitewash, and they were guarding a balloon, my last. My grin vanished.

The moment the balloon came loose, I had won. I stood, swaying on my feet. My bottom was throbbing with pain, feeling fat and swollen behind me, hot and ready for penetration, up either hole, or both. I still wanted Sophie to get it, my determination outweighing my need for submission. I knew it wouldn't last.

I started forward, my huge shoes slapping on the concrete, the paintball dye squelching in my clown suit. They got ready for me, arms spread, manic red grins and goggle eyes fixed to my body. We met. Sophie grabbed me, and Emmeline. I wrenched myself forward. One let go, the other didn't. I swung around, clutching for the balloon string and missing by inches. Jade grappled my arm.

They had me, Jade and Sophie, clinging to my arms. I struggled, kicking out, wiggling my bottom in a frantic, futile effort to stop Emmeline getting the whitewash down my trousers. Jade twisted my arm, hard. I squeaked in pain as it was forced high up my back and locked in place, one-handed. I was held, still kicking and wriggling, but helpless. Jade laughed as she took hold of the waistband of my panties.

I hung my head in defeat as she pulled open the back of my panties, holding them out with her hand. Emmeline chuckled, then grunted with effort as she lifted the bucket, and tipped. In went the whitewash, cold and, as it splashed over my bottom, my eyes screwed up in disgust, male laughter sounded from behind me, and female, my persecutors dissolving in giggles as my panty pouch filled and overflowed.

They gave me the whole bucket, poured slowly down the back of my panties, with my pouch overflowing to run down the inside of my clown trousers. It had quickly soaked in between my bum cheeks, and over my pussy, to trickle down my thighs and drip from the front of my knicks. My face stayed screwed up throughout, set in disgust and humiliation, until at last I was done and Emmeline put the whitewash bucket on my head.

Even when they let go I just slumped down, totally defeated, with the whitewash squelching in my sodden panties and trickling slowly down my neck and into my clown head through the breathing holes. Only when somebody took the bucket off my head did I rise, to grope for the balloon string and tweak it free. A cheer went up from the boys.

I pulled my clown head off with aching arms. I was soiled, exhausted and bruised. I was also aroused, and ready for fucking, but with six balloons I knew I hadn't lost. There would be no gang-bang for me, but I was too exhausted to calculate what was going to happen.

Fat Jeff lent me a shoulder as we staggered back to the first warehouse. There was water there, and I washed my face, but was stopped by Gavin when I began to remove my clown outfit.

'Punishments first,' he said, wagging a finger at me.

'You're going to have us like this?' I demanded.

'Oh, yes,' he answered happily.

'You are a pervert, Gavin Bulmer.'

He just grinned. The others were no better. Monty was rubbing his hands in glee. Fat Jeff was picking bits of custard and pie crust off his goggles but he was still smiling. The others looked nervous but excited. I sat down and immediately regretted it as the mess in my panties squelched underneath me, filling the mouth of my pussy with thick, cold whitewash.

'Let's see, then,' Gavin stated, turning to the circle. 'Six balloons, Penny? Nice work, you'd be good at urban guerrilla games, you would. Still, you got the pie and the whitewash, so six minus fifteen gives you a score of minus nine. Whoops.'

He nodded and made a mark in the notebook he had pulled from a pocket, then went on.

'Jade, two balloons and a face full, so two less five makes minus three. Not bad. Sophie, one balloon and the full works, and one minus fifteen is minus fourteen. Not good. Emmeline, no balloons and the whitewash, but you saved your face. Zero minus ten is minus ten. We get Sophie, boys!'

Every single one of them had turned to her, some lustful, some shifty or guilty, every one eager, every one with his eyes fixed to where the rounded balls of her breasts showed beneath the sodden blue costume. She had taken her clown head off, revealing her face, streaked with sweat, her make-up a ruin, her blonde hair plastered to her cheeks and forehead. Her mouth came open as she took in the eight men who were going to fuck her, then she turned to me.

'I'll get you for this, Penny Birch.'

I shrugged. Gavin stepped forward, holding a small knife. Taking the front of Sophie's costume, he cut a careful slit, then pulled it wide, ripping the cloth. She gasped as her chest was exposed, but there was more arousal than shock in her tone. I made myself as comfortable as I could, eager to watch, and at once wishing it was me and extremely grateful that it wasn't.

Most of the boys weren't used to it, I could tell. Monty was more than happy, with his cock ands balls hanging out of his fly, nursing himself to erection as he admired Sophie's body. Gavin and the two Jeffs were squeezing their cocks through their trousers, but the others looked pretty sheepish, while Emmeline's boyfriend was having a whispered and urgent conversation with her in one corner.

Sophie saw the problem. She sighed, walked over to a chair beside the stack of beer cases and sat down. She pushed her bottom out. Her bum cheeks peeled apart with a sticky sound as she pushed it all out through the hole in her clown costume. The pose left her pussy showing, her pubic hair clogged white and filthy, the hole an oval of pink flesh at the centre. Her bumhole showed too, pink and glossy with sweat, then hidden as a trickle of whitewash ran into it. Her ring tightened at the cool touch, then opened again. A little bubble appeared briefly in the whitewash before bursting to leaving the pink dimple at the very centre of her anus showing once more, even as whitewash trickled into her open pussy hole. She smiled and winked at Gavin, then spoke.

'Well, boys? Come and get me, if you're man enough.'

I could see what she was doing. A lot of laddish types simply can't handle rude, open female sexuality. They wanted her willing but pliable, a pretty doll to stick their cocks in, not aggressive.

Sometimes it might have worked, but not now. She'd had her back to Monty, and his cock was already stiff in his hand. He didn't wait to be invited twice, but lumbered up behind her, wanking as he came. She only realised when he was about a foot away, and turned with a squeak of surprise. The next moment he had her by the hips and was pulling her towards him. She squeaked again as his erection pressed between her slimy bottom cheeks, and as he lifted her bodily. He was already rutting in her bum crease as he lowered her to the floor, and her weak protests were completely ignored as he adjusted himself and slid his cock up into her body.

'Ah, cunt!' he sighed, and began to fuck her.

It broke the spell on the others, most hurrying forward to get their places. Gavin got there first, only to be shouldered aside by Fat Jeff. Both hurried to get their cocks out, but Gavin was first and had quickly pulled Sophie's head around by the hair. A fresh squeak of protest from her broke off as her mouth was filled with cock, and Jeff was forced to content himself with fondling one dangling boob as he wanked at his penis.

Monty was going strong, his fat gut quivering to his pushes along with the flesh of Sophie's bottom as she was fucked, his face red and sweating with the effort. Jeff Jones had come close, and was watching Sophie's buttocks move as he stroked his still hidden cock. Another man came beside her, to feel her spare tit.

I was beginning to want to get my hands down my panties, but I didn't need to, not when pretty little Emmeline had to lick my pussy for me. She looked uncertain, kneeling to one side in wide-eyed shock as she watched Sophie fucked. I could only pray she wouldn't chicken out, and enjoy the view.

It was getting good. Monty was absolutely hammering into her, his face the colour of a beetroot. He was jamming her body back and forth so hard that she was having serious trouble sucking Gavin's cock, except that he had her by the hair and was fucking her head. I really wasn't sure if Monty was going to make it, but he did, whipping his cock out at the last second to spray come all over Sophie's slimy bottom, both on the glossy, whitewashed cheeks, in the crease and over her pussy. He finished off rubbing his cock on her bumhole and flopped back, to sit wheezing on the ground.

None of the others seemed all that keen on sticking their cocks in her sperm-sodden pussy, except Fat Jeff, who had scrambled around in an instant. There was a loud squelch and a truly obscene bubbling noise as he jammed himself up her, and she was being fucked once more, as hard as before. He'd barely got his rhythm when Gavin came, jerking her head back to do it in her face and catching her in both eyes. She was left blinded, with two thick lenses of come rolling slowly down over her scrunched-up eyelids and a long streak joining them across her nose.

Jeff Jones didn't even give her a chance to wipe her eyes, but stuck his already hard cock in her mouth. She tried to pull back, but he took her by the ears, holding her head onto his erection with her cheeks bulging like a chipmunk's. He had it well in, and it didn't surprise me at all when she started to gag on it. She began to bat on the floor with her hands, but he was lost to the world, his head thrown back in ecstasy as her throat went into spasm on his cock. He groaned; I realised he'd come. The next second a great gush of sperm and saliva and mucus exploded from Sophie's nose and around her lips, then from the mouth of her cunt as Fat Jeff spunked inside her. Both pulled back, to leave Sophie coughing and spluttering on the floor, sperm and juice running from mouth, nose and cunt, blinded and choking.

The others held back, uncertain, one looking pretty angrily at Gavin and Jeff Jones, who were laughing together over Sophie's plight. It didn't stop him putting his cock in her mouth the instant she'd recovered her breath. She took it like a brave girl, sucking, and a moment later wiggling her bottom to invite rear entry. I gave her a clap and a cheer, which she deserved, and Jade joined in.

Emmeline didn't, because she was down on Andy's cock, kneeling at his feet with as much of his erection as would go in her mouth. He looked ready, and I thought he was going to come when he gently detached himself from her and walked quickly to

Sophie. He didn't fuck her, but began to jerk his cock over her upturned bum as his eyes feasted on the slimy, sperm-soiled globes of her cheeks. A moment later he'd added his own sperm to Monty's.

That left two, the least confident. One was at least trying to get his cock hard, the other just standing there, looking feeble. The guy in Sophie's mouth came, she swallowed and released him, then sat back to use the sleeve of her clown costume to wipe the sperm from her eyes. One eye seemed to be gummed shut. The other came open a crack. She beckoned to the last two men. Both came. Sophie twitched her thumb back to indicate her bottom to the one who was wanking himself, and opened her mouth for the other. He obliged, pulling out a big, limp penis, which she took in.

Before long the other man was in her, and they were rocking her slowly between them. She had begun to masturbate, and I wanted the same. I put up my legs, opening them wide, and leaned back against the wall, my pussy open. Emmeline had been watching Jade and me, and went abruptly red. I beckoned to her. She came, on faltering steps and biting her lips. Hoping I could simply take charge, I clicked my fingers and pointed to my pussy. She went down, right down, curled up with her little bottom stuck out behind her, her face just inches from my sex.

She wasn't going to do it, not without prompting; she needed the responsibility taken out of her hands. I was glad to take it, and took her gently by the hair to pull her in to my sex. Her nose touched, her lips, her tongue, and she was licking. I relaxed, holding her gently in place and wondering if I dared make her lick my anus. The answer was probably no, but I didn't need it. I was too close.

The men were getting busy with Sophie, rocking her body between them as her flesh quivered in time.

Her boobs were swinging, the hard nipples swaying back and forth, and her little tummy shivering to each push where it hung from the tattered clown costume the man up her pussy was holding onto. She did look good, sweet despite everything, despite her inane costume, despite being covered in spunk and dye and whitewash. Her face still looked innocent, even with a fat cock stuck in her mouth, but no more innocent than the pretty, freckled visage pressed to my pussy.

I was in a sorry state myself, but with Emmeline licking my pussy and Sophie with a cock in each end I knew that for once my orgasm was not going to be over my submission. It was great to watch Sophie used, and I was thinking of the way the men's sperm had exploded from so many orifices at once when the two Jeffs had come up her. It was just a shame she hadn't had a good thick cock wedged up her bumhole at the same time. Then there was Emmeline, so sweet and pretty, with her freckles and glasses and big brown eyes. I was fairly sure she'd never licked pussy before, or not often, and now I was making her do me, holding her head in place as her tongue worked inexpertly on my clitty.

Clumsy it was, but I was going to come. My bottom cheeks started to tighten, and my thighs, my pussy to give little jolts of pleasure with each flick of Emmeline's tongue. I fixed my gaze on Sophie, delighting in how rude they had been with her, in how ridiculous she looked, how utterly degraded, sucking and fucking with come and mess dripping from every part of her body, her sole garment the wrecked blue clown outfit, and that torn to show what mattered to the men, her fat little boobs, her bum . . .

I was right at the edge when the man up her pussy grunted and pulled out. I thought he was going to come over her bottom, and that would have been enough. Instead he growled a complaint about her cunt being sloppy and pushed his erect cock to her bumhole. Up he went, hard, forcing her ring, which must have been slimy and loose already. She'd been in ecstasy, close to orgasm as she rubbed, but her single open eye popped wide as her anus was invaded. The cock flew from her mouth as it came wide in protest, only to be grabbed, jerked, and a great fountain of come to erupt full in her face. She cried out in shock, caught the second spurt in her open mouth and went into a coughing fit again, spunk spraying from around her lips. At that moment the man in her bum came, even as he struggled to force himself deeper. She was already slumping down, and as his cock slipped free her anus closed, ejecting a little spurt of dirty brown spunk.

My orgasm just hit me. It was so dirty, so utterly dirty, the perfect climax to her gang-bang, lewd and filthy and out of control. Even as she collapsed in the pool of mess beneath her I was riding a wave of pure ecstasy, with my hand locked tight in Emmeline's hair as I used her mouth and nose to frig on. Sophie was on her side by the time I'd finished, lying despoiled, thoroughly used, too far gone to even try and get up. Then it was over, and I remembered that I now had to go and suck a dirty old man's cock.

I always seem to get that, and I was smiling as I left the warehouse. There was even a trace of regret that I hadn't been given the full treatment, but not much, because I wouldn't have missed being licked by Emmeline for anything. She was so sweet, for all her lack of expertise, and clearly not at all used to licking pussy. That was nice, to think I might have been her first.

It was getting cold, and I'd taken my ordinary clothes in a bundle, despite Gavin's insistence that I go to Dave in the clown outfit. I was seriously uncomfortable, with my panties sticking to my skin, while my whole body ached and my bumhole and feet were itching unbearably. Just before I reached Dave's hut I stopped for a scratch, which was sheer bliss, although I discovered that my crease and all the little hairs around my hole were clogged with whitewash. I felt a lot better for it anyway, and I took off my shoes as well, which felt better still.

I needed to find the loos for a proper wash, but Dave had to be seen to first. He was in his hut, and had been watching me approach. He was ready too, with an open copy of *Razzle* on his desk and his cock already out. I got straight down, taking it in my mouth and struggling not to gag at the taste of hair grease and dirt. For a moment he watched me suck, then went back to *Razzle*, admiring a picture of an over-endowed blonde girl with her legs spread wide as I attended to his penis.

Being made to suck off a dirty old man is bad enough, but having him read a pornographic magazine while I do it was just too much for my sense of humiliation. I was going to masturbate, and had even put my fingers to the sticky mess of my pussy, when his cock jerked and filled my mouth with sperm. That was it, crude, quick and dirty. I decided my second orgasm could wait, and intended to give him a few pointers on basic etiquette, principally that when being sucked it is polite to pay attention to the girl doing the sucking.

I never did. Even as I began to stand the interior of the hut flared bright to approaching headlights, then blue. Dave jerked back in his seat.

'Fuck! It's the pigs!'

He didn't need to tell me. I just ran.

Eight

I had come terrifyingly close to disaster.

When I awoke the next morning, back in my flat, all I could do was stare up at the ceiling, think of what might have happened and worry if it would not still come home to roost.

The memory of my escape and journey home was like a bad dream; running down alleys in my socks with my bum bare behind, expecting the wash of headlights on my back at any moment; hiding, then dressing in the dark and damp of a tumbledown shed by some canal; finding a group of truckers gathered around a coffee stall; yellow lights flickering over my legs as I lay slumped in exhaustion in the cab of a long haul driver; taking his cock in my mouth on a lay-by somewhere along the A4.

I'd done it, through sheer determination and a big slice of luck, and it really brought home to me how big a risk I was taking. So many things could have gone wrong. If I hadn't made my little foray outside the estate, I wouldn't have known how to get away. If Dave the gateman had taken his time with me they might even have caught me down on him, and masturbating into the bargain. If I'd rescued just two fewer balloons I'd probably have been licking Jade's pussy when they arrived. Those were just a few of many possibilities.

It was my own stupid fault anyway. I hadn't even been drunk, stone cold sober in fact, just high on adrenaline from excitement and fear and the anticipation of dirty, rude sex. I could have played by the rules, taken my fair punishment if I'd lost. No, I'd had to be clever, and gang up on Sophie, then go outside to get the balloons. Presumably the couple in the car who had seen me had reported the presence of a lunatic dressed in a clown costume.

On the other hand, it might have been the noises of the paintball guns and the girls' screams that drew the attention. I didn't know, but I was very, very glad not to have been caught. The others had been, undoubtedly, and that was a serious worry.

It had been nearly midday before I woke up, and I rang Gavin Bulmer immediately. My relief on hearing his voice was immense, but nothing compared to that when he told me they had not been arrested. Apparently it had been a close thing but, for all the mess, nobody had actually been naked when the police appeared. Emmeline had still been down on Jade when they heard the car coming and saw the lights, but Sophie had managed to cover herself up in time, presumably with one of the men's coats, as her clown costume had been a write-off. It was just fortunate they were such a bunch of perverts that they'd wanted us to have sex with our clown costumes still on, not naked.

Not that it was all bad, but the good side only sank in slowly as I sat in bed drinking coffee. Gavin, both Jeffs and the other Razorback boys had been given a serious shock. All their events were cancelled, indefinitely. It was a shame, because I'd had some very strong experiences with them, but it solved one of my five problems. I unearthed my list and solemnly crossed Razorback Paintball off.

I was not in good condition. It had taken ages to get the whitewash and dye off my body, and had left me bright pink all over. That, along with my paint-ball bruises, made me look as if I'd contracted some weird infectious disease. The bruises were round, each about a centimetre across, and concentrated on my bum and around my boobs, which said a lot for the boys' shooting as I'd been jumping about like a mad rabbit. My face was all right, thanks to the clown head, but it was one more piece of good luck that had saved my hands.

Jade called me in the late afternoon, to tell me off for making her worry. I apologised and made a joke of it, suggesting she spank me next time we met up. Her answer was oddly coy, but I thought nothing of it, still too tired to worry. She'd slept with Sophie, which didn't surprise me or worry me, our relationship being completely open.

The week passed uneventfully. Tuesday was embarrassing because of my spotted bottom. Elaine accepted it with her normal patience and understanding, but did me in the kitchen with a wooden spoon instead of her hand. Afterwards I spent an hour arranging my spanking room. It had a window seat, ideal for cushions, so I could be put over there, or on the bed, or a chair. As it was only sensible to make it a functional spare room, I added a chest of drawers and prettied it up a little.

Just the knowledge that there now existed a room furnished specifically for me to be spanked in was so appealing that I stopped on the way home for a sneaky frig. It was done parked in a lonely lane with my hand down the front of my panties, and took seconds. The orgasm left me feeling more content than ever, and I knew that the next time I got it across Aunt Elaine's knee I would feel safe. Back at home I crossed her off the list after no more than a moment's hesitation.

On the Thursday I saw Marjorie Burgess, who congratulated me on my progress, as condescending as ever. I was a little surprised, as I hadn't done anything that could be considered progress except for my regular visit to Gabrielle. Certainly the rest of my weekend's activities were anything but progress from her point of view, not that she knew.

Friday delivered a nasty shock. Jade rang, full of enthusiasm as always, to say that we were going to a party, with Sophie. Unfortunately it was at the Rathwells'. I'd explained to her, and Sophie knew too, but both of them seemed to think I should get it over and done with. I tried to explain that it was all very well for her and Sophie, but she pointed out that it was my fault in the first place, implying that I should take my medicine. We ended up arguing, and with her telling me she was going with Sophie anyway and that I could do as I pleased. By then I was so angry I was shaking. I was even tempted to cross her off the list as well, telling myself I should find a quieter, more sensible girlfriend.

I couldn't bring myself to do it, but nor could I bring myself to go to the Rathwells' party. It wasn't like the six I'd attended in order to pay my debt off, supposedly. They'd been spanking parties, each with a dozen or more men, who had paid to be able to dish out bare bottom spankings to girls. I didn't really approve, as I find the idea of paid sex distasteful. Not that I'd been paid. I'd been tricked. After going over more men's laps than I could reliably count, Morris Rathwell had told me that, while he considered my debt paid, Melody didn't. So it had been for nothing, and I could not possibly go to the party, which was strictly for friends. That meant Melody firmly in charge, and my head shaved.

There was still my appointment with Gabrielle, and I had to return their clothes, so I went into London anyway, thinking black thoughts about Jade, Sophie and Melody as I stared out of the carriage window at the driving rain. It was windy too, pretty depressing weather, with the last few leaves coming down from the trees and everything looking grey and wet. By the time I got to Victoria I was completely fed up, and soaked, my umbrella having turned inside out when a gust caught me in the Buckingham Palace Road.

Monty wasn't there, which was just as well as I was simply not in the mood for him. He had been, so they already knew about the Night of the Clowns. Gabrielle and Poppy were as sympathetic as ever, listening to what I had to say and providing sensible advice where they could. At the end she suggested an afternoon in her special bedroom. I wasn't sure about it. She finds being in a nappy soothing. I find it humiliating. On the other hand, the idea of a few hours of complete peace, with Poppy on call as nurse and no responsibilities whatsoever, was seriously tempting. I voiced my reservations, to be told that what mattered was how I felt, that the nappy was optional. She told me that there was a plastic sheet on the bed anyway if I needed to wet myself, and asked if I needed spanking. I told her I might, and she understood.

So I went, stripping naked and Poppy taking all of my clothes, shutting the curtains and locking the door. The effect was immediate. It was warm, the light dim and a rich pink, while the faint sound of the rain outside only served to enhance the feeling of cosy security. I tend to think too much, my brain always full of ideas and emotions, and constantly considering the ifs and buts of life and work. The whole idea of Gabrielle's nursery environment was not to think, to relax completely.

I tried, but it was not easy. She could do it, I knew, becoming so detached that she could suck her thumb or a dummy, let Poppy feed her, wet her nappy or even do her dung in it, without feeling even slightly self-conscious. I didn't feel I could achieve that, but lying naked and curled up in her bed, I understood enough to want the same feeling.

Her aim is to escape the obligations of her place in the world, of the social pressures of simply living as we do. To the outside world her behaviour is immaculate, exactly what is expected of a successful, modern young woman. I try to be the same, but I love to break society's taboos, especially those put upon us by the papers, the women's magazines, the style fascists. Gabrielle prefers not to break them but to dispense with them, to forget them, and in her room she can.

A thumb in my mouth felt good, but slightly silly. I sucked anyway, trying to let my thoughts drift and to enjoy the feelings of warmth and security. Naked and locked in, I felt submissive, in the sense of being protected, and I let the idea grow. I knew Poppy would nurse me, change the sheets if I made a mess, wash me, powder me, spank me if she felt I needed it. I realised it was working even as I began to slip towards sleep.

When I woke up I had no idea if I'd been asleep ten minutes, or for hours. There was no clock, deliberately, and I had no idea of the time, or any way of finding out. Dim light was still filtering through the heavy curtains, and it was still raining outside. Still half-asleep, I felt delightfully warm, wonderfully snug, and so protected. I caught the faint sound of Gabrielle's voice from beyond my door and my feelings of protection grew stronger still. My thumb was still in my mouth, and I kept sucking, no longer self-conscious, just perfectly comfortable.

I must have lain like that for hours, half-awake, just watching the slow shift of the light; the murmur of the girls' voices and the patter of rain the only sounds I was conscious of. I was curled up, my knees high, one hand tucked around my waist, the other at my face, my thumb deep in my mouth. My tummy had begun to feel a little tense, my insides heavy, but I took no notice. I didn't need it.

It began to grow dark, the light fading ever so slowly, and my sense of detachment growing with the darkness. When the time came to pee, I just let it come, trickling down over my thigh, then squirting out behind me with a hiss. My mouth came open in sheer bliss at the sensation, so good, so unrestrained. My bumhole was pouting too. I didn't try and stop it, but let nature take its course. My ring came open, gaping to the gentle pressure, stretching wide. Out it came, a fat, heavy lump, squeezing between my cheeks and cutting off as my hole closed. I didn't stop, but let go the full contents of my rectum, slowly, not pushed, not held back, each piece rolling slow and sticky down my bum cheek and onto the sheet beneath. I was still peeing as I did it, a gush, then a trickle, and a last little squirt as my bumhole finally closed.

Until that moment it had been simple abandonment, but as I finished the arousal hit me like a tidal wave. I was sobbing with pleasure and shaking my head as I rolled onto my back. My bum went right in it, the mess squashing out over my cheeks, one bit lodging firmly between them. I had to touch. My hand went down, to find my pussy, moist and sensitive, a little wet with piddle but more with my natural juice. I spread my legs, wide. My other hand went down, lower, to touch the warm, tingling skin of my slippery anus, then the fat, firm lump wedged between my cheeks. One finger went up my hot, slimy bumhole, my thumb went up my pussy and I was masturbating.

There was no fantasy, no need to focus on anything but what I'd done and how it felt, not at first. With my bottom hot and wet and squashy in my own mess, my clitty burning under my finger, my head swimming with that wonderful sense of abandonment, that was all I needed. Gabrielle would have come like that. I didn't. My own dirty mind took over. I began to wish there was more, an impossible amount, enough to sit in, enough to wallow in. My dirty finger pushed in deeper, seeking in the hot embrace of my rectum, and finding.

I pushed. It started to come, squeezing down my tube. My finger came out of my hole, to the mouth, feeling my dirty little ring spread slowly open. Out it came, into my hand as my whole body started to jerk in helpless contractions. I squashed it between my cheeks, back up my filthy, slimy hole, and I was screaming, bucking and thrashing on the bed, my bottom squelching in the mess beneath me, my clitoris on fire.

My bumhole opened once more as the orgasm exploded in my head. I stuffed what came out back up, with all four fingers, penetrating myself, deep, still screaming, still writhing, my muscles locked hard, my mind fixed on the wet squashy feeling that covered my whole bottom and the burning of my sex. Peak after peak hit me, all the while with my pussy and bumhole contracting on my fingers, over and over.

It never did break, but faded, in a series of little jolts, to leaving me smiling, eyes closed, body limp, my fingers still well up myself. It felt so good, so dirty, and I even gave my bottom a little wiggle to feel the mess and remind myself I'd really done it. I had, providing a truly sublime orgasm, and I didn't even have to clean up. Even as my mind turned to Gabrielle and Poppy I heard the grate of the key as it turned in the lock. Light flooded the room and I opened my eyes, to find that it was Poppy, looking down on me, one hand on her hip. She spoke first.

'Have you . . .'

'Messed myself? Yes.'

She nodded, and disappeared, leaving the door wide open. I lay still, so happy I wanted to purr, to laugh. Gabrielle had been right, it had been exactly what I needed, and if I'd done it my own special way, then no doubt that was what she had expected. Finally enough common sense filtered back for me to realise I ought to do something.

My legs were still up, and I hadn't even messed the covers. I kicked them off, but it was all I dared. Poppy came back at that moment, now in rubber gloves and holding a big bowl. She made a face as she saw the state I was in, but came to kneel beside me.

She didn't say a word as she cleaned me up, simply doing what was necessary with a brisk, matter-of-fact efficiency. I'd been expecting giggles, jokes at my expense, empathy for the way I felt. There was none of it, and I realised that just because I'd come it didn't mean I was finished with, just the therapy. I was not going to resist. I was theirs, for anything they wanted of me. It would be a small price for what they had given me, even if I didn't take pleasure in it myself, which was unlikely.

Once she'd mopped me up I was turned off the bed, onto a plastic sheet, and sent into the bathroom, where I was told to wait. Gabrielle was in the clinic, looking very cool and demure, and barely spared me more than a glance over the top of her glasses. Despite my orgasm, I still had the delicious sense of protected submission, and waited meekly for Poppy. She soon came, to clean up, then turn to me.

'In the shower, young lady.'

I went, letting the plastic sheet fall as she turned the water on. It came, cool enough to make me start. I took the soap, intending to clean up, only for Poppy to smack my hand gently and take it away.

'None of that. I want it done properly. Hands on your head.'

I obeyed, already trembling slightly as my arms went up. She still had the gloves on, and there was no compunction about touching where she needed to, rubbery fingers quickly sliding between my bum cheeks and up into my hole. It was all I could do to control myself, with her finger wiggling about up my bottom, but I held back, letting her clean me. Every crease and fold of my bottom and sex was attended to, then the rest of my body, soaped and rinsed, soaped again and rinsed a final time. Only when I was absolutely spick and span did she let me out of the shower.

Gabrielle appeared in the doorway to watch Poppy finish up. I was towelled down, and made to bend to have my bumhole and pussy powdered. She finished with cream, slipping a finger just one joint deep up my bumhole. It was as brisk and efficient as before, even as she fingered me, but I noticed she made sure Gabrielle got a good view.

At last I was done, clean and dry, naked, powdered and creamed. Poppy took off her gloves and finished the last few tasks, never speaking, until she returned to the bathroom. She sat down on the loo and patted her lap. I was going to be spanked.

'Over my knee.'

It was less an order than a statement, delivered with absolute certainty that I would do as I was told.

I went, my bum towards Gabrielle, shivering slightly as I draped myself over my nurse's legs. She took me gently around the waist and gave me a pat on my freshly powdered bottom cheeks.

'Now,' she said. 'When you were put to bed, what did I say?'

'I . . . I don't know,' I answered, genuinely unsure what she was talking about.

'I said,' she went on, speaking slowly and with a pause between each word, 'I said that there was a plastic sheet on the bed in case you wet yourself. Wet yourself, Penny, not dirtied yourself, wet yourself. And what did you do?'

'I . . . I dirtied myself,' I managed.

'Yes,' she said. 'You dirtied yourself, didn't you? All over your sheets, and all over your bottom. You should have called for me. You should have let me put you in a nappy. But no, you didn't, did you? You are dirty, disgusting, and disobedient, so now I am going to have to spank you.'

She began, laying a firm swat across my bottom, another, and more, to set up a steady rhythm on my bare bum cheeks. It was just hard enough to make my muscles jump and draw a little grunt of shock from my mouth with each one, and as she spanked, she talked.

'You see what happens when you make a mess, Penny? Do you see what happens? You end up with a warm bottom, that's what happens. You get spanked, spanked like the dirty little brat you are!'

It got harder, and faster, the slaps of hand on bum flesh loud in the room. I began to kick my legs, and spread my thighs to the pain, heedless of what I was showing, because it simply didn't matter, not in front of her.

'I'll teach you!' she said. 'I really will. Now get that fat bottom up, high!'

I struggled to lift my bottom, desperate to show I was obedient. My cheeks spread and I was showing her my bumhole, the little rude dimple she'd just had to clean, because I was such a dirty slut.

'Good!' she snapped as she kicked a leg up to make sure my bum stayed well spread as the punishment went on. 'Show it to Gabby. Show her your spanked bottom. She gets the same. Maybe she'll learn something if she knows what she looks like while she's being spanked, how rude she looks, how silly she looks . . .'

She was right. I did look rude. I did look silly. My thighs were pumping, my cheeks bouncing wildly to the smacks, my tits quivering, my hair jumping. Worse, my pussy showed, every little pink wrinkle and fold, clit and lips and hole; and my bumhole, pink and wrinkly, winking lewdly as I abandoned myself to my pain.

'Dirty, dirty, dirty little brat!' Poppy snapped, now laying into my poor bum with all her force. 'This is going to be a lesson, such a lesson, you brat, you dirty-bottomed little tramp! Right, on your knees!'

I went, scrambling down and around, to kneel at her feet in front of the lavatory. She stood, her fingers shaking as she popped the button of her jeans wide. They came down, pushed all the way to the floor, her panties with them. Her pussy was shaved, pink and smooth, the crease moist with her need. She reached back, to lift the toilet seat, and sat down.

'That was your punishment,' she told me. 'Now you say sorry.'

My response was a weak nod. She had cocked her knees wide and slid forward, spreading her sex for my attention. I went down, poking out my tongue as I found her pussy, to lick at her pouted lips and the tiny bud between. She sighed and put her hand on my head, stroking me as I gave her what she obviously so badly needed. My bottom was warm, my head spinning with the pleasure of my own submission, my own punishment, what she'd said to me. She went on, her voice now thick with passion.

'Sorry I had to spank you, Penny. You know I had to, though, don't you? You know you need it?'

I nodded, too busy licking to answer. She made a little purring noise and cupped my head gently in her hand, holding me in place.

'You did deserve it,' she sighed. 'You deserved more, a lot more, not just having that fat little bum of yours shown off to Gabby. You like that too much, far too much ... Even if I'd used the bath brush you'd have liked it. I bet you'd have cried ... I bet you'd have blubbered, but you'd still have liked it. I should have really done you ... I should have made you clean up yourself, naked ... Yes, that's right, naked on your knees, and I should have shown you what you'd done first, like you do with dogs. Yes, that's it, I should have taken you by the scruff of your neck and shown you what you'd done ... I should have scragged you and smacked you, and held your head right over it ... and pushed your face right in the middle of the whole filthy mess! Oh Penny, you filthy, darling little slut!'

Her voice broke off, into a cry of pure, high ecstasy and she was coming, her fingers locking in my hair, her pussy in contraction in my face. I stuck to my task, licking busily and letting her build her own fantasy, my job to do as I'd been told and not make a fuss.

As she came down she gave a long, satisfied sigh. My head was pulled gently away from between her thighs and I sat back. She was smiling, as happy as I'd been myself after my own orgasm. After a long time, she spoke.

'Thank you. That was lovely, beautiful.'

'It was, and very dirty. Bad girl.'

'Look who's talking!'

I just smiled. I was thoroughly content, my bottom warm, my feelings of arousal and submission pleasantly high. It wasn't over, I was sure. Gabrielle had been very cool, watching and doing nothing, saying nothing, but I knew it would have got to her. As I stood up, she reached for my hand. Poppy followed as I was led from the room.

We went back to her special bedroom. The bed was now made again, as fresh and clean as when I'd first got in. Gabrielle sat down, and very calmly began to undress. I watched, enjoying the exposure of her slender, elegant body, her little breasts and neatly rounded bottom. Like Poppy, she was shaved, her pussy completely denuded, with just a hint of her inner labia showing between the outer.

I waited, wondering what she wanted, until she was nude. Poppy had stripped too, leaving the three of us stark naked. She went to a dresser, to pull out three fat, pink and white adult nappies. One went to Gabby, one to me. I put it on, watching Gabby to see how it was done properly, with the bulk clasped between my thighs and held in place as I did up the tabs at either side.

It felt strange, the bulging material heavy around my hips, making me very self-conscious of the fact that I was in a nappy. Gabrielle had opened her arms and I came into them, cuddling her, our flesh pressed together, her breasts pushed to mine. She rolled, pulling me in underneath her, and I spread my legs to let her get onto me. For an instant she was looking into my face, bright-eyed and smiling, and then we were kissing, our mouths open, our tongues entwined. Beside us, Poppy was putting her own nappy on.

I felt truly privileged, to be taken in by them, as an equal in their play, and I was determined to give of my best. Poppy climbed on and there were three of us on the bed, tumbling together, kissing and stroking, rubbing each other's boobs and feeling the puffy nappy material over each other's bottoms. I wanted to make Gabrielle come, to say thank you to her.

Before long I had my chance. She was on me, head to tail, her thighs wide over my head, the seat of her nappy just inches from my face. I took hold of her hips, to rub my face into the soft white material, then to pull it aside, exposing her pussy, pink and glistening and bare. My face went in and I was licking, deep in her hole, then on her clitoris. She sighed and wiggled her bottom, eager for more. I gave it, holding her firmly as I tongued her, the big nappy squashed out in my face.

She sat up, queening me, her pert bottom spread over my features, my nose pressed to her bumhole, my face smothered in thick, puffy nappy material. Poppy climbed on, to sit over my hips, pinning me down as she and Gabrielle began to kiss. It felt great, at the bottom a pile, where I belong, sexually. That they were girlfriends made it better still, with me serving them, ready to lick, as ordered.

Gabby shifted on my face and I was tonguing her bumhole, deep up, and completely abandoned to her needs. She wiggled, already sighing. I pushed my tongue deeper, pulling her hard onto my face. I felt a change in her weight, then her nappy was pulled harder against my face and I knew her hand was down the front. I kept licking, eager to make her come with my tongue up her bottom, to really say thank you, properly, the way I like to when another woman has taken me to ecstasy. She lifted, pulling against my grip. I held tight, pulling her back onto my face.

'Let me up,' she gasped. 'I need to be full . . . I want you to watch.'

'Anything,' I promised.

Her hand came back, to adjust the nappy over the swell of her bottom. She began to climb off, but Poppy spoke.

'No, Gabby, sit over her, like you are. I'll hold her down for you . . .'

'I couldn't, not if . . .'

'Do it,' I said. 'You don't need to hold me down, Poppy, you know you don't.'

'I know, but I want to . . . I want you helpless, tied . . .'

I nodded my head, reached up and opened my legs, spread-eagling myself on the bed. Gabby sat up, into a kneeling position across my waist, legs wide, bottom stuck out, the nappy thick and white and curving smoothly around her own elegant shape. She was stroking herself, slowly and gently, just enough to stay fully on heat, with one little tit cupped in a hand, her hair hanging down her back in a cascade of soft brown.

Poppy had got down, and was burrowing in a drawer. She began to pull out ribbons, thick, pink ones, made of heavy satin. I put my wrists to the bed posts, my ankles too. My breathing was getting heavy, my excitement rising, and theirs too, Gabrielle masturbating, Poppy working with quick, urgent movements as she began to fix me to the bed.

I'd told the truth, she didn't have to. It made sense though, to keep me down, to make sure that I had to comply with whatever was wanted of me, to do whatever Gabrielle needed. It would stop me frigging too, and diluting Gabby's experience by attending to my own needs. One wrist was tied off, Poppy using a big bow, pretty, but secure, too tight and too well tied to allow me to escape. My other wrist followed, then my ankles and I was helpless, Gabrielle stroking herself all the while and watching patiently as I was made ready for her.

Poppy stood back as she tugged off the last bow. Her eyes were bright with excitement, her face shining. Gabrielle was getting urgent, the long, sleek muscles of her thighs starting to tense. I swallowed hard, my eyes fixed to the seat of her nappy, and the twin slices of creamy bum cheek peeping out at either side. I could see between her legs, with the nappy material shivering to the motion of her fingers as she masturbated.

She stopped suddenly. Her hands came out of her nappy and down from her breasts, to her hips. She pulled her back in, sinking a little, to a squat, her bottom pushed out, round and feminine, the smooth white nappy round over her behind. I heard her sob, and the hiss of her pee as she let her bladder go. I saw the muscles of her pert little bottom change shape as she let her anus pout, and I knew she was doing it, filling her nappy with dirt.

Again she sobbed, louder, and suddenly her nappy seat was no longer so smooth, a lump growing right over where I knew her bumhole was hidden. The lump grew, swelling as she pushed her mess out, growing rounder, and bigger still, to a fat, globular bulge. She was sobbing in raw emotion as she let it come, her flesh quivering, the muscle of one leg twitching. Still the bulge grew, ever rounder and ever fatter, until the weight of her mess became too much. Her load moved, to hang, heavy and bulbous between her thighs.

'That's it,' she gasped. 'That's all.'

'Now come,' Poppy breathed. 'Go on, do it.'

Gabby nodded. Her pee had spilled a little, droplets running down her thighs, but no more. Her legs were open across me, touching, and I felt the wet as one tiny trickle reached me. I was barely able to control my breathing, the urge to stuff a hand down my own nappy and masturbate irresistible. Save for the ribbons securing me firmly to the bed, it would have been too much not to. The straining seat of Gabby's nappy was right over my tits, hanging heavy and round, a sight so dirty, so delightfully improper, that just to see was enough to set the muscles of my pussy twitching in anticipation.

She steadied herself. Her hands went back as before, to pussy and tit, stroking, teasing herself. Then she was rubbing and the bulge in her nappy had begun to quiver, moving to the rhythm of her fingers. She got faster, her legs went tight and loose again. Her breathing was audible, slow and deep, but growing faster. She began to pant, then to sob. Her bottom cheeks started to contract, her bulge began to wobble as she picked up her pace, now frigging herself with desperate urgency. She cried out, a single, ecstatic sob as she threw her head back, and she had sat down, full on my chest.

I felt her load squashed out between my boobs as her weight settled onto me. Suddenly I was struggling in my bonds, desperate to escape, to get at my pussy, to grab her, to give myself the same glorious feelings she was having. I could do nothing, only lie helpless as she gasped and sobbed her way through orgasm, her full nappy squashed out over my bare boobs, her bottom wriggling in the mess.

Poppy took pity on me as Gabby started to come down to earth. A hand slid down the front of my nappy and I was being masturbated, her skilled, gentle fingers working between the folds of my sex to rub at my clitty. Gabby stayed put, sat firmly on my chest, her full nappy heavy and fat and squashy between my little boobs. I was gasping in moments, and shaking my head, then coming, and at the last, perfect moment Gabby lifted her bum, sat back, and pushed the bulging, loaded nappy seat right in my face.

Nine

I was very glad indeed that I'd stayed with Gabrielle and Poppy. What we'd done had been truly, utterly filthy, yet also safe, fully and completely consenting, and private. It also left me without any marks, even my smacked bum pristine by the morning.

It had been something I could never, ever have done with men around, or most women. With them it had been possible, if not easy. I'd needed a while to get into the right head-space, but once there, I'd been able to let myself go completely. Both had been so sweet too, kissing and cuddling as we cleaned Gabrielle up, without a trace of guilt. There hadn't even been any humiliation, at least until that last awful, perfect moment when she sat on my head. Then it had come in a massive rush, completely overpowering and in perfect tune with my orgasm, despite the fact that her nappy seat had only pressed gently to my face.

Whatever had happened at Rathwell's I knew it could not have been as powerful, at least not without leaving me marked. They'd have beaten me, they always did, and I was getting tired of having to turn up for my Aunt Elaine with my bottom bruised when the whole idea was that she should take care of my needs. In all likelihood I'd have had my head shaved as well, which really would have been the final straw.

It was a shame about Jade but, if she was going to get in with Sophie, then it was going to be impossible to maintain our relationship the way it had been. True, if she thought I was bad about making her do things with men, then she had a serious shock coming with Sophie. Yet her protestations of lesbianism had been becoming both weaker and more convenient with time. Possibly she could now handle it.

By the time I'd reached home on the Sunday evening I had decided that if she wanted to further explore her sexuality with Sophie, then I would stay away. It was the only sensible decision. I would take a break, avoiding sadistic lesbians, crazed dominas, dirty old men and all the other assorted perverts who took so much pleasure in abusing my body.

I could do it too, taking my sexual satisfaction across my aunt's knee once a weak and with Gabrielle and Poppy as invited. If Jade got upset I knew I'd be running to her in an instant, but just possibly the emotional crisis would allow me to bargain with her.

She didn't get upset. She sent me a long email telling me I was a silly cow for not coming to the Rathwells', and describing the party in glowing detail. I had to admit it sounded good. Just about all my friends had been there, even my ex, Amber, along with her new girlfriend, Kay. They'd put on a show, Kay getting a public knickers-down spanking, to everybody's delight, although Amber had apparently been fiercely protective otherwise. Jade and Sophie had been maids, in uniform, including little flounced skirts and frilly panties. There had been one for me.

Melody had been in fine form, spanking the maids and teasing Amber into dealing with Kay, making her own sister lick her pussy in front of everybody, and generally acting the high and mighty domina. She'd been in leather, her custom-made cat suit that left her big, dark breasts bare and buttoned down over her pussy, the same one she had worn for her 'Black Goddess' picture. I could just imagine it. The thought left me weak at the knees, but only partly through my sense of submission. She would have had me, I knew, naked and soundly whipped, penetrated in both holes, tied-up and finally shaved bald.

Despite my own encounter, reading the email left me feeling frustrated and fed up. I knew I'd done the right thing, rationally, and I knew I wouldn't have missed the grown-up baby-girl session for anything. I still wished I could have gone, and ended up masturbating over the thought of being dominated by Melody, coming at the instant my fantasy reached the part where her razor touched the skin of my scalp.

There was enough going on at the department to keep my mind fully occupied on the Monday. In addition to lectures and a practical there was a meeting about the allocation of room space during which I had to face down no less than five of my male colleagues, all senior to me. I succeeded, but at the expense of taking on responsibility for more practicals, which cut into my research time. It still left me feeling pretty triumphant, but I couldn't help but wonder if I'd have been able to swing it with a bald head and slap marks on my face. Jade didn't ring, or email.

Tuesday was spent making sure that the decision reached on Monday actually happened, which was exhausting. By leaving time I needed to let somebody else take control for a while very badly indeed, which was just as well. That evening I was given my first session in my spanking room.

Aunt Elaine had added a few touches, purely decorative, but enough to set her own stamp on it. That was right, because it stressed her status, her right to make the choices, and to punish me. There were several pieces of linen, flowers, and watercolour prints of the Thames Valley. The result was homely, very domestic, and old-fashioned, in many ways the ideal situation in which to spank a girl.

I got it across her knee, in the window seat, my woollen skirt turned high and my tights and panties tugged down to my thighs. As always, it was firm and deliberate, maybe a hundred solid swats delivered to my naked cheeks, to leave me full of warm pain, contrite and happy. She left as soon as I was done, and I masturbated on the bed, face down, stroking my hot bottom and teasing my anus as I came.

Afterwards, my feelings of catharsis were as strong as ever. On the way home I found myself viewing my situation in a clearer, more detached way, and a great deal happier about my decision to take a break. Back at my flat, there was still no message from Jade. I crossed her off the list, with reluctance, but less than I would have expected. That left the Rathwells, and Marjorie Burgess.

Marjorie was on her way out. I'd got it right, playing the penitent sinner, so that she could feel superior. That meant she saw me as low, and therefore she was not going to try and foist off her ghastly nephew on me, or any of her other male acquaintances. All it needed was a little more time. Once she was satisfied that I was 'cured' there was still the risk of rumours and gossip, but there was absolutely nothing I could do about that.

I hesitated, tempted to cross the Rathwells off on the grounds that as long as I wasn't at any of the London parties, Melody wouldn't catch up with me. She had her little pet, Annabelle, who she kept bald in a gesture of vicarious revenge. She had her twin sister, Harmony, also Sophie, Jade if I was any judge of character, and as many other playmates as she could possibly have wanted.

Unfortunately, that wasn't the way Mel worked. She loved to play spider and fly, and the more I struggled to evade her web the more she would relish it. It might be ages before she acted. It had already been over a year, and there was no doubt in my mind that she was enjoying drawing out my agony. Yet it would happen, eventually.

My decisions had lifted a great deal of worry, and I felt happy and light-hearted for the rest of the week. I saw Marjorie Burgess on the Thursday and she again congratulated me on my progress, despite not knowing that there was any. Again it puzzled me, but I was too busy to give it much attention.

By Friday night I was looking forward to my appointment with Gabrielle. Jade had finally chosen to communicate, sending an email to say that she was taking Sophie to Whispers and asking if I'd like to go. I declined, regretfully, but sure that an afternoon with Gabby and Poppy would more than make up for it.

It didn't happen. I went up to London with my sense of anticipation absolutely soaring. We spent a half-hour chatting and discussing what could be done with me that afternoon, and then Gabrielle's bell went. It was somebody called Jo Warren, who had worked herself up into a serious state over something. Gabrielle let her up and Poppy and I retired to a nearby coffee bar. One hour passed, and another, with our conversation getting increasingly giggly and increasingly naughty. She was going to put me through a routine, alternate spanking and suckling at her breast, which sounded absolutely heavenly.

By the time Gabrielle finally rang Poppy's mobile my panty crotch was soaking and my skin tingling all over, my bum and boobs especially, with my nipples at rigid attention. Poppy was no different, and we walked back hand in hand, absolutely floating, to find Gabrielle in a state of utter panic. Her mother had rung, from France, to say that she and Gabby's father were coming over on the Eurostar and would be there by the evening.

Her parents knew she was a lesbian, but felt it was something she would get over with time. They knew nothing whatever about her predilection for being put in nappies. They also expected her to put them up, so the special bedroom had to be converted into an unremarkable guest room, in approximately five hours.

I had to help, naturally, and so spent what should have been an afternoon of dirty, passionate and loving sex doing an instant room makeover. It didn't help that Gabrielle was close to tears, which was not like her at all. So I ended up doing most of it, including persuading Natasha Linnet to house several hundred stuffed toys and the entire collection of grown-up baby-girl accessories in her flat.

That alone took four trips between Victoria and Primrose Hill, and left Natasha in a foul temper and with a nasty prick in her hand from a nappy pin that had come open. We made it though, and by the time the light had started to fade the room was innocent, if still somewhat too pink for most tastes.

We did a final, frantic last search, finding one over-sized dummy, and the bell went. I stuffed the dummy in my pocket. Sure enough it was her parents, and I was given a brief kiss to say thank you and hustled out into the chilly evening. As I stood on the pavement, the most appalling frustration began to well up in me. It should have been so good, and now I had nothing.

I considered going to Whispers, and probably would have done had I not felt quite so sweaty and sticky after all my work, not to mention exhausted. It would have been asking for trouble anyway, but it was really my lack of energy that decided me. So I went back home, to watch a bad film on TV and ponder on what might have been. Even in bed I found it impossible to masturbate properly, with the knowledge of what I should, or could, have been up to.

Sunday was dull, a wet, slow day, with time hanging heavy on my hands. I was in a bad mood, and couldn't shake it, whatever I tried. I was frustrated but not turned on. I was missing Jade, but I knew that she would be sleeping off the effects of a night out at Whispers, probably in Sophie's arms. I was angry with Marjorie Burgess, and myself, the world in general. That evening I came on my period, which really put the cap on things.

It made me feel a little better, emotionally, but it wasn't going to do much for my Tuesday evening. By mutual agreement my panties stayed up when I was on, and it was never quite as satisfying. I felt I needed them pulled down, badly, and to be spanked really hard. I was going to be in tears, and I wanted to be, and for those tears to come freely, and fast. In the end I decided to ask her to pull my panties up between my cheeks, for all the embarrassment it would cause to do so, and also to really wallop me.

My luck was out. With Christmas approaching, my mother had decided to come up to discuss the family festivities, so for the second time in a few days what should have been an erotic experience ended up as mundane. I had to stay too, adding my contribution to a four-hour discussion that could perfectly well have been done in five minutes on the phone.

I ended up driving my mother back to her house, and that was that. I went unspanked. I couldn't do Wednesday evening because of a departmental party

I could not afford to back out of. By Thursday I was climbing the walls, and feeling so awful that I had begun to wonder if Marjorie Burgess was right, that I was hopelessly addicted to sex and was now in some sort of post-erotic cold turkey.

What I needed was a bloody good spanking, but I'd worked myself into such a state I didn't even want to phone Elaine. Instead I spent the evening surfing the sex-addiction sites and trying to be as objective as possible about them. There were dozens, all basically similar, and it was one o'clock in the morning before I finally turned off the computer.

The result was a relief. They were drivel, without exception. Some were Christian drivel, some pseudo-scientific drivel, some just plain old-fashioned complete drivel, but all were drivel. The only unifying factor was the authors' inability to come to terms with human sexuality, their own and more especially other people's.

Their norm was a state of self-righteous denial and repression, something I had got over a long time ago, either by simple rejection, or by learning to take pleasure in the breach of ingrained taboos. Unfortunately I'd reached a level of sexual liberation well ahead of that considered acceptable by society at large. I was still right. My problem did not lie in myself, but in society. Marjorie Burgess was right. I was a 'filthy, dirty, perverted little nymphomaniac tart', and I was proud of it.

In the morning I was filled with a new determination. I was not going to let Marjorie Burgess, or any other smug, self-satisfied prude, destroy what I had achieved for myself. Nor was I going to put myself at the mercy of thoughtless dominants. I would keep control. Gabrielle's parents were still with her, but I'd manage something at the weekend, something safe, exquisite and utterly filthy.

I was wondering what to actually do as I ate my lunch in the university canteen. My morning had run late, and the people I'd initially joined had left, but I had nothing on until two o'clock and felt like indulging my imagination over a slow coffee. Not a minute after I'd sat down again, Marjorie Burgess appeared. She was absolutely beaming as she made for my table. I smiled and greeted her, diplomatic as ever, despite the urge to push her plate of macaroni cheese right in her face.

'I am so proud of you, Penny,' she announced as she sat down.

'Thank you . . . but why?' I managed, wondering what on earth she was talking about.

'Now, now, there's no need to hide your light under a bushel,' she went on. 'Not from me. Miss Gabrielle Salinger must be thanked, of course, but I do feel you should take at least a measure of the credit.'

So she had been speaking to Gabrielle.

'Well . . . I've been trying, yes . . . But, what did Gabrielle . . . Miss Salinger have to say?'

'Oh, I haven't been in touch . . . not really. I did speak, yesterday, but she seemed to think it a breach of confidentiality to discuss your case directly with me. You will have to tell her that I am to be trusted, of course. That was not what I was thinking of, but of your behaviour.'

'How do you mean?'

'I can tell you now, I think, as you will want to thank me. When I called to clean up your computer, I installed a little program to monitor any attempts to access pornographic sites, and to report on which sites you have accessed. Now I know you have not only resisted temptation, but been devoting a great deal of time to the understanding of your addiction.'

She gave a little, satisfied smile and began to eat. I could only stare. She had planted a program in my PC, a virus effectively, to report what I did. That was bad enough, but she was not only proud of this appalling breach of my privacy, but expected me to be thankful!

I am not hot-tempered, but I nearly broke. One swift movement and the macaroni cheese would have been in her face and I'd have had a nice clear minute to give her my exact opinion of her behaviour and her character. I didn't do it, common sense prevailing at the last second, but it was as close as I'd come in my life to assault.

She just went on eating, entirely complacent. I fought my anger down, hiding my emotions behind my coffee cup until I had regained control and could say what she wanted to hear.

'I see . . . I didn't realise. Thank you.'

'It needed to be done, Penny. Is there anything else you want to say, any other thanks you should give?'

I was left puzzled, not at all sure what she was talking about, until I remembered that she was a Christian.

'I shall go to pray this evening,' I promised. 'At St Boniface's.'

It was the only church I could remember the name of, and that because it was at the end of my street and had one of those huge signboards outside with a thermometer to show the progress of the fund for the roof or whatever it might be.

'You must, yes,' she agreed, 'but that was not what I meant. Should you not also thank me for saving you from yourself?'

I nodded, because it was all I could do for a good ten seconds before I recovered my voice. When I did speak, it came out in a thin squeak.

'Yes.'

Fortunately she took my tone for humility or something, not shock and outrage. She smiled and went on.

'Then I think we may think of you as one of us again. You are to continue the therapy, of course, and I shall see Father David and make sure you are attending at St Boniface's regularly. I shall be keeping an eye on you myself too, naturally.'

She went back to her macaroni cheese, leaving me to curse myself for trying to be too clever. I hadn't had to give the name of a church. I hadn't had to say I would go and pray. I'd done it, and inevitably she turned out to know the priest who ran the wretched place, probably along with every other sanctimonious Bible-basher south of Birmingham.

For the rest of the afternoon I was in a state of near demented fury. I couldn't concentrate on anything, and delivered my two o'clock lecture in a flat monotone, straight from the notes. What she had done was totally and utterly unacceptable, yet there was nothing I could do about it. I still wanted revenge, but it could not be open, or malicious. I wanted it to be, but I simply had too much to lose. It would have to be something abstract, even if it was only spending hours surfing for the worst kind of porn I could possibly find with my laptop.

I went to church, of course, too cowardly to risk the lecture I'd get if I didn't, and sure she would have rung ahead. She had. Father David was waiting for me, a tall, grey-haired man with an air of uncompromising severity, and one of Morris Rathwell's dirty old men.

There was no doubt about it. He had been at two of the six parties I'd attended to pay off my debt. He'd even spanked me, bottom bared across his knee with my panties in my mouth to keep my squeals down. The last time I'd seen him, Sophie had been leading him out of the room by the hand, to have his cock sucked.

He spoke a single word, my name, and went silent. We just stared at each other, his face working through successive emotions of surprise, embarrassment and outright fear. I could see what was going through his mind. Marjorie would have told him I was a repentant sinner, if not why. Now he knew why, and it made me very dangerous indeed to his position. The instant I found my voice I hastened to reassure him.

'I repent nothing, David.'

He was white in the face as he answered me.

'Mrs . . . Marjorie Burgess, she . . .'

'. . . is a bigoted old fool. I can keep a secret, David, and I'm sure you can too.'

'Yes . . . absolutely . . . of course.'

'Good. Now, are you going to take me somewhere private, and pull my panties off, and stuff them in my mouth, and spank my naughty bottom, and . . . and . . . just abuse me . . . make me feel dirty . . . make me feel rude . . . come on, David, now!'

He hesitated for an instant, and then he was striding down the nave towards the door. It shut with a clang that rang through the empty church, the huge iron key rasped in the lock, and we were alone. I waited, my heart hammering, my lower lip trembling. I needed it so badly, as I had all week, and longer. Now I was going to get it.

There was fear as he walked towards me, that delicious, toe-curling fear which comes when you know you're going to get a spanking, when you want it so badly but can imagine the coming pain, and that dreadful, wonderful humiliation that never seems to fade. He was smiling now, just faintly, so stern, so full of authority. I hung my head, waiting, his to punish as he pleased.

He took my hand as he reached me, to lead me up the nave of the church, our footsteps echoing in the huge, silent building. I really thought he'd take me into some side room, a vestry or something, but he simply walked to the front pew, directly below the pulpit. He released my hand and sat down, looking up into my eyes. I was going to be spanked in a church.

'Take off your shoes, socks and trousers,' he ordered. 'Place each garment neatly beside me on the pew.'

He'd been the same at Rathwell's, harsh, cold. It was fantasy, but still a wonderful way to act as he gave me discipline. I nodded and bent to my shoes. He spoke immediately.

'What do you say?'

'Yes, sir. Sorry, sir,' I responded quickly.

'Not "sir", Penny. Say "Reverend".'

'Yes, Reverend.'

'Good, now do as I told you to.'

I undid my shoe, my fingers shaking as hard as ever. He was going to spank me, to take down my panties and spank me, in a church, his own church. I may be an atheist, but I spent an awful lot of time in church, at school mostly. I am not immune to the concept of sacrilege.

One shoe came off, and the other. I took off my socks and folded each. They went into my shoes, which I placed together on the pew. The stone felt cold beneath my bare feet, and it was more than I could do not to wriggle my toes with the tension building up inside me as I put my fingers to the button of my jeans.

He just watched as I opened my fly, cool and aloof, betraying no hint of emotion. I pushed the jeans down, over my bum, off my thighs and low, to the ground and I was showing my panties. Still he failed to react. I folded the jeans, nearly dropping them in my clumsiness, placed them on the pew and stepped back in front of him, to stand, my hands crossed over the gentle bulge of white cotton at the front of my knickers. He looked at me, and nodded, then spoke.

'Come across my knee.'

I went down, into classic spanking position, my favourite beyond doubt, draped over a man or woman's knee, helpless, passive, my lifted bottom the focus of my body. My toes were on the cold stone of the floor, my fingertips too, until he took one arm and pulled it up into the small of my back, twisting until I squeaked in pain.

'Quiet,' he ordered, as he casually tucked my jumper and blouse up under my arm.

'Yes . . . yes, Reverend . . .' I managed. 'I . . . I'm sorry.'

'You will be, believe me, Penny. I intend to punish you well, Penny. I fully intend to make you cry.'

'Yes, Reverend . . . thank you, Reverend.'

'Oh, you won't thank me, I don't think so.'

'No, Reverend.'

I was choking with emotion, his words bringing my sense of humiliation ever higher. He began to stroke the seat of my panties and I let out an audible sob, completely overcome. He chuckled and spoke again, all the while stroking my bottom through the thin white cotton of my knicks.

'No, Penny, I don't think you'll thank me at all, but you will be sorry, very sorry.'

It was turning me on, the lingering familiarity of his touch, the knowledge that he could explore my bottom as he pleased, and for as long as he pleased, the certainty that in his own good time he would be going to take my panties down. He really drew it out, fondling me with ever more intrusive intimacy, squeezing my bottom cheeks, pinching the softness of my flesh, tracing the edges of my knickers with his fingers. Soon I was dizzy with erotic humiliation, dreading the moment my panties would come down, yet at the same time in desperate need of exactly that. Finally he spoke again, still stroking and teasing my bum cheeks and crease.

'So, Penny, shall I spare your blushes?'

'No . . . Reverend.'

My first word came out as a little, choking sob. We both knew my panties were coming down, and we both knew that was no reason not to torture me about it.

'No?' he queried. 'Why, you immodest little tart! Or is it that you know you deserve this, that you know they ought to come down . . . that they have to come down. Yes, that's it. A girl's knickers always have to come down in the end, don't they?'

'Yes . . .'

'Yes, what?'

'Yes, Reverend.'

'Yes, no matter how good she is, no matter how much she struggles to avoid it, every girl knows that her knickers will have to come down in the end, either so that she can have her bottom smacked, or for a good, honest fucking!'

Suddenly his hand was between my legs, cupping the plump, wet bulge of panty cotton that hid my sex. He squeezed, firmly, pushing a piece of fabric into my hole with his thumb. He was rubbing on my clit too, and it was more than I could do to hold back a gasp. He began to frig me through my panties, rubbing hard, until I was panting and pushing my bottom up for more. He went on, his voice loud with excitement, reverberating around the empty church.

'But that's not what you're getting, is it? Not sex, Penny, no, not what you're supposed to get . . . what you'd like to get! What you're getting is a spanking, and you're getting it with your knickers down and that big round bottom bare to the air, in fact your whole rear view bare, cunt and all!'

He stopped frigging me as he finished, and the next instant my panties had been whipped down and I was bare, my pussy showing behind, rude and wet and ready. He didn't content himself with pulling them down either, but took them right off, jerking them down my legs and off my ankles with a peal of gleeful laughter as I came bare, nude from the waist down, my pussy . . . my cunt, as he so crudely called it, bare and vulnerable.

Not that he'd finished with it. Still holding me tight, he pushed his hand in between my thighs, spreading them, and more, my sex lips, to show the wet, puffy pussy flesh and my now gaping hole. He slid his thumb up, to wiggle it inside me, and spend a moment easing it in and out, just long enough to set me sighing with pleasure. Then he let go, and once more adjusted my body into the ideal spanking position.

'You're a tart,' he told me happily, 'a slut, a trollop. Imagine getting a wet cunt because a man is going to spank you! You should be utterly ashamed of yourself, not aroused! Still, tart or otherwise, I seem to remember you tend to howl, and we already know how to deal with girls who howl, don't we?'

'Yes, Reverend.'

'And what is it, Penny?'

'They get gagged, Reverend.'

'Exactly!'

I knew what was coming. Sure enough, my panties were being offered to my mouth, crumpled into a convenient ball, with the soggy gusset at the top.

'Open wide, Penny.'

My mouth came open, as far as it would go. The panties were crammed in, firmly, the dry cotton harsh in my mouth as they went, the taste of my own sex suddenly strong in my head. He wedged them right in, and took hold of my jaw to force me to close my mouth, leaving me with my cheeks bulging and my eyes popping as I struggled to make saliva. He gave another of his little quiet chuckles as he let go.

His coldness was gone, a pose dissolved in the sheer delight of having me pliant and naked across his lap. I no longer cared, aroused beyond the point where the sudden change in play role mattered. He was going to spank me, and that was all.

He was actually laughing as he changed his grip again, and then it had begun. I gasped into my panty gag at the first smack, caught off guard by the sheer power of it. My legs flew apart at the second and I was kicking at the third, all delivered so fast and so hard I had no chance to catch my breath. I just dissolved, making a totally undignified display of myself, thrashing and kicking and waving my free arm about, my hair jumping to the smacks, his laughter and the slap of hand on female bum flesh echoing and re-echoing around the church.

The pain, and my helpless, pitiable display lasted just moments, and then the heat in my bum had taken over. I was still a mess, a truly pathetic mess, with snot bubbling out of my nose as I struggled to breathe, my hair everywhere and my bum wide enough to show my anus most of the time. There were no tears though, I was too turned on, too well warmed up with his groping and his casual, lewd investigation of my sex. He was firm, really firm, delivering the walloping I'd been craving for days, and he talked too, adding to my humiliation as I was beaten.

'... rosy and bare, stripped and spanked, oh, what a way to be! How does it feel, you bouncy little tart, bare bottom over my knee, your cunt showing to the world! Oh, how I wish I could do this in front of my congregation, oh that would be fine, to let the whole po-faced mob of them get a full view of your great fat wobbly bottom as you're spanked over my knee, you gorgeous little tart! And just look at the state it's got you in!'

It stopped. I hung limp, panting, my legs cocked wide. A hand touched my thighs, my sex, and his finger went into my pussy with a wet sound. He began to probe, opening me, exploring me, his upturned thumb pressing between my bum cheeks, just an inch from my anus. I gasped in pleasure and my soggy panties fell out of my mouth. I pushed my bottom up, hoping to get his thumb up the hole and be held, cunt and bum, in his fingers, maybe spanked like that. He continued to probe me, slipping a second finger into my pussy hole, and again he began to speak.

'Yes, you'd like that, wouldn't you? I bet you would, to be spanked in front of an audience, not like Rathwell's mob, but an audience who think it's real discipline, who think you're getting your spanking because you've been naughty, because you deserve it ...'

'Yes, please ...'

It was straight out of a spanking magazine, but it was good, a classic, English discipline fantasy. I lifted on my toes, eager to get a hand to my pussy if he was going to run through his fantasy while he punished me. He saw what I was trying to do and lifted his knee higher to stop me.

'Oh, no, you don't, Miss Tart. I decide when that happens.'

He pulled his hand from my pussy and my hole closed with a loud farting nose, bringing me a fresh jolt of humiliation as he laughed in response.

'Please!' I begged. 'Let me . . . let me rub while you spank me . . .'

'No.'

'Please! I beg you! I'll suck your cock afterwards . . . you can fuck me . . . bugger me . . .'

'Yes,' he said with absolute, concrete certainty. 'I can, can't I?'

'Yes, anything, just . . .'

He changed his grip, abruptly, letting go of my twisted arm and curling his own around under my body, to find my pussy. I moaned in pleasure, utterly helpless in his grip, about to be masturbated to orgasm as he beat me, then made to suck him, to take him in my pussy, up my bum . . .

'Here goes!' he crowed.

'Please . . . yes . . . and talk . . . tell me how you'd spank me in public.'

He chuckled. His hand settled on my bottom for a moment, and then he had begun to spank again, more slowly now, heavy, well placed swats placed right over my bumhole.

'Yes,' he said, 'in front of my congregation, ideal. How you'd hate it, how you'd fight to stop your knickers being dropped, how you'd howl once they were down!'

He laughed, enjoying the image as it filled me with humiliation – deeply personal humiliation. I tried to bite the thought down, but I couldn't. I was thinking what he was, only with Marjorie Burgess right up in front of the congregation, her face set in her most self-righteous smile as my bum came bare for punishment. It was the last thing I wanted to think about. I hated her, but it was going to happen. I just couldn't help it, with his fingers working in my sex and my bum on fire to the swats.

'No!' I cried, forcing my mind to a more acceptable humiliation, being done on the church steps, for everyone in the street to watch.

'Yes,' he said. 'In front of everyone, a full church . . . That's right, I'd publish it in the parish magazine, announce that I was going to spank a tart, a fat-bottomed little tart! That would bring them in, wouldn't it? It would, by the hundred, all to see your knickers taken down, Penny, all to see you get what you deserve, spanked in public . . . spanked till you howl . . . spanked with your big fat bum wobbling behind and your cunt on show!'

I cried out as I started to come. He was really laying in, smack after vicious, heavy smack, jolting my whole body as he rubbed at my pussy . . . my cunt. In my head I was outside, stripped bare on the church steps, my legs pumping in my pain, my thighs wide, my bum cheeks bouncing crazily, my wet cunt flaunted, my bumhole winking . . .

. . . and Marjorie Burgess right behind me, smug, calm, superior as I blubbered my way through a well-deserved punishment, a spanking for my dirty behaviour, a spanking for being a tart . . .

I screamed as I came, hating my fantasy, but quite unable to stop it. Right at the peak I burst into tears, and he had made me cry, as he'd promised. Then the spanking had stopped and I was coming down, snivelling, angry with myself but unable to deny the force of my orgasm.

'Are you all right?' he asked.

I nodded as I slipped from his lap, to kneel, panting on the floor. My bottom was ablaze, hot, throbbing and undoubtedly bruised. He'd been hard, really hard, dealing with me the way I should be dealt with, thoroughly spanked, by hand, and any pathetic protests I might make just ignored. My hands went back, to cup my smacked behind, feeling the hot, roughened skin and that strange, heavy feeling, as if my bum cheeks were made of lead.

'Not too hard?'

I shook my head.

'Good. Then you can take my penis in your mouth.'

I nodded. It wasn't his fault I'd come over Marjorie Burgess. He deserved his treat. Suddenly it occurred to me that if she knew, she would be absolutely outraged, and I was smiling again. I gave my bottom a little jiggle, wondering if I should ask for his cock in my pussy, up my dirty little bumhole or stick to sucking.

He had lifted his robe, revealing lean, muscular legs, very hairy, and no pants, just his cock and balls, lolling against his thigh. He was getting stiff, his helmet showing red through the wrinkled hole in the end of his foreskin, wet with bubbles of pre-come. I gave him my brightest smile.

'Do you usually go naked under your robes?'

'Yes. Now put it in your mouth.'

I shuffled forward, my mouth open, to take him in.

'Good girl,' he said as his cock filled my mouth. 'Do it well and, who knows, I might give you sixpence.'

It was an offer of money, disguised but real. I shook my head on my mouthful of penis. I didn't want money. I wanted to suck his cock.

Being spanked and then made to perform oral sex is so me. It really is close to the final humiliation, to strip a girl's bum, spank her, and then expect her to go down on cock or pussy, using her mouth and tongue to bring the person who had just punished her to orgasm. I don't need to be paid to do it.

He was right to call me a tart anyway. Not being paid just made me the cheapest possible tart, a free tart, which was how I felt as I squatted, splay-legged and bare from the waist down, sucking on the penis of the man who had just spanked me. I wanted to come again, and it made a good fantasy, to think of myself as a tart, his tart, giving sex for some trivial favour, or just because I'd been told to.

I was still feeling my bum, and I let my fingers go between my cheeks, to my hole, teasing the sweaty little dimple and thinking of how the cock in my mouth would feel up my back passage. Spanked and buggered is better even than spanked and sucking, the really final humiliation to inflict on a spanked girl, to stick a cock up her bumhole. I put my finger in, sucking harder and wondering if he'd take the hint or whether I'd have to make him an offer, maybe sit in his lap and let him watch as he penetrated my hole. He could fuck me too, first, just to make sure he'd had me properly.

'Could you fuck me?' I asked as I came off his cock.

He nodded eagerly. His cock was rock hard, and glossy with my saliva, more than ready for my body. I stood, turned, gave him a wiggle of my smacked bum and sat slowly down in his lap, taking his cock to guide it into my pussy. My passage was soaking, but quite tight after orgasm, and felt well stretched by the time he was in.

I wiggled, happy to have his cock up me, and spread my thighs so that I could play with myself as I was fucked. His hands took my hips, helping as I began to move myself up and down on his erection. It would have been easy to come, just as I was, my bottom smacked, his cock inside me, enjoying my cunt because he could, because I was a little tart, and once spanked, could be fucked at will.

'I'm going to come,' he grunted.

'No! Not now, not in my pussy!'

I lifted, snatching at his cock. He gave a yelp of surprise as I put the head to my bumhole. I was sloppy, with sweat and juice, and he went in, his helmet popping my ring even as his cock jerked in my hand, and suddenly I was pumping spunk up my own bottom. I kept at it, tugging hard on his shaft as my hole filled, spurt after spurt of thick, hot sperm erupting into my anus. It got me sloppy in an instant, and he was sliding up, deep into me, still coming as his cock stretched out my rectum to capacity.

As my bottom settled into his lap I was sighing with pleasure. He was up my bum, right up, my pussy pressed to his ball sack, my crease slippery with sperm and my own juice. I began to rub again, thinking of how I was, no clothes on below my waist, my bottom spanked, my cunt fucked, and finally buggered. It was right, the best treatment for me, to spank me and bugger me, to call me a tart as I was used, as I was stripped, as my bottom was slapped up, as my dirty little bumhole was filled with cock . . .

I came, crying out as before, my mind fixed on how I was, on what I was, a well-buggered little tart.

Ten

I left St Boniface's feeling immensely pleased with myself, if a little sore. It was a clear rule at Rathwell's spanking parties that you never asked the men about themselves, and discussed their lives only if they volunteered information. Most were businessmen, like Rathwell himself. I knew the others included members of most of the principal professions, but I had never thought one might be a vicar.

It was extremely funny, and thoroughly satisfying, in particular how Marjorie Burgess would have felt if she had known what we'd done, and in the church as well. Her outrage would have known no bounds. She would have been blind with fury, speechless with indignation, breathless with shock. In short, she would have felt much as I did about the way she had behaved towards me.

Sadly I couldn't tell her, and not only for my sake. David would be in bigger trouble than me if he got outed, much bigger. So it was going to be our secret, and that meant I could rely on him as an ally. She evidently had a good deal of respect for him, personally and as a clergyman, which was magnificently ironic. She would also take his word, and I didn't even mind dropping into the church occasionally if it meant a good, solid bottom-warming and maybe one up the bum instead of meaningless prayer.

Back at my flat I solemnly crossed her off my list. It was done, everything I could, my supposed sin forgiven, my defences in place. I would still be deemed unworthy of nephew Graeme, and I had added to my list of safe, local spankers. It was well worth a celebration, and once I'd eaten I went down to the local off-licence and treated myself to a bottle of vintage Champagne.

I drank it in the bath, up to my neck in hot water with the bottle in easy reach. My bottom ached just a little, and the skin of my cheeks was still rough to the touch, keeping me in mind of my spanking. I'd been well done, thoroughly roasted. It was going to bruise, but not much, probably not even enough to make me worry about Tuesday.

David was good. He had taken complete charge, made me feel as if my will was totally unimportant, yet fulfilled my needs. I like a man who'll really take trouble over punishing me. He had made such a big deal over taking my panties down, so that I felt utterly humiliated before the spanking even began, physically, and because he'd made me feel I deserved it. If there was a fault, he could have paid more attention to my anus, as I'd more or less had to bugger myself. He scored at least eight out of ten, maybe nine as a spanker.

He was interesting too, born in the late Fifties, for all that his grey hair made him look older, and into a family for which the church was everything. There had never been any question of him taking any other course than that of his father and his grandfather before that. He had hated every minute of it, the church schools he'd attended in particular. Too intelligent to blindly follow the faith, he had nevertheless gone along with it, ending up ordained. Since then he had made the best of it, confining his rebellion to the occasional indulgence of his love of spanking girls.

Not daring to try and find a spanking partner, he had confined himself to professional services, and always in London, which he felt was a safe distance. Morris Rathwell had approached him while he was leafing guiltily through a spanking magazine in a Soho shop, and that had been that. It was a thoroughly seedy story, although it amused me and I could certainly sympathise. I'd rescued him too, in a sense, which was another reason to feel good, as before I'd left we had agreed to see each other on a regular basis.

I was thoroughly drunk by the time I'd finished the Champagne, and slumped on my bed in just a towel, for a slow, leisurely frig over what we'd done. The computer was still on, and I went to check my mail. There was the usual assortment of spam, a couple of straightforward messages, and an invitation, to the Rathwells' big Christmas party. I was so drunk and so pleased with myself that I briefly considered accepting and trying to face Melody down. Even after a whole bottle of Champagne inside me I knew she'd just laugh at me, and I sent a polite rejection.

By the time I woke up it was nearly eleven. There was a brief moment of panic as I realised I was supposed to be with Gabrielle, and then I remembered her parents. I rang anyway, to make sure she was on for the following Saturday, and returned to bed with a mug of coffee. I felt so much better for my visit to the church, and when Jade rang in the afternoon I felt better still, after a friendly conversation that finished with us agreeing to be occasional playmates away from the main clubs and parties.

She was going to the Rathwells', and so, it seemed, was just about everybody else, including Zoe, Monty Hartle and the main Razorback boys. It was the next Saturday, and I was going to be with Gabrielle and Poppy, which would keep me from feeling bad about it. Then there was Tuesday, and the potential offered by David. It was enough, varied, thoroughly rude, yet safe and under my control. I'd done it, finding a balance to satisfy my need without taking undue risks.

The week went well. Tuesday was a delight, an experience that left me feeling fresh and happy and absolutely right about myself. I drove up as usual, with butterflies in my stomach, but none of the misgivings that had always troubled me before. We ate dinner, and talked, until it was time. My aunt then took me gently by the hand and led me upstairs, to the special room. I was put across her knee, in the window, my jeans and panties taken down and my bottom spanked. By the end I was crying softly, feeling penitent, and cleansed, and fully aroused. She kissed me on the forehead as I climbed onto the bed, and left me to masturbate myself to a series of dizzying orgasms.

I was due back at Elaine's for Sunday lunch, which was a full family affair, with myself, my mother, my cousins Kate and Susan, Kate's husband Jeremy and their girls, Pippa and Jemima. Elaine even made a dry joke about my behaviour at the party as I left, implying that she might spank me in front of all of them. I laughed, although the idea of having the dinner in the room I'd so frequently taken my punishments in was more than a little unsettling.

On Wednesday I saw Marjorie Burgess, which was just funny. I'd left my computer on-line the night before, on the nuttiest of the Christian sex-addiction sites, which was therefore what she thought I'd been doing while in reality I was getting my spanking. David had spoken glowingly of my behaviour as well.

Thursday was David's night, another spanking, and a leisurely suck of his cock, this time in his vestry at the back of the church. I let him put me in a surplice, which was fun, me looking ever so demure until the back was turned up to reveal my bum, already bare for spanking. As before, he made me come while he spanked me, bringing a girl to orgasm under punishment being something he particularly enjoyed.

Once we'd finished he walked back down the church with me, and we said goodbye on the steps. I kissed him and turned towards my flat, to find my mother standing outside the door, looking straight at me. She was a fair way off, but not so far that she wouldn't have seen me kiss David, or noticed his dog collar. I waved, detached myself from David and started towards her.

'Mum, hi,' I greeted her as we came together.

'Your young man?' she asked as I quickly pushed the key into the lock.

'No . . . yes . . . well, in a way,' I stammered. 'We, er . . . only met last week.'

'A vicar? I am surprised, I must say, considering your opinions. Still, I must say . . .'

I was given the full lecture, about how it was about time I settled down and started producing grandchildren, and gave my standard answers.

'. . . so hopefully in this man you have at last found somebody suitable,' she finished. 'How old is he, by the way?'

'I haven't asked, Mother! Less than fifty.'

She sighed, a note of mild exasperation familiar to me for as long as I could remember. I shrugged. She went on.

'What I came to say is, that you must speak to Susan.'

I groaned inwardly. Since I left university either she or Elaine had frequently wanted me to 'speak to Susan', generally when Susan had chosen some unacceptable boyfriend and was refusing to take any notice of Elaine. I never managed to make any difference anyway. Sure enough.

'She wants to bring her boyfriend on Sunday,' my mother went on, her tone suggesting that the man had to be a cannibalistic serial killer at the very least, 'and I really don't think it is appropriate. Nor does Elaine.'

'Is that the singer?'

'Yes. He calls himself Fungus, apparently. The band, so I'm told, is called Leprous Death. I really don't know where they get these names from, and he certainly doesn't sound the sort of person one would want in the house.'

'She won't take any notice of me, Mum, you know that.'

'You must speak with her, Penny. It's bad enough with both Pippa and Jemima expecting to bring friends . . .'

Sudden inspiration struck me.

'Perhaps I should ask David . . . my vicar friend, if we can hire the church hall? It's huge, he's desperate for funds and we could cook some of the food here. That way Fungus can't pinch the silver.'

She paused, then spoke.

'Well, it is a thought, but . . .'

'I won't change Susan's mind, Mum, and it will keep the girls happy, and mean a great deal less mess.'

'Perhaps, yes . . . Very well, you can organise everything, and I'll tell Elaine. You might want to ask your young man too. David, you say his name is?'

'Yes, David Cartwright.'

She gave an approving tut and disappeared into my kitchen, a sure hint that I should make tea. I followed. It had been an inspired idea. Not only did it save me the trouble of a fruitless argument with Susan, but it meant not eating dinner with the entire family in a room in which I had been spanked bare perhaps as many as fifty times. Just the knowledge would have been painfully embarrassing, especially with Pippa and Jemima there. The change of venue also gave me perhaps an hour extra to get back if I stayed over with Poppy and Gabrielle, which I had been invited to do.

Friday was the end of term, with all the attendant chaos. I managed to book the hall in the morning, and spent the rest of the day dealing with all the little odds and ends that needed clearing up in the department. There was a party too, and it was close to midnight by the time I got back to my flat. There were several messages, both on my phone and email, all urging me to go to the Rathwells' party, including one from Melody herself, promising not to shave my head. I was not falling for it, and before I turned off I quickly dropped in on her Black Goddess femdom internet community to leave a cheeky message. In bed, I set the alarm, thinking of Poppy and Gabrielle and how it was going to feel to spend most of the next day in nappies.

That was what I was expecting, to be introduced to more of their highly developed grown-up baby-girl fantasies, and not to be spared even the dirtiest and most humiliating details. Mainly I wanted things done to me, but I was prepared to take my turn in charge, even if it meant changing their dirty nappies, a prospect which gave me a very curious mixture of emotions indeed.

I left in plenty of time, with my fantasies growing stronger and more detailed as the train pulled me in towards London, so that by the time I rang on Gabrielle's bell I was absolutely squirming in my panties. I was buzzed up, and reached the landing to find Poppy waiting for me, her head sticking out around the door.

'Ah, yes, just the girl we want to see!' she greeted me.

'I'm here. What's up?'

'What's up, Penny Birch, is that thanks to your dirty behaviour, Monty expects to dob us both . . .'

I was already laughing. She went on.

'. . . with a chocolate sponge cake.'

'Sounds yummy. Can I watch?'

'No, Penny, you can't watch. We watch. You get dobbed.'

She moved quickly back, letting me in. I followed. She was in one of her baby-dolls, pink, with a fluffy trim and panties to match, also see-through, giving me the expected view of her wiggling bottom as she turned. Sure enough, Monty was there, sat on the sofa with the chocolate cake on a box in his lap, also Gabrielle, stark naked and looking slightly sulky.

'Penny's going to do it,' Poppy announced, propelling me forward with a slap to my bum. 'Come on, girl, clothes off, get to work, and you're to eat it up, all of it.'

'I not sure . . .' I managed, eyeing the cake.

It was the soft kind, moist chocolate sponge smothered in thick brown icing with the texture of whipped cream. The words 'Happy Birthday' had been picked out on the top in white. It was huge, it was simply too much. Monty might have been able to eat it, just, so might Fat Jeff, but not me.

'It's not my birthday until January,' I pointed out.

'Strip!' Poppy ordered.

'At least let me have a coffee!' I protested. 'I only just got here.'

'Strip!'

'Please? I thought it would be just us, anyway . . .'

'Strip!'

'Oh, all right!'

I hadn't expected to be sucking cock within five minutes of my arrival, or at all, but that looked like what was going to happen. Monty was watching, his fat face split into an expectant grin, as I started to strip. I was trying not to look too resentful as I did it, and to get my head around the sudden change of plan. I'd dressed sensibly, jumper, thick skirt, tights and all, which seemed to fascinate Monty as he watched me peel. When I got to my bra he put the chocolate cake down and took his cock out. By the time I was down to just my panties he was half-erect.

'Bum out, peel 'em down,' Monty demanded.

I sighed, but turned my back to him, sticking my bottom well out and easing them slowly down to show him. I'd chosen big, white cotton panties with little pink flowers as that seemed to suit Gabrielle's taste, which made having to show them to Monty especially humiliating, never mind pulling them down for him to wank over.

'Cute arsehole,' he remarked as I pulled them off my ankles, fully bent to give him the view he obviously wanted. 'Nice cunt too. I like 'em hairy. Gimme those.'

I passed him the discarded panties. He sniffed them, then wrapped them around his cock, shutting his eyes in bliss as he rubbed himself. I knelt down.

'Hands behind your back,' Poppy ordered. 'Fetch a ribbon, would you, Gabby?'

'Not tied!' I protested. 'Why do I have to be tied?'

'Because it's more fun,' Poppy pointed out, 'for us, that is, and because that way we'll have less nonsense out of you.'

'Okay,' I sighed.

Gabrielle had gone, and came back immediately, holding a wide, pink ribbon. Monty was still enjoying his 'panty wank', and watching as I crossed my hands behind my back. Poppy came behind me and I felt the ribbon twisted around my wrists, then between, before being knotted off in a neat bow. It left me feeling like a Christmas present, Monty's Christmas present.

He was grinning as he put down my panties. I gave him a resigned smile and shuffled forward into cock-sucking position, ready to be dobbed. He'd been lying back, his great belly quivering to the motions of his masturbation. Now he moved, forward, spreading his massive thighs to push his cock close to my face. He paused to tug off his jumper and the top beneath, exposing the full bulk of his torso, with his vast gut lolling forward, a great mass of pasty white flesh with his cock protruding obscenely from beneath.

Poppy stepped in to take the cake, carefully positioning it beneath Monty's cock. He took hold of his erection, which was so stiff he had trouble pushing it down. It went though, the bloated helmet plunged into the soft brown icing, and through, deep into the mass of the cake. For a moment he wanked himself into the cake, clearly enjoying the feel of it. His hand found my hair as his cock came up, brown and sticky and thick, the chocolate icing collapsing slowly down to either side of his helmet. He pulled me in, suddenly, so that I didn't get my mouth open quite in time and some went on my nose before I could take it in my mouth. Then it was in. I sucked, drawing the thick, soft cake off the hard mass of his penis. It was delicious, the richest chocolate and rum too, if slightly spoiled by the taste of cock that managed to permeate through it. I slurped it up anyway, and swallowed my mouthful. Monty immediately stuck his cock back in, to pull up a yet fatter lump and back it went, straight into my mouth.

He fed me, force-fed me really, controlling me by the hair as I was made to eat scoop after scoop of chocolate cake. I wasn't even allowed to suck properly, and he was far too urgent, smearing cake on his belly and in my face to the tune of Poppy's delighted giggles. Gabrielle was quieter, but riveted to the scene as I was forced to eat mouthful after mouthful.

I tried to be good, taking in as much as I could, but I soon had chocolate icing and bits of cake squeezing from my lips every time Monty put his cock in my face. Each time I'd struggle to swallow with my mouth still penetrated, which he loved, and I was gasping for air between each portion. In no time I was feeling sick, and bloated, but still I tried to be good, riding the submissive high I'd been building up and thinking of my utter humiliation if I was actually sick.

Still he kept on, mouthful after mouthful, utterly merciless as he used my body. Not even half the cake was gone, and I knew I could not possibly finish, not without throwing up. I had a nasty feeling that wouldn't stop Monty. He would make me eat it all. I kept going, until for all the strength of my submissive feelings I was close to breaking.

My stomach was in pain and my eyes had started to water by the time he had scooped out the heart of the cake. I was beginning to retch, the muscles of my abdomen and chest jerking in reflex each time the fat, cake-laden penis was thrust into my mouth. Suddenly I could take no more. It was going to happen, if he didn't stop, all over his belly and cock and balls and the floor . . .

'Amber!' I gasped, my slow word, when I finally realised that one more mouthful was going to bring the rest up.

Monty chuckled and pushed his cock back into the cake, to stir, breaking bits from the edges.

'Full, are we?' Poppy asked.

I nodded. Immediately my stomach tightened, but I held it down.

'She is going to be sick,' Gabrielle said. 'Enough, Monty.'

'Oh, I don't know,' Monty said. 'I really wanted to make her eat it all.'

'I will be sick,' I managed. 'I can't take another mouthful, I really can't!'

'Could you make the loo?' Monty asked. 'After a few more mouthfuls?'

'I . . . maybe . . .' I admitted.

'Do not,' Gabrielle advised. 'He will stick your head down into the bowl and fuck you while you're being sick.'

'I will not!' Monty protested.

Gabrielle merely raised her eyebrows. Monty was looking sulky as he scooped up another cock load of cake and icing.

'One more,' he demanded. 'Eat up.'

I gaped wide as he pulled my head in. His cock went in, smearing cake over my lips and nose, and my mouth was full, the sweet, rich cake now just sickly. I struggled to swallow, managing a little even as my stomach and gullet twitched in protest. He stuck his cock deeper in, holding me firmly by the hair. I shook my head in frantic protest as my stomach heaved. This time I couldn't hold it. My mouth filled with hot, liquid mess, bulging out my cheeks and making my eyes pop as I fought to hold it in.

'Nice!' Monty sighed. 'She's been sick on my cock, a Reverse Carl! I love it when they do that.'

'Dirty bastard!' Poppy said.

Monty took no notice, holding me still as I forced myself to swallow what was in my mouth. I thought he would come, and I knew that a mouthful of sperm really would be the last straw. I'd bring the lot up, all over him, which would be no more than he deserved. He didn't, but pulled his cock slowly free, to leave me gagging and dizzy, with brown spittle running from the corners of my mouth.

I only stopped it happening by a desperate effort of self-control. He had put the cake down and sat back, still holding his cock. I'd eaten maybe three-quarters of it, more than I would have thought possible, and I felt that if I so much as moved it was going to come up again, that or I would simply burst.

His cock was still filthy with chocolate icing, pulled into long streaks and wet smudges by my lips. There were bits of cake in his pubic hair too, and on the great, white bulge of his gut. I was no better, worse maybe, my face filthy, my hair soiled, my boobs and tummy stained with blobs of the soft icing and sticky, rum-soaked crumbs. He was smiling too, my mouth was slack, with brown drool running down over my lower lip. I looked up, wondering if he was going to force me to finish him off in my mouth, or perhaps over my face. That wasn't enough for him.

'Cunt time!' he announced happily. 'On your knees, bum up.'

I shook my head. I physically couldn't do it. Instead I forced myself to rise and collapsed onto the sofa. My tummy was so full, bulging upwards so that it looked as if I was several months pregnant as I lay groaning on my back with my legs pulled up to take the strain off my middle. Monty stood, to look down on me, grinning, and suddenly he had grabbed my ankles.

I squealed in protest as I was rolled up, but too late. His cock had already found my pussy, and he pushed it up, the chocolate cake squashing out around my hole as he filled me. He began to fuck me, my legs spread wide around his huge belly. It hurt, his body jamming onto my swollen stomach so that I felt I was going to pop, and my weight on my bound wrists. I didn't want to spoil his fun, but I had to say something.

'Stop it, Monty, you're hurting me!'

'Sure.'

He moved back. I sighed with relief as his weight came off me and his cock slid from my pussy. He was still holding my legs, but he let go of one, to take a firm hold on his cock, jerk, grunt, and eject a great, thick streamer of spunk across my upturned belly. I could only sigh in resignation as he milked himself off over me. My pussy was full of chocolate cake, my face and boobs smeared brown and sticky, and now I had what looked like a week's worth of spunk trickling slowly down over my distended belly. Poppy started to clap.

'Well done, Penny, but I'm glad that wasn't me!'

All I could manage was a moan. Poppy pushed on my shoulder, to roll me over and tweak the bow that bound my wrists loose. It came, and she held out her hand to me. I took it, and let her help me up from the sofa as she pressed a tissue to my messy tummy.

'Time we got you cleaned up and in your nappy,' she said. 'Come along.'

She led me to the bathroom, where most of their stuff was, with the special bedroom still out of commission. Feeling the way I did, I was more than happy to let her take over, and meekly followed her orders as I was washed, powdered, creamed and put in one of the adult nappies, one with a border of pink animals.

Topless, with nothing on but the puffy pink and white nappy around my hips and my distended belly pushing out the front, it was impossible not to let my feelings surface. It felt wonderfully naughty, and made me want further humiliation, and punishment too. All I needed was an hour or so to let the strain in my stomach subside and I would be ready and willing.

I got it, slumped in an armchair with a dummy in my mouth as Monty ate the rest of the chocolate and Poppy turned her attention to Gabrielle. The plan seemed to be that Gabby and I would be the baby-girls, Poppy something halfway between a nurse and baby-sitter, Monty just Monty. It was going to mean spankings, probably being put to his cock again, and eventually filling my nappy in some way that was sure to be deeply humiliating.

By the time Gabby had been stripped, gently spanked across Poppy's knee with her sex showing from behind and put into her nappy, I was game to at least follow orders. Monty had begun to talk about lunch.

'We should get a Vacherin cheese,' he was saying. 'That shop will be open, maybe Penny . . .'

'No, Monty, please!' I cut in. 'Not more dobbing, I really couldn't . . .'

'Not dobbing,' he laughed. 'I was going to say you should come with me, in your clothes, but with the nappy on underneath.'

'Yes, make her,' Poppy agreed immediately. 'Do it, Penny, and you're to wet yourself while you're out.'

'I'm not really ready,' I protested, 'and I . . .'

'Just do it,' she cut me off. 'Come on.'

I couldn't help but smile. It would be nice, undeniably, to have the nappy on under my coat, and better still to wet myself in the street and come back with it all soggy around my bum and between my legs. I nodded and went to my clothes.

My panties had disappeared, presumably pocketed by Monty as a keepsake, but I didn't really need them anyway. Tights were a must. I pulled them on, and up, over my nappy, which felt very strange indeed, and naughtier even than being in the nappy alone. I put my bra back on, as I wanted to be as normal as possible except for the nappy, and my jumper, skirt and boots.

Looking in the mirror, it was blatantly obvious that I had a nappy on, with my skirt bulging out around my hips. Just to look at myself like that was delightfully humiliating, and it was more than I could resist not to pull up my skirt, first in front, then at the back, to show off how I could be exposed. Just the idea put a lump in my throat. I imagined being caught, made to take my coat off and lift my skirt, to show a crowd of complete strangers that I was in a nappy, or bending, and having someone see my bulging tights.

Poppy handed me a big mug of milk. I drank it, thinking of how I was deliberately contributing to my own downfall, to wetting myself. I was going to do it too, no question. Monty was ready, and holding my coat for me. I put it on, which hid my nappy bulge completely, but I was still feeling deliciously naughty as I made my way down the stairs. I looked completely normal, but I wasn't. I could feel the nappy, soft and full between my thighs, hugging the contours of my hips, bottom and tummy. Monty kept patting my bottom too, to keep me in mind of my condition.

I had no idea where the shops he wanted were, so I let him lead, down one street, then another, and into a narrow alley with a high brick wall on one side and the massive concrete side of some huge building on the other. I was feeling so naughty I was tempted to flash, and had even started to undo my coat when a man climbed out of a car in front of me. I stifled a giggle, blushing, then stopped. It was Fat Jeff. He was holding a sack.

Monty's huge arms had closed around my body before I could react. One massive, flabby hand closed on my mouth, pressed something to my lips, the chocolate-smeared panties he had taken earlier. I fought, struggling in his arms and trying to speak, only to have the dirty panties forced hard into my mouth. He lifted me as Fat Jeff reached us, both of them ignoring my kicking legs as I was bundled into the sack, upright, and forced down into the boot of the car. Monty let go of my mouth for an instant and I tried to spit the panties out, only to have a thick band of tape pressed into place across my mouth. It was Jeff, and I could only stare in helpless consternation as my head was taped up, the reel wound twice around and torn off, to leave me gagged. More tape went around the neck of the sack and I was truly helpless.

I was still kicking, fighting in the sack and struggling to make myself understood, but nothing would come out. They just grinned back, thoroughly pleased with themselves, sure that for all my struggles I was theirs to do with as they pleased, and that I would enjoy it. Only they were wrong. I was aroused, yes, but I didn't want to be taken away from Gabrielle and Poppy. It wasn't fair, and it was also stupid, to kidnap me when with a little effort they could have had all three of us.

The truth sank in even as Jeff spoke.

'Sorry, babe, but no party is complete without you.'

'You ought to be flattered,' Monty added.

I managed to make a muffled gurgling noise, but I was ignored. The boot slammed and I was in utter darkness. They hadn't kidnapped me for their own dirty amusement. They had kidnapped me to take me to the Rathwells' party.

That was worse, far worse. They could have done the most beastly things to me, spanked me until I was a grovelling, tear-stained mess with a bottom like a ripe plum, peed on me, sat on may face, buggered me and fed me off their cocks, anything. I'd still have ended up accepting it. The Rathwells' was worse, far worse, with the family party the next day, at which I'd be arriving stark, staring bald . . .

I caught another voice, from outside the car, female, and yet another. It was Jade, and Sophie. I began to make muffled squeaking noises again, desperate to draw their attention to my plight. They obviously weren't going to be told I was there until we reached the Rathwells', by which time it would be too late, but if I could just attract their attention. I began to bang against the boot, kicking feebly within the confines of the sack.

'Shut up, Penny.'

It was Jade. She knew I was there. She was in on it. Sophie spoke next.

'Be a good girl and lie still, Penny, and remember, you brought this on yourself. You deserted poor Jade, and you know you're just being silly about the party.'

I struggled to speak, nearly choking on the balled-up panties, but nothing intelligible came out. She went on.

'Mel's not going to shave your head, so stop being such a baby! Jade and Zoe and me let her have us for a whole night . . . which is another sore bum I owe you, by the way. She gave her word she wouldn't shave you, in writing, and witnessed by Harmony, Morris and that lawyer bloke, Montague.'

Still I struggled to make myself understood. Montague was a pretty high-powered lawyer. He was also one of Morris' spankers, and something of a favourite with Mel. I might be able to trust him, but it was simply not a risk I could afford to take. I continued to kick. Sophie spoke.

'Just shut up, Penny!'

The engine started. I rolled in the sack as the car pulled out and was forced to brace myself with my knees and elbows. One of the girls spoke, but I could no longer make out the words. It was hopeless to fight, and as I let my muscles go limp I was wondering how long I could hold in the pint or so of milk Poppy had given me.

Long enough was the answer, so long as they went straight to the Rathwells'. It was in Hampstead, maybe an hour's drive in bad traffic, and I wasn't straining at all. My bladder wasn't anyway. My tummy was still painfully tight, but I knew I could make it without having an accident. If they went to Jeff's, or Jade's, and left me, then I was in real trouble. It seemed to take for ever, but I made it, my worry subsiding as I heard Jeff speak into an intercom, but not my fear. It meant we had reached the Rathwells' gates. We drove through, parked, and I heard Morris' voice.

'Have you got Penny?'

'Yeah, no problem,' Jeff answered. 'It worked a treat.'

'Nice one, boys, and girls,' another voice answered,

feminine, silky and cruel. Melody Rathwell. 'Hi Sophie, hi Jade.'

'She's in the boot. In a sack,' Monty put in with great relish.

'I'll get her out, yeah?' Jeff said.

'Yes, do that,' Melody answered. 'Don't let her out, just stick her in one of the bedrooms.'

'Got it.'

Jeff's key clicked in the lock and the boot came open, flooding me with light. He stood above me, Monty next to him. I tried to plead with my eyes and made more muffled noises through my panty gag. They ignored me, reaching in to lift me by the sack. Melody paid no attention whatever as I was hauled up onto Jeff's shoulder, but she led the way into the house and up the stairs. The others followed, to a spare bedroom, where I was dumped down. Jeff was puffing a little, but was grinning as he turned to Melody.

'One bitch, as ordered,' he said.

'And now we get our blow-jobs, yeah?' Monty demanded.

'Of course,' Melody answered sweetly. 'Sophie, Jade, see to the boys.'

Sophie took Jeff's hand, Jade took Monty's and they left. Melody came to look down on me, her full lips curled up into a cruel smile, her eyes shining with pleasure. She spoke.

'So, Penny, now I get even.'

Eleven

I lay helpless in front of Melody Rathwell, gagged and sacked up. My whole body was shaking, my heart hammering, and I was telling myself over and over that I had to stay in control, and not let her dominance get to me.

It was not easy. She had punished me so many times, spanked me, caned me, peed on me, made me lick her pussy and bumhole. I'd given her the same, though, once or twice, and I forced myself to remember how she'd looked tied, with head shaved and an apple stuck in her mouth so she could be served as a suckling pig.

She nodded, her cruel, dark eyes moving down the sack to where my bottom was pushed against it. Her hand came out, to pat me though the sack, firmly. Her expression changed to puzzlement as she felt the soft, thick padding over my skin. She spoke.

'You're dressed, aren't you?'

I nodded.

'In what, a quilted jacket? It's not that cold out. Hey . . .'

Her wicked grin grew that much broader as she realised why I was so well padded.

'You're in a nappy, aren't you?'

I gave a single, forlorn nod, my attempts to hold myself as her equal dissolving in ruin. She chuckled, and began to work on the tape at the neck of the sack, still speaking, her voice full of laughter.

'So who put you in a nappy? Poppy and this Gabrielle girl?'

I nodded again. She went on.

'Playing your dirty little games, eh? You are a filthy bitch, you know that, don't you? You're what Jeff Bellbird calls you, aren't you? A dirtbag bitch. So maybe I'll let you keep your nappy on this evening. I bet you'd like that?'

I shook my head frantically. She made a face, expressing mock pity. Being in a nappy was special, for Poppy and Gabrielle, nobody else. Melody didn't know, and if I told her she would only laugh.

She had unfastened my neck, and she stood to tip me out of the bag, my boots coming with it, leaving me to stretch on the bed in an effort to ease the stiffness of my knees and hips. I put my hands to my gag, determined to have my say, but she caught my wrists, twisting both to force me face down on the bed.

'Tut, tut, Penny, none of that. Diss me and you are in big, big trouble. Now are you going to let me undress you, or do we have to make a fight of this? You know I can do it, Penny, and you know it's fair.'

I shook my head frantically, but I had gone limp, knowing I was going to stripped whether I liked it or not. Maybe it would be nude, maybe just down to my nappy, but it was going to happen. She continued to talk as she began to fiddle with the buttons of my coat, one hand holding my twisted arms, the other beneath me.

'It is fair, Penny, and you know it. You did me up good and proper, and now you'll get yours. So you whored for Morris, and yeah, I know you hate that stuff, but you love the spanking, and all that male attention, and don't try me with any of that goodie-two-shoes bullshit. I know.'

I could only nod my head in miserable agreement as my coat came open. She took the sleeves and pulled it off behind me, revealing my skirt and the bulge beneath.

'Oh, very ladylike!' she laughed, and planted a firm smack on my seat. 'Yeah, I know you, Penny Birch. You are the dirtiest slut out, no competition! Going out in a nappy, yeah? And I bet you were going to shit in it? You make Sophie look pure, you do.'

She laughed again, as she popped the button on the back of my skirt. It came loose, the zip was slid quickly down. Her hands took hold of the hem and it was pulled down my legs, and off, exposing the seat of my tights, stretched out around the puffy nappy material.

'Pink rabbits?' she commented. 'And ducks too, and little baby puppy-dogs, how sweet! Let's get a better look.'

Her hands locked in my tights and they followed my skirt, down and off, to leave me in just my nappy below the waist.

'Nice,' she said. 'The boys are going to love you tonight.'

I shook my head frantically, and turned to plead with my eyes. She wagged a finger at me and rolled me over onto my back. Taking a firm grip on my upper clothes, jumper and top together, she hauled it all up, lifting me as she did so, to pull the lot over my head. My bra had become disarranged, one tit peeping over out of her cup. Melody tucked it back in, only to snip my catch open and pull my whole bra off.

As before, I was topless in a nappy, only now it didn't feel naughty and free, it felt vulnerable and thoroughly humiliating. I was really trembling, and I wanted so badly to give in to her, utterly. She began to touch, tweaking one already hard nipple, then running a hand down over the curve of my waist and around to my swollen tummy. Abruptly she moved her hand, to cup the crotch of my nappy.

'Still dry, I see,' she remarked.

I nodded.

'Not for long, I suspect,' she went on. 'So, are you going to be a good girl?'

Again I nodded.

'I'm very glad to hear it, Penny. I promised your fellow little tarts that I wouldn't shave your head, and as you know, I always keep my word. You needn't worry about that but, to make up for it, I want you to be my slave this evening, and maid for the party.'

I nodded once more, but I didn't believe it. It was too easy, and nothing she wouldn't have asked of me anyway.

'When I say maid,' she went on, 'I don't just mean serving the drinkers and letting the guests have an occasional feel. I mean being ready for service, for everybody, all night. That means men and women, for whatever they want, subject to my choice. No stop word or, if you do use it, I'll have your head as bald as your buns in five minutes.'

This time my nod was less eager. I could cope, maybe, but there were some things beyond my limits, and she knew them. All she had to do was pick some maniac who would demand something totally unacceptable, and I'd be done. I wanted to tell her it wasn't fair, that I couldn't play that sort of game, that I had a responsible job, anything. I couldn't, which was clearly why she'd left me gagged.

'Good,' she said. 'First off, I think I'll have you greet the guests just as you are, in your nappy. You can stand at the door and serve drinks. Your clothes stay here, so I can trust you. Put them in that wardrobe.'

I obeyed, hanging my coat up and folding the rest beneath it. Melody watched, lounging on the bed. She was in a simple black dress, leather, as powerful and languid as ever. I considered trying to bargain with her, to let me remove her gag, perhaps to have my face sat on in return for being allowed to take the nappy off. Nude was better, for me, in front of their guests. She knew that, and I knew that if I tried to bargain I'd be lucky to get my bottom roasted before I was sent downstairs.

When I'd finished she locked the wardrobe, then led me to another room, one they'd done out as a play room, with a thing like a miniature vaulting horse for girls to be bent over for whippings, a great wooden cross, and an iron cage. There was also plenty of equipment, all designed for the punishment, control, restraint or humiliation of girls. I stood biting my lip and looking dumbly at the line up of canes, whips and paddles, wondering how many were going to be applied to my bottom before the night was out, and how hard.

Melody had ducked down, to open a chest. The inside was full of compartments, each lined in red velvet, each containing a device, in stainless steel, bright chrome or even silver. She chose one, a solid metal torc with a long chain link lead attached to it. I tilted my chin up, surrendering to her, and it was fitted around my neck, the catch clipped off and a tiny key twisted into the lock.

She had collared me, but she wasn't finished. Again she bent, this time to pick up a silver tray with a short length of chain and a cuff at each side. I sighed as I put my wrists out, again giving in to her without thought for my likes and dislikes. I could bear it, I knew, both serving and being made to go near naked, even with the added humiliation of the nappy. By the end I would come to take pleasure in it, I knew, in certainty at my reaction to erotic humiliation.

As the first cuff was locked off onto my wrist I heard footsteps in the corridor, then the voice of Melody's twin sister, Harmony. She had their pet with her, Annabelle, who was stark naked, her hair no more than a short blonde frizz on her scalp, her pussy shaved, with her slave tattoo clearly visible. A horrible thought occurred to me, that Melody might force me to choose between shaving or having my own pussy tattooed, or worse . . .

I'd be running to fetch the razor myself.

'Cute,' Harmony remarked, running her eyes down my body. 'What's with the nappy?'

'She was already in it,' Melody explained.

'Slut,' Annabelle remarked, and immediately squealed as Harmony's hand met her bottom.

'Shouldn't she be able to greet the guests?' Harmony asked.

'No, keep her gagged. She talks far too much.'

'What if some guy wants her to suck him?'

'He can fuck her, whatever.'

Harmony shrugged and ducked down to pull a collar from the chest. Annabelle was evidently my fellow maid, only she would be nude.

'Where's Sophie?' Harmony asked.

'Sucking one of the guys who got Penny,' Melody answered. 'Jade too. Deal with them, would you? I'm going to put this one front of house.'

'Nobody'll be here for quite a while.'

'So?'

She had taken my lead, and pulled me after her as she left the room. I pointed as we passed the loo, to the door, then between my legs.

'Wet yourself, that's what the nappy's for, isn't it?' she laughed, and pulled me on down the corridor.

I followed, resigned to being maid, but determined not to wet my nappy, let alone fill it. She'd leave me soggy, I knew, and I'd smell. That was unbearable, with so many people there who just wouldn't understand, for all their love of spanking, bondage or whatever it might be. In front of Gabrielle and Poppy was one thing. They understood. In front of the Rathwells' guests was another thing again, too much, more than I could take.

Melody led me down stairs, into the huge, vulgar entrance hall. There were pillars to either side of the door, to match the Greek portico at the front of the house. Both had a double twist of soft, heavy rope around them, with a steel ring fixed into the knot. My lead was clipped to one and Melody walked away, her heels ringing on the marble floor.

The lead wasn't locked, and for a moment I considered pulling the gag off and unfastening myself. It was pointless, as I'd still have the collar on, the tray fixed to my wrists and my clothes locked away upstairs. I couldn't find it in myself to face Morris and Melody down either, because I knew in my heart that I didn't want to. All I needed to do was stay calm and pray she would play fair. She had before, or I would never have been able to shave her in the first place. With luck she would again, or I could make my stand when the time came, or fight and struggle and kick until it finally sank in that they just could not do it to me . . .

I brought myself back from the edge of hysteria with an effort. I told myself that I had choices, but I simply didn't want to make them now. What I could do was visit the downstairs loo. It was just a few metres away, and I could be in and out in maybe two or three minutes, with the nappy back on and nobody any the wiser. Not that I was yet in any danger of actually wetting myself, but the milk had come through and I could feel the urge building up. If I was caught it would mean a spanking, maybe the cane, but I was going to get beaten anyway, doubtless several times. It was tempting, too tempting . . .

Harmony appeared on the staircase even as I turned to unclip my lead. She was leading Annabelle, who was collared but had no tray. I hung my head in submission and if she had noticed she didn't react, simply clipping Annabelle into place opposite me. Like me, Annabelle had been gagged, her neat, pretty mouth open around the red ball held in by a leather strap. Slender, naked, with her tattoo on plain view, she looked extremely vulnerable, yet elegant. She was in five-inch patent leather heels connected by a thin silver chain, enhancing her long legs and muscular little bottom, while her trim waist, neatly rounded little belly and small, firm breasts added to her appearance as a true icon of the submissive female. I tried to remind myself of how much more popular I was than her among the spankers, both male and female, but found myself looking down at my bare feet and the bulky nappy around my hips.

Harmony left us, walking away, only to turn as she reached the bottom of the stairs, and speak.

'The bathroom's locked, Penny, so don't bother.'

She clattered away up the stairs. I exchanged a look with Annabelle, and she raised her eyebrows in return. Again I glanced to the ring on which my lead was clipped off, wondering if I could make it upstairs, only for Morris himself to appear, carrying a case of Champagne. He barely glanced towards us, but I realised it was hopeless. The girls would be making up, and there was Morris too, and Monty and Jeff. I'd be caught before I made it.

I gave in, resting against the pillar. I had no idea of the time, but it was still full daylight outside, and couldn't be much past one o'clock, if that. If it was an evening party, I'd have maybe six or seven hours to wait, and I would have wet myself long before then. I tried to remember what time it had said on the invitation, but I'd barely glanced at it before refusing, and I knew it might be one, or the other.

When the intercom went, maybe half-an-hour later, maybe longer, I was actually relieved. Sophie appeared, naked, collared and with a tray like mine, but attached to only one wrist and laden with full Champagne flutes. She began to giggle as she saw me, then spoke quickly into the intercom and pressed the button. I straightened up, holding out my tray and she began to unload flutes onto it.

Now I was really stuck. There was no way I could put the tray down and deal with my nappy even if I did get to the loo. The glasses would fall, the lot. Not that I gave a damn for the Rathwells' glassware, but I was in no state to be surrounded by broken glass, barefoot. I'd just have to try and hold on.

It was Gavin Bulmer, along with Andy and Emmeline. I found myself blushing as their eyes moved immediately to my nappy, and more for Emmeline than either of the men. They looked amused. She looked shocked. It was going to get worse, I knew.

Sure enough, more people soon began to arrive. Morris came to the door, offering the guests Champagne from my tray and instructing them to give their coats to Annabelle, who was hanging them on a rack behind the pillar. All of them looked at her, in admiration, envy, open lust. All of them looked at me, in amusement, derision, shock. Many of them made a joke, mostly to do with incontinence. The pressure in my bladder grew steadily.

By the time the house had began to fill up I flushed pink from my face to my chest, and my obvious embarrassment had begun to draw even greater amusement and even worse jokes. They began to grope me too, touching my breasts to make my nipples erect, tilting my head up by the chin, stroking my hair or the skin of my tummy. I was soon dizzy with both arousal and humiliation, and didn't know if I wanted to come, or cry, or both.

A group arrived, all men, all middle-aged, but not Morris' regular spankers. I didn't know any of them, they were loud and red faced with drink. As they came closer I realised that they were German. I wasn't surprised. I'd known Morris to invite men he wanted to impress or influence before, men who didn't understand the subtleties of etiquette. I stiffened, more aware than ever of my nappy, and held out my drinks tray, perfectly still.

'Pretty, yes,' one remarked to Morris, his eyes lingering on Annabelle's body.

'My wife's slave,' Morris said casually.

'Ah yes,' the man said as his gaze reached Annabelle's tattoo. 'You are marked, little one. That is good.'

He had given her his coat, but stopped her as she turned to hang it up, holding her arm. Morris did nothing, but watched with a quiet smile as the man put his finger to Annabelle's sex, and up. She stiffened, and her eyes closed as she was penetrated. He chuckled, and said something to his friends, in German. They laughed.

I knew the sort, their knowledge of SM restricted to bad dungeon videos and maybe the *Story of 'O'*. As one turned to me, the biggest, a real bear of a man, I found myself trembling.

'And what is this?' he said. 'In a diaper?'

Another laughed, the man who had been inspecting Annabelle turned to me, the fourth, a short, fat man with a receding hairline, came behind me. I held absolutely still as the big man began to grope my breasts, his huge fingers splayed beneath them, his thumbs rubbing over my nipples. I shut my eyes, my body trembling, my self control right at the edge as his beer-laden breath washed over me.

'Do you like me?' he growled, his accent thick, his voice harsh.

He let go of one boob and took hold of my chin, tilting my head up. I was shaking, and would have been unable to answer even without my gag in. After a moment's more groping he spoke again.

'Maybe I will fuck you, yes?'

I still couldn't answer, but I was thinking of his huge body on top of mine, his cock inside me. He was looking right into my eyes, his own strangely pale, a milky grey. He was going to fuck me, I was sure of it, and Melody would make sure I let him, maybe hold me for him, maybe tie me down for him to use just as he pleased . . .

My half-scared, half-excited fantasy broke as the little fat man behind me took hold of the waistband of my nappy. I jerked instinctively, my muscles reacting to the touch, and to the knowledge that he was peering down the seat of my nappy, at my bare bum. He spoke.

'Yes, it is good to fuck her. She is clean down her nappy.'

'You say she is clean?' another said. 'She will not be when Carl has finished with her.'

They burst into laughter. I burst into tears.

It was just too much, to be molested, teased, made to feel as if my will was nothing, all that I could handle. To have my nappy inspected to see if I was clean or dirty was too much, from him, from someone who only wanted to make a joke of it.

In an instant the tears were running down my face in streams, accompanied by great racking sobs as the full depth of my feelings burst to the surface. A moment later Morris' arm was around me. He spoke as he began to dab at my cheeks with a handkerchief.

'Hey, that's not like you, Penny. What's the matter?'

He didn't wait for me to try and answer, but began to pull the tape from my face. I let him, still in tears, my vision too hazy to do more than make out the rough shapes of the people around me. I winced as the tape was pulled from my skin, and off the hairs on the back of my neck, but it came. Morris hugged me closer as I spat out my panties, now sodden. They fell on the floor with a wet plop.

'Do come in, gentlemen,' Morris addressed the Germans.

They moved on, still laughing and joking among themselves, and obviously at my expense. I just stood there, snivelling pathetically with snot running down my face and crying so hard I couldn't see at all. I heard a click as Morris unclipped my lead, then his voice.

'Sophie! Take over on the door. Harmony, take Penny upstairs, give her a cuddle, spank her bottom for her, rub her cunt, whatever. I tell you, what did I say earlier, warm them up!'

'Mel was with her,' Harmony answered, but Morris had already turned to greet a new guest.

Sophie had come, and took my glasses, leaving Harmony to lead me upstairs. It was so easy to relax into her body, to let her comfort me, even when I knew full well she would be firmly on her sister's side. That didn't matter. I needed to be held, and she was there, stroking my hair and whispering soothing things to me as she led me to the master bedroom.

I knew she wouldn't stand any nonsense, and I was in no condition to give any. As she sat down on the bed I simply melted into her arms, unsure if I was to be cuddled, or spanked. What she did was to cradle my head and back, and put me to her breast. She was already bare, in a tightly laced corset of bright green silk that thrust her big, dark breasts out. I took her nipple in, suckling, my emotions still raw, the tears still trickling form my eyes.

I gave in completely, my eyes closed as I mouthed on her nipple, surrendered to her as she brought my feelings back into balance. It was soothing, at first, nothing more, but I knew what she was doing, and how I would react. She was touching the back of my neck, gentle, easy caresses, and stroking my back as she held me. Slowly, steadily, my arousal began to come back. My tears stopped, I began to feed more eagerly on her teat.

She changed her grip, her hand slid down the front of my nappy and she was masturbating me. I just let it happen, still sobbing as her fingers probed my body; two sliding deep into me to hold me by my pussy, two splaying my bum cheeks, to stretch my anus out. My legs came apart, wide, spread to her fingers. I took more breast flesh into my mouth. She cradled me closer, pulling my face to the abundant softness of her chest. Her thumb began to work on my clitty.

I was going to come. She had me completely, surrendered to her, body and mind, feeling warm and safe as I suckled her and her fingers worked on my sex and neck. Already I could feel my pussy muscles tightening, my bumhole twitching. She knew me too, changing her grip once more, to rub my anus with a finger still juicy from my sex – my cunt.

She penetrated my bumhole as I started to come, popping my ring just at the right moment, so I felt it tighten on her. My pussy clamped too, hard on the intruding digit and I was there, mouthing on her boob, rubbing my face into the softness of her chest, squirming in her arms. For one blissful moment all my bad feelings were gone and there was nothing but pleasure. I held the feeling, as long as I could, and she went on frigging, holding me as I jerked and trembled in her arms.

It finished, eventually, to leave me limp and a little drained. The need to pee had gone, but came back immediately, stronger than before. I almost gave in, knowing that I could do it with her, and that the worst I would get would be a smacked bum.

'That's better, isn't it?' she said, ruffling my hair. 'Now let's see about your bottom.'

I gave a little squeak of surprise, not having expected to get spanked after I'd come, but she was already rolling me over. I went, unresisting, bum up over her lap. Her fingers found my nappy tabs and it was being opened, one side, the other, and the back pulled down over my bum, to leave my cheeks bare and ready.

She began to spank, immediately, the slaps ringing out around the room, then my cries as it got harder. I knew she was being nice, warming my bum so I could cope with my job as maid, but it still hurt, and I couldn't help but kick and wriggle and squeak. She kept going, holding me firmly in place as my cheeks bounced and spread, until my whole bottom was suffused with a warm glow and I had begun to stick it up for more. Immediately she stopped.

'There we are, now back to work with you.'

'Okay,' I answered. 'I will. Can I go without my nappy?'

'I suppose so . . . yes, why not? People ought to be able to see your red bum.'

I nodded as I climbed up. I felt so much better, infinitely more confident, even to wanting to show off my red cheeks to my friends and the guests. Harmony gave me a final swat as I stood, and followed me from the room. I considered asking her about Melody's intentions, but didn't, sure that she would only say what her sister had told her to.

What I could do was go to the loo. Not easily, with the tray handcuffed to my wrists, but I could manage. Unfortunately Morris had locked his private bathroom, and the main upstairs one was very much in use, with the door fastened and ecstatic grunting and sighs coming from within. So I went downstairs, only to find a queue. I waited, now wriggling a bit but sure I could hold on. Morris appeared, smiling, and glancing at my bottom with an appreciative nod.

'Sorry about our German friends, Penny,' he said, 'but you're all right now?'

'Just about,' I said. 'It just got too much for me. I . . .'

'I understand, and you know I'll look after you, don't you?'

'Yes . . .'

'And you'll give them a bit of action later, yeah?'

'Morris! I . . .'

'Good girl, they're well into you.'

'But Morris . . . oh, never mind. Look, Morris, about Mel and this head-shaving thing? I . . .'

I stopped. Melody herself was approaching, with a man I had never met before; young, very good-looking, with an air of smug arrogance. He was in a suit, immaculate and clearly expensive. Morris immediately broke into a real crocodile grin and stepped towards them. There was music, and I didn't catch their words, but Morris gestured to me and Melody nodded. They started towards me. Morris gave me a sign from behind their backs, the circled fingers he always used when he wanted a man shown particular favour.

'What a pretty slave,' the man remarked to Mel as they came close. 'Is she yours?'

'Yes,' Melody answered and I felt my mouth twitch in instinctive protest.

'Still impudent, I see,' he said, 'and no tattoo. New?'

'Yes,' Mel repeated.

He looked at me, downwards.

'Turn around, girl.'

I stifled a sigh as I obeyed.

'Not bad,' he remarked as I presented my bottom to him. 'Well formed, certainly, if perhaps a little fleshy. Do you know what I'd do, if she was mine? I wouldn't tattoo her, I'd brand her.'

He was another of the same, like the Germans, full of rubbish he'd picked up from videos and such. Either that or he was a genuine psychopath. Nobody in their right mind brands girls.

'Recently spanked too,' he said as his hand found my bottom, 'but not very hard. If I were to beat you, girl, I'd do a proper job of it. In fact, I think I just might.'

I jumped as he planted a sudden, stinging slap on my bottom. It sent a jolt to my bladder, reminding me how badly I needed to go.

'Where should I take her?' he asked, addressing Melody.

'Anywhere you like,' she answered casually. 'Do her in private, or in front of everyone. It's up to you.'

'Up to me, of course,' he said, and turned to me.

'So, slave, tell me your name?' he demanded. 'And you can turn around now, I'll be seeing plenty more of your bottom soon enough, and so will everybody else.'

'It's Penny,' I told him.

'Well, Penny,' he went on. 'I'm going to smack your bottom, in public, and then maybe I'll take you upstairs and fuck the living daylights out of you, if it amuses me. How does that feel?'

'I . . .' I began, and caught Melody's warning look as she stepped away. 'I'm a little scared . . . I haven't much experience . . .'

He gave me a smug little grin that told me it had been the right thing to say. I was pressing my legs together to ease the growing pain in my bladder, the bathroom was vacant. It couldn't wait, and I certainly couldn't get through another spanking.

'I need to go to the loo first,' I babbled. 'Please?'

'Is that any way to address me?' he answered coolly. 'You call me Master. You should know that.'

I would have called him Supreme Ruler of the Universe to be allowed to run to the loo. Master was fine.

'Please, Master.'

'Please what, slave?'

'Please may I go to the loo, Master?'

'Hum . . . I'm not sure. Maybe . . . Yes, why not? It will amuse me to watch you.'

I didn't care if he watched me or not. I didn't care if he made me suck his cock afterwards, or fucked me, buggered me, anything. I just wanted the loo. He pulled on my chain, towards the toilet door. I was going to make it, just. My bladder gave a sudden, sharp twinge, but I held on, hobbling towards the loo behind him, my thighs crossed, my hand pressed to my tummy, biting my lip against the pain in my bladder. He stopped.

'Or maybe not,' he said. 'I shall spank you first.'

'No, please . . . please, Master, I can't . . . Ow!'

He had jerked on my chain, pulling me down even as he took a seat on one of the chairs put out specifically to make it convenient to spank the girls. I went, down over his knee, bum high, and as he kicked my legs apart to get me showing from the rear I just exploded.

I gasped as it happened, loud, but no louder than the sound of the piss as it squirted from my spread pussy. He cried out in genuine anger as it spurted over his trouser leg, and then he had dropped me. I went down on my bum, the pee still squirting out, in a high fountain as I sprawled on the floor. He was cursing, and slapping at the huge pee stain on his leg, but I simply didn't care. It was too late to stop, and I just lay there, on my back, legs spread, with the piddle hissing and bubbling out of me, all over the floor.

Even when I finally stopped I made no effort to get up, but just lay there, with my bum in the enormous puddle I'd made. He'd gone, too furious to hold his supposed role as a dominant, but other people quickly began to gather round. Most of them were thoroughly amused, a few shocked. I was wondering if any would have the guts to simply fuck me where I lay, or give me a wet spanking, when Melody pushed through the crowd. She was holding a bucket and a big yellow sponge.

'Mop it up, Penny,' she sighed. 'Honestly, can't you keep yourself under control for five minutes? That was one of Morris' most important clients.'

I opened my mouth to speak, struck so hard by the sheer injustice of her words that it was threatening to start the tears in my eyes again. She had turned away before I could bring myself to say anything, and I was left to mop up my pee, with a good dozen people watching me. I took the sponge, only to discover that with the tray attached to my wrists it was almost impossible to use it.

Someone began to laugh at my efforts, then another. I bit down my feelings, determined not to get in a state again, but to let my humiliation become erotic. I was mopping up piss, my own piss, which I'd done in front of the people now watching me. It didn't matter who they were, so long as it turned them on. I hung my head as I began to scrub one-handed, holding the tray with the other.

I'd splashed all over the place, making a long, ragged pool, with bits a good few metres away where I'd squirted as I'd been put over his knee. I was wet with it too, my thighs and bum soaked, as well as my knees, and my lead was hanging in it. All I could do was scrub, and think about the show I was making from the rear, with my red behind wobbling behind me as I worked, my pussy on plain view, and available to anyone with the guts to just stick his cock up me. No one dared, too shy, or too precious, to just get down and use me. I couldn't ask. I needed to be taken, fucked, buggered even . . .

I turned as a male voice sounded behind me, a lewd drawl.

'Fucking nice! Stick it up, Pen.'

It was Monty. He just didn't care that he'd have to kneel in my piss pool to fuck me, that other people were watching. All he cared about was the display I was making of my bum, and what that did to his cock, no more precious or shy than a rampant bull.

He got down, right in the pee, gripping me by the hips. I put the sponge down and braced myself, folding my arms on the tray. His zip came down with a rasping sound, his knuckles brushed between my bum cheeks, then his cock, resting in the shallow groove, his balls hot and ticklish against my pussy. He began to rut, his cock already hardening as the fat shaft began to move in my crease.

'Fucking nice!' he repeated. 'I love it, rubbed up a bum slit. What's it to be, Penny, cunt, or up the dirt box?'

I closed my eyes, the sheer crudity of his words enough to send a shock right through me. He was going to do me, properly, with people watching, and he knew I'd like it up the bum, but he was going to make me choose, force me to say the dirty words . . .

'My . . . my bum, please, Monty,' I managed, my voice a hoarse croak.

Someone in the crowd called me a dirty slut, but he didn't leave. More had packed in behind the front row, so that we were in a circle of gawping men, girls too, Jade among them, a lover, watching a man rut in my crease, about to watch me buggered, by a man . . . actually by the same man the little tart had sucked off not so long before.

'Bum it is,' Monty said cheerfully, his cock now a stiff rod between my cheeks.

He took his cock, pushing it down to my sex, and in, not deep, and only to scoop up some juice from one to hole to grease the other. It felt good anyway, and I was sighing and gasping to the motion as he began to plaster the wet from my pussy up over my anus. I let myself go loose, pushing a little, then hastily tightening my ring as I realised it was not such a good idea. I was full, and it was going to get messy, something better done in private.

Nobody had told Monty, and it was too late to stop him. He'd put his cock to my bumhole, and he must have realised, because it went in easily, with a distinct squelch. Nobody could see, with his huge belly lying on top of my bum, but they could hear, and I felt the blood rush to my face in embarrassment, even as Monty gave his second push.

I gasped in reaction as a good two or three inches of thick, hard penis were abruptly jammed into my already packed rectum. Monty grunted in pleasure and tightened his grip on my flesh. I put my head down, grovelling in my pee as I was buggered, at once utterly ashamed and utterly delighted, ecstatic and in an agony of embarrassment, with a man's cock up in my already bloated rectum and so many others looking on.

Monty just did not care. He simply forced the rest of his cock up my bum, bit by bit, until his balls were hanging against my vacant pussy, and began to pump into me, making a disgusting squashy noise with each push. I kept my eyes closed, concentrating on the breathless ecstasy of a really good buggering, and the bulging, helpless feeling in my packed gut. I didn't even know Jeff was there until I heard his voice.

'Nice one, Monty, you dirty snerd nurgler!'

He was right next to me, and even as I looked up he had taken me by the hair.

'Shouldn't have let your nappy go, should you?' he said, nodding to the pee pool.

He laughed, and abruptly pushed my face down, right into the pee, catching me off guard. For a moment my face was being rubbed on the floor, with my lips spread out in the piss and my nose pressed down hard. Then he had brought my head up again, and was tugging at his fly. It came. His hand went in, and his fat cock came out, even as my head was dragged towards it.

'Suck it!' he ordered.

I didn't need to be told. My mouth was already wide, my lips pushed out. His cock went in and I was sucking, the thick taste of male mixing with that of my own pee. He still had my hair, and began to tug on in, forcing me to let him control the rhythm as he fed his cock in and out of my mouth. After a moment he adjusted himself, leaning back so that he could fuck my head at leisure and stay clear of the pee.

Monty had kept himself moving up my bum as Jeff got in place, but as I started to suck he got faster, and harder. I'd seldom felt so bloated with a cock up me, and I knew I was going to have to run the moment he pulled out. For now, I couldn't, but only let them use me, a cock in each end, my body a toy for their use, my dignity nothing, my feelings nothing.

Jeff was soon hard, and had begun to force his erection into my throat, to make me gag on his helmet. I wanted to frig, to come as they used me, to feel Jeff spunk in my mouth, and know Monty had done it up my bum, to let the audience know that I wasn't just willing, but really enjoying it. I tried to get my arms back, but I couldn't, slipping in my piddle and unable to hold myself up with the tray on my wrists.

'Stop arseing around, Penny!' Jeff ordered, as I slipped for the third time. 'Leave your cunt alone, you dirty bitch!'

'No,' Monty grunted. 'Let her. I like the way their arseholes tighten when they come.'

'Nah, make her a Corn Fed Chicken, that's the best.'

Monty laughed, and stopped, suddenly. I tried to look round, but he was already pulling his cock from my hole. As the head popped free I remembered what a Cord Fed Chicken was. Jeff laughed. I tried to protest around my mouthful of cock, but I couldn't, not in earnest. I knew I wanted it, and I couldn't stop myself, for the agonising wave of self-pity and disgust that swept over me as Monty took a firm hold of my body and twisted.

I came, sliding around in the piss, and I was gaping before I could stop myself. My eyes popped as his cock was stuffed firmly in my mouth, and then I was sucking up my own mess, with tears of humiliation spraying from my eyes as I jammed them shut, unable to bear the thought of being watched suck on the penis that had only a moment before been jammed to the hilt up my dirty bottom.

'Fucking little slut bitch!' Monty sighed. 'That is good!'

He had taken my head, to hold me on his cock, making sure I couldn't get away. I didn't want to. I was sucking with desperate eagerness, my pussy twitching even without the touch of my fingers. I had to come, instantly, before the moment was lost. My arms went back, heedless of the tray, to snatch at my aching cunt. Monty grabbed me as I went down, holding me firmly, and I was frigging, even as Jeff's cock head found my bumhole. He went straight up, my anus slack, my rectum an easy, sloppy passage, into which he jammed the full length of his erection in two firm shoves.

Monty grunted, and came, full in my mouth, adding a mouthful of slimy spunk to my woes. My anus clamped on Jeff's cock and I was coming too, sucking in desperation, wriggling my bottom on the huge erection inside it, snatching frantically at my sex as my pleasure rose, up and up and up. I heard Jeff grunt as his cock erupted up my pulsing bumhole. My whole body went tight, painfully tight, and I had swallowed what was in my mouth, to bring myself to a second peak, higher, more powerful than the last.

I just collapsed, completely, sliding off their cocks before they had pulled back themselves. Everybody was staring, silent, the man whose suit I had peed over included, his mouth open in amazement. On some rebellious impulse I gave him a casual V sign as I pulled myself up onto one elbow, but he continued to stare.

'Nice,' Monty sighed. 'You are one dirty bitch!'

Jeff nodded. I managed a weak smile. Monty shifted his weight, and winced.

'Ah, my fucking legs!' he complained.

'Dead right,' Jeff agreed. 'I hate doggy position. Be a doll and clean up, Pen.'

He slapped my bum as he rose. I could only shake my head. My mouth was still thick with the taste of my own bottom, and it wasn't so good after the orgasm. There was a bottle of rum on a table nearby. I caught it up, upended it over my mouth, rinsed, and spat into the bucket I'd been using for the floor. The crowd had begun to disperse, and I followed Monty and Jeff into the bathroom to wash. I'd meant to give them a piece of my mind for kidnapping me, but I simply couldn't bring myself to argue. Instead I managed a single question.

'Did you two perverts tell Gabrielle and Poppy you'd taken me?'

'Yeah, sure,' Monty answered. 'I sent a text. What do you think we are, irresponsible or something?'

I shook my head and went back to the rum. My bumhole was sore, and my cheeks still felt sensitive. I needed some time in the loo, alone, as well. I was clearly not going to get it downstairs, with the house now pretty well full to capacity, and they had enema equipment upstairs, something I badly needed if people were going to expect to bugger me. So I gave the boys a kiss each to thank them and made for the stairs, only to find Sophie in the corridor, mopping up my mess. She immediately threw the sponge at me.

'Clean up you own mess, you!' she said as I dodged.

I just stuck my tongue out, but went for the sponge, as it was only fair. She stood up.

'I owe you such a spanking,' she said, 'and you are not going to get away with it.'

'You do not!' I protested as I got down once more, squatting so I didn't get too messy. 'You helped Monty and Jeff kidnap me, Sophie!'

'Yeah, and?'

'And that makes us even after my trick at the Night of the Clowns, that's what!'

'Oh, no, it does not! I got had by eight men – eight!'

'Yes, and you loved every second of it.'

'Like you then, and . . .'

She stopped. Melody was coming towards us.

'Sophie, get back to serving,' Mel ordered. 'Penny, what are you doing?'

'Cleaning up.'

'For half an hour?'

'I . . . I got waylaid.'

'So I heard, buggered by Monty Hartle and Fat Jeff. You're supposed to be serving drinks.'

'Yes, but I had to clean up, you said, and . . . sorry, Mel.'

I hung my head, expecting my face slapped, maybe to be turned over her knee. Nothing happened.

'Slut,' she remarked. 'Now get on with it, and from now on, stick to quick blow jobs. There are nearly twice as many people here as we expected. Nobody seems to understand what RSVP stands for any more.'

She stormed off, leaving me to finish up. I did it as quickly as I could and went to the kitchen, reasoning that it would be better to do as I was told. With my tray laden with flutes once more, I began to circulate. It was not easy, with barely a gap between the knots of people and nobody watching what they were doing. Having my bum constantly pinched and my boobs molested didn't help either. Then there were the spankings, with kicking legs sticking out in all sorts of unexpected places as one girl or another had her bottom reddened.

It was still a break, and I took several opportunities to refresh myself, even though it meant balancing my tray and bending over to get my lips to the glass, which was just asking for trouble. Before long I was pleasantly tipsy, and had even begun to feel confident. Mel not only seemed to be good for her word, but was far too busy playing hostess to worry about me. If anything, she was more interested in my ex, Amber, trying to tease her into taking a spanking, or lending out the winsome Kay, who was firmly attached to a lead.

Amber had been with me the night I shaved Melody's head, and I went over to see if she had picked up anything, curtseying as I offered the Champagne. Both accepted, Kay giving me her shy smile as she took hers. She was achingly pretty, and I still felt a touch of jealousy as she took a firm hold on Amber's arm.

Mel had said nothing, and after talking for a while I moved on, more sure of myself than ever. There was a cabaret coming up, a caning competition, to see who could produce the most perfect set of lines across a girl's bum, and give the best display while doing it. That was presumably the highlight of the evening. I was safe.

I still needed my visit to the loo, preferably for an enema, but I held it off until I had began to wriggle. With the competition in half-an-hour, I made my way upstairs, only to find the bathroom locked again. Irritated, I knocked on the door. A voice called out from inside, female.

'Girl or boy?'

'Girl,' I answered. 'Can I come in please?'

'Alone?'

'Yes.'

I hadn't recognised the voice, but when the door opened I recognised them. It was Jade's tormentors, Naomi, Sam, and the butchest of all, AJ. AJ and Sam were in the giant Jacuzzi Morris had installed, relaxing back against the edge and drinking beer from the bottle. Naomi had let me in, and as I entered she shut the door behind me, at the same moment I realised Jade and Zoe were there as well.

They had been hung from the shower rail, their arms stretched high above their heads, their wrists linked, their toes barely touching the tiles. Zoe's skin was prickled with sweat and she looked scared. Jade was bleary-eyed with sensation, her hair matted around her face, her cheeks and both fat breasts red with smack marks, her mouth slack, her sex running juice. Behind me the latch clicked shut on the door.

AJ looked up at me. She was naked, her lean, muscular body hazy beneath the water, boobs and hips showing her as a girl, but her short cropped hair, tattoos and the hard look to her face taking her a long way from what people think of as feminine. Sam was looking at me too, prettier, less butch, but every bit as aggressive. Suddenly I wanted to be somewhere else, anywhere else. AJ spoke.

'Well, if it isn't Little Miss Muffet.'

'I . . . sorry,' I managed. 'I . . . just came in to . . . I'm busy, serving drinks.'

'Stick around,' she said. 'Watch what we're doing to your girlfriend.'

Naomi pushed me, and I stumbled forward. I managed a smile and backed up against the wall. Jade looked up, her eyes half-lidded, and managed a feeble smile.

'Watch, please, Penny darling,' she slurred.

I nodded.

'Finish Dumplings off, Naomi,' AJ ordered. 'All the way.'

Naomi stepped forward. She was dressed in tatty jeans so low-slung the back of her knickers showed, a black leather crop top, and gloves. Jade flinched, then jerked and cried out as Naomi's hand landed across her face in a full-blown slap. AJ chuckled and moved closer to Sam. They kissed as Naomi put in a second slap, this time across one of Jade's breasts, to set the fat globe wobbling and leave a red handprint on the already darkened skin.

AJ's legs had come up, and I saw that Sam was masturbating her, but both had their eyes fixed on Jade. Naomi struck a third time, slapping Jade full in the face, and a fourth, to the other cheek. Each time Jade gasped and her body jerked in reaction but, for all her pain, she was pushing her belly out. Naomi responded, cupping Jade's sex with one hand, to rub at the sopping pussy. Jade sighed, her head lolling to one side, only to jerk back as a smack caught her full across her cheek.

The next was across Jade's breasts, harder still, to make her meat flatten to her chest, the next to her face, her breasts again, and her face, as Naomi laid in, slapping fast to the sound of Jade's cries of pain, harder, and faster, until Jade was screaming, and thrashing as she hung, her breasts and buttocks wobbling frantically, her legs kicking, her mouth wide, her flesh distorting to smack after smack . . .

She came, her screams suddenly taking on a new tone, a blend of agony and ecstasy that had my stomach fluttering and made my bladder feel weak. It looked awful, the way her soft flesh bulged and bounced to the smacks, the mess of discoloured skin over her chest and face, yet she was there, in orgasm, and when Naomi stopped a fraction too soon, for one instant she was begging for more. Naomi slashed her hand in with every ounce of her strength, to send a spray of spittle from Jade's mouth as the gloved hand caught her across the face, and it was done.

Jade hung limp, for an instant, her full weight on her wrists, before she could recover herself enough to stand. Naomi reached to untie her, but was stopped by a gesture from AJ, who was as before, leaning back, her thighs spread as Sam rubbed her pussy. Her voice was hoarse as she spoke.

'Leave her. Do Zoe. I want to come.'

'No, please,' Zoe answered. 'Not like Jade, I couldn't . . .'

'Yeah,' AJ cut in. 'I want to see you get it . . . I want to see you come like your bitch friend. It's good.'

'No!' Zoe pleaded. 'I don't want it done to me, I want to do it, I want to . . .'

'You want to dish it out, learn to take it,' Sam said. 'Just do her, Naomi.'

'I don't want to be done!' Zoe whined. 'Please, AJ, what's my mum going to think?'

AJ sighed, then spoke.

'Fucking baby dykes. Okay, Naomi, string Penny up, do her instead.'

'No,' I answered, 'you can't, not like that anyway. Spank me, fine . . . or would you like me to lick you?'

'You'll do as you're fucking told!' she snapped. 'God I hate whiney subs. Just get up there, you little bitch!'

'Look, AJ . . .'

I trailed off. It was hopeless, and the only sensible thing to do was get away. I backed for the door, but Naomi moved to cut me off, catching me by the hair as I fumbled for the latch.

'Ow! Let go! Naomi, please!'

'Shut it, bitch, you'll love this, and you know it.'

'No! I can't . . . Naomi . . . no . . . not my face, anyway . . . my breasts, yes, but not my face . . . not my face!'

She was dragging me to the shower, her hand twisted viciously into my hair. Zoe gave me a frightened look, her lower lip trembling, and Jade mumbled something I didn't make out. Naomi took my arm, twisting it to force me to turn the tray over. I held still, shaking and wondering if I should just scream. Her hand went to the thick leather belt holding up her jeans, to pull it free, and I realised I was to be beaten with it, only for her to push the prong of the buckle into the last link of my tray chain and twist. It came open, my other arm was caught and twisted and the opposing link broken in turn. The tray fell to the tiles with a clang.

'Up,' she ordered.

'No, Naomi, I . . . Ow!'

She had cracked the belt across my back, hard, and my arm was jerked high before I could recover. Then I was babbling.

'No, please, no, no . . . I'll bend . . . I'll . . . anything Naomi . . . spank me . . . piss on me . . .'

'Shut up, bitch.'

Her hand lashed out, at my face. I jerked back, just in time, squealing.

'No, Naomi! Not my face, I said . . .'

'She said to shut up,' AJ cut in. 'Now shut up, or you get worse. I want to watch you smacked up while I come, and that's what's happening.'

I glanced at Jade, and the purple bruises discolouring her face and breasts. She seemed half-conscious, and if I knew she had been treated the same way before, I'd never seen it. It was terrifying. I shut up, but was shaking hard as Naomi tied the broken chain off, twisting them together above the shower rail to leave me as helpless as the others, on my toes, with the whole of my body vulnerable.

'In the face,' AJ said calmly, and I was screaming, for Melody, for Morris, for Amber, and then just screaming as Naomi's hand caught the side of my boob with a stinging, full-bodied slap.

The door handle twisted, twisted again and went still. There was a sharp knock.

'Piss off!' Sam called out.

The answer came immediately

'This is Melody Rathwell. Open the door.'

'Mel, help!' I yelled.

'You are such a fucking baby!' Naomi snapped, but she had already turned for the door.

Melody entered as soon as the latch had come up, annoyance showing in her face as she took in the scene, then puzzlement.

'What's the matter?' she demanded.

'They were going to torture me,' I explained, 'the same way Jade's been done.'

'Oh, right . . . what about it? You don't want to?'

'I can't let that happen!' I exclaimed. 'You know that, Mel!'

'Whatever. Look, stop mucking about. You're supposed to be serving, and the caning competition is starting. Are you lot coming? Hey, hang on, what happened to Penny's tray? Who the fuck did that?'

She looked up, and there was anger in her glance now. Nobody spoke, but the answer was obvious. Jade, Zoe and I were hung on the shower rail, AJ and Sam were in the bath. Naomi had put on a face, but it looked more sulky than tough.

'You fucking little bitch!' Mel spat, and came forward.

Naomi threw her arms up, protecting her face, but that wasn't what Melody was after. One powerful black arm shot out, around Naomi's waist, and she squealed in shock as she was taken hard by the back of the knickers and hauled in as Melody sat down on the loo. Naomi went straight over, with one long squeal of indignant shock as she realised her fate and a short, pained one as her panties were wrenched high to lift her bum into spanking position.

'No, you can't! Not me, you can't do this!' she yelled as Mel's hand grasped the back of her jeans, and pulled.

Without the belt, the jeans came straight down, exposing the pink globe of Naomi's bottom, with the panties pulled up so tight her pussy lips were splayed out to the sides of a strip of bright red cotton. I could even see her clitty, squashed out to one side. Mel laid in, jamming Naomi's whole body forward with the first smack.

Naomi went wild, kicking and scratching and thrashing about, but to no avail whatever as the spanking got under way, fast and furious, slap after slap, the round pink buttocks bouncing and quivering, and both bright red in moments. It lasted seconds, no more, maybe thirty or so spanks, but when Naomi was finally dropped, her face was streaked with mascara-blackened tears, and her hard look had turned to a rueful pout.

'You shouldn't . . .' she began as she tugged the panties out of her crease.

'No,' Mel cut in. 'You shouldn't. You shouldn't abuse my hospitality. Now get downstairs, or get out!'

She glanced around. AJ met her gaze, and for one moment I thought AJ was going to stand up for herself, and then she was smiling and simpering, no tougher or more dominant than Sophie or Jade.

'Sorry, Mel, we'll mend it, yeah? It wasn't meant bad or anything, we just got a bit carried away.'

'Whatever,' Melody answered, turning for the door. 'Just make sure you watch what you're doing.'

'Can you get me down, please?' I said, suddenly terrified I was going to be left after all.

'Yeah, sure, Penny,' she answered. 'I need you anyway. We've got a load of guys downstairs who want to see some girls get the cane, and half the girls are getting prissy about it because most of the crowd are businessmen, and mostly pissed.'

She had began to work on my chains, and quickly had them open. I dropped down, grimacing as the blood flowed back into my arms.

'Me too, please,' Zoe asked.

Mel turned to her, still speaking.

'So we need bums, pretty ones.'

She paused, to crane her head around Zoe and inspect Jade's bottom. It was unmarked, and she nodded in satisfaction as she went on.

'You three for starters, how about you others?'

'No way!' AJ answered, in utter indignation. 'Never, ever, do I go down . . .'

'Not in front of men!' Sam added.

'Pathetic,' Mel stated as Zoe's wrist straps came open. 'Naomi?'

'I . . . I can't, I'm . . .'

'Butch, I know,' Mel answered, turning her attention to Jade. 'Okay, you won't take it in front of men, fair enough. Come down anyway, yeah?'

Zoe was rubbing her wrists, and Mel quickly tweaked open the buckle on Jade's bondage strap. Naomi was standing by the loo, ruefully rubbing at her smacked bottom, but AJ was climbing from the bath.

'I'll do Jade,' she said, 'just give us five to get dressed.'

Mel nodded as I made for the door. Zoe tried to follow, but Sam reached out to grab her ankle.

'You're mine,' she said, 'and don't throw one, it's just your bum.'

Zoe made a face but didn't try to get loose and a moment later I was through the door and safe, except that I was about to have my bum caned. That didn't matter, not beside what they'd been about to do to me, and I was actually feeling grateful as I followed Melody down the stairs.

The competition had already started, in Rathwell's living room, which has as much floor area as my entire flat, but was still packed. He'd put a small stage up, more a block, really, but I still couldn't see through the solid wall of male backs blocking our way. I heard the coarse laughter, and the dirty remarks as some girl or other was put up to be beaten, and my stomach began to flutter again. Only when Mel had forced her way through the press did I realise who it was, little Emmeline.

She looked absolutely terrified, with her huge eyes wide and her mouth a little open as she stared at the crowd who were about to see her stripped and beaten. Not that there was much more stripping to do. She'd been in a schoolgirl outfit, but was now topless; down to her skirt, long white socks and shiny black shoes, presumably with panties on underneath. Her little rosy nipples were stiff, and her face and chest flushed pink. Andy was standing beside her, next to a whipping stool, cane in hand. As Mel hustled me in with the other girls in a roped off area, he spoke.

'Bend over.'

Emmeline gave him a brief, pleading glance, which was ignored, and went, very slowly, with what had to be real reluctance, as she turned her back on the audience and draped herself across the stool. She was so short she had to go up on tiptoe to get over properly, and when she did she lost her balance and ended up right over, with her feet off the ground and her bum stuck well up in the air in a ball of red tartan.

Her panties showed too, pure white and very tight, the width of the crotch taut across her pussy, but stained wet in a harp shape where her juice had leaked through. I could see her face, upside down in a frame of hair, her eyes now closed, her teeth showing as she bit at her lip. Andy reached the cane out, to twitch her school skirt up and put the full width of her panty seat on show, the tight white cotton seat absolutely bulging with cheeky young bottom. I caught a sigh of appreciation from the assembled men. Andy tapped the cane across Emmeline's panty seat. Her legs stiffened and closed, leaving her sex a plump bulge of white material between her thighs. Somebody in the audience called out.

'Not that way, mate, pull 'em down!'

'Yeah,' another called, 'like the others, or it's not fair.'

'Yes, on the bare,' a third demanded.

Andy hesitated, uncertainty showing in his face. Obviously Emmeline had asked for her panties to be left up, but the demand for her to be stripped had risen to a chant. He pursed his lips, glanced to her, to the audience and back.

'Do her bare!' a voice yelled, louder than the others, deep and heavily accented. 'Do her bare or we come and take them down for her!'

There was an immediate gale of laughter. I looked round, to see the huge German who had said he would fuck me. He had spoken, and he looked as if he meant it. Andy was still hesitant, and he looked seriously worried, but he stepped forward suddenly, took a firm hold of Emmeline's panties, and twitched them down. She gave a despairing sob as her bum came bare and the crowd roared in appreciation.

I just stared, my gaze riveted on her pretty, pale bottom, with her rose pink anal star on blatant view between her opened cheeks, and her little chubby pussy peeping out from between her thighs, as bald as an egg, with the string of a tampon hanging down between her sex lips. As I realised, my mouth came open. Then I had hidden my face in my hands, unable to look out of sympathy for the awful embarrassment I knew she would be feeling.

Only when I heard the thwack of the cane on her naked flesh and her answering scream did I peep. I just had to, and I kept watching, my eyes riveted to that tiny piece of white string, and the red line now decorating her poor, sweet bottom. I wanted to run up and cuddle her, to kiss her better, to hold her as she was beaten. I also wanted it done to her, and it was no good denying my feelings. As the second stroke smacked into her flesh I put my hand to my pussy, to give myself a gentle squeeze. It was tempting to masturbate, then and there as I watched, but I knew my own caning would be far easier to take if I was excited. So I stuck with stroking myself, just gently.

Emmeline had screamed with the first two strokes, and she kept screaming, tight, high sounds of pain and fear, with each stroke of the six. It actually made me feel guilty, but she stayed down, and she stayed in position, not even trying to cover the rude show she was making of bumhole and pussy, although she must have known how she looked, and that her string was hanging out.

When he had finished he pulled up her panties first, then helped her down. She was shaking, and red-faced, with a single tear showing on one cheek, but she smiled as the audience burst into cheers and clapping, and even managed a little curtsey as she stepped down from the block.

For the first time I turned my attention to the other girls in the ring with me. Sophie was there, but her bottom was already decorated with six well-placed cane welts, all parallel, and obviously delivered just so across her bottom. She had her arm around Harmony, who'd also been whacked, but less expertly, with two of the cane cuts running down onto her thigh and a third curled onto her hip, to end in a blob of rich purple against the brown of her skin. There were two others, a tall, brown-haired girl I didn't know, and Annabelle. As the tall girl turned to speak to Emmeline, I realised that she too had been caned. Annabelle was close to pristine, her little egg-shaped bottom cheeks flushed with the pink of a gentle warm-up spanking, no more. I was next, or one after at best.

I had no idea who was going to do me. Amber would have been my choice, but she was one of the judges, along with the lawyer Montague and Morris himself. It was not my choice anyway, and I found myself glancing around in serious apprehension, scared that I might get some drunken idiot. Mel reappeared, now holding a clipboard, and I hurried over to her.

'Who's caning me?' I demanded.

She didn't even look up.

'Sophie.'

'Sophie? But . . .'

'But nothing,' Sophie said from beside me. 'I owe you this.'

'But you've been caned yourself,' I said, realising that it was a completely stupid statement even as it came out.

'So?'

I sighed, reflecting that it could have been a lot worse. She might have it in for me, but she was small, female and experienced. She wouldn't miss.

'Up,' Melody ordered, jerking her thumb towards the stage.

I went, on my own accord for a couple of steps and then hauled after Sophie as she took me firmly by the ear. I squeaked in protest as a ripple of laughter spread over the audience, and then I was being pulled up onto the block and found myself looking out over a sea of faces. My ear was released and I stood, more conscious than ever of my nudity, of the collar at my throat and the cuffs on my wrists, of my boobs and belly and the puff of fur between my legs.

They were all staring at me, a hundred odd pairs of greedy, lecherous male eyes, and all keen to enjoy my discomfort, both physical and mental. There were women too, one to every three men or so, a few obvious dominas, more looking sweet and sexy but a little smug, those who'd backed out, and who now would probably enjoy my suffering more than any of the others.

A face caught my eye, a delicate oval framed in a neat blonde bob, smiling, right at me – my cousin Susan. I hadn't known she was coming, for all that she'd been to Razorback events with me. I managed a weak smile as my level of embarrassment went up another notch. I moved as Morris stepped up onto the block, to put an arm around me as Sophie flexed the cane he had given her.

'Ladies, Gentlemen, sluts, slaves and whoever else has managed to get in here,' he called out. 'A big hand for our fifth couple, Miss Sophie, whose other end we have already seen, but who will now be dishing it out, and Penny, her bottom.'

He jumped down, returning quickly to his seat. There was a huge lump in my throat as I turned to Sophie, and I was shaking hard. It had been a while since I'd felt the cane, and it hurts, a lot. She was smiling, her eyes bright with pleasure.

'Kneel,' she ordered.

I went straight down, determined to obey exactly and not give her an excuse to give me any extra strokes. She stuck out one dainty foot, bare and dirty underneath.

'Kiss,' she ordered.

I bent forward, to kiss her foot, pressing my lips gently to her skin. She swapped feet and I repeated the gesture, then turned. I swallowed my lump as she stuck out her bum, and planted a gentle peck on each cheek. She took hold of them, and spread them wide, right in my face, stretching out the rude pink star of her bumhole. I puckered up once more, put my face to her open crease and kissed her anus, tasting her as my lips met the sticky, sweat-slick flesh.

'Up, slut,' she ordered, 'and over you go.'

I stood, a little unsteady, but now thoroughly aroused. Being made to kiss her bumhole was so right for me, and the lewd, intrusive stares of the audience were suddenly welcome, no less humiliating than before, but welcome, because I wanted to be humiliated, utterly. I went to the stool, and bent myself over, making sure my position was as rude as it could be, with my cheeks open behind to show off my bumhole and my thighs well apart to give my pussy a good airing.

'What a good girl,' Sophie said, 'an utter slut, but still a good girl. Oh and look, folks, she's been spanked already, and pinched a fair bit too.'

She touched my bottom, on the tuck of one cheek, where a man had goosed me particularly hard. I realised it must have bruised. Sophie went on.

'Who saw her get buggered?'

There was an immediate chorus from the audience, confirmation, rude remarks, a few disappointed questions. Most of them had seen, and what I'd done for Monty.

'Well,' Sophie said, 'while she was having her fun, I was serving drinks, and she should have been doing the same, not sucking cocks that had just been up her fat backside.'

There was a ripple of laughter as a hot flush suffused my face. Sophie prodded my bumhole with the cane tip, to make my ring twitch.

'Look at her wink! She's so used to getting it up the bum she opens automatically!'

She poked me again, and once more my bumhole opened a little, an involuntary response I'd had for years. My face was burning, and I must have been crimson with embarrassment. Again she prodded my hole, egged on by laughter and cat-calling in the crowd, then stood back.

'So now I'm going to cane her,' Sophie said happily. 'And here goes.'

I tensed, by instinct. The cane whistled and struck, laying a line of fire across my bare bum and drawing a mewl of pain from my lips.

'One,' Sophie said. 'How many was that, Penny?'

'One,' I answered. 'One, Miss Sophie.'

'Good girl,' she said, 'she knows her place, you see, folks, at the bottom. I mean, look at her, she even kisses my bum.'

There was another burst of laughter, the whistle of the cane, the smack as it caught my meat and I was squealing and jumping on my toes, caught completely off guard by her.

'Two, Miss Sophie,' I managed, still kicking.

She laughed to see me wriggling and cut in again,

harder still. Once more I jumped as the pain hit me, and screamed this time.

'Three, Miss Sophie,' I gasped.

A bubble of helpless frustration had begun to rise in my head, and it burst as she pressed down on my back to make me spread my bottom once more and show off my anus. I burst into tears even as she gave me the fourth stroke, making water splash from my eyes as I once more went into my ridiculous little routine of hopping and kicking, but this time blubbering too.

'Four, Miss Sophie,' I sniffed. 'Ow!'

There was immediate laughter from the audience. Sophie chuckled and put her hand to my bum, quickly rubbing my cane stripes to make them come up. I winced, then gasped as for a brief moment her finger stole onto my bumhole, and back, tickling, and I was giggling stupidly and wriggling over the stool. More laughter greeted my reaction, then silence as her finger slid up into my bumhole.

For a moment she probed me, deep in, feeling about inside my rectum. I shut my eyes in burning humiliation. I knew what was coming. Sure enough, her finger left my bumhole and she ducked down, to offer it to my mouth.

'Open wide,' she ordered. 'Suck my finger clean, and I promise I won't go over the six.'

I opened my mouth. Her finger went in, rich with the taste of my well-loaded bum. She laughed, in delight and derision.

'That's right, suck it up, you little slut. She's sucking my dirty finger, boys, yuck!'

There was a another chorus of laughter, cat-calls and filthy suggestions. I was sucking, my face screwed up in misery, my head burning with my humiliation, but I was sucking, and swallowing my saliva. She made me do it properly too, keeping her finger in my mouth until I was good and finished, and wiping it on my cheek afterwards. She stood again, and I forced myself to let my body go limp.

'How many was that?' she asked.

'Four . . .' I answered. 'Four strokes, Miss Sophie.'

She knew, she could count them on my bottom, easily. Still she hesitated, my bottom twitching in my apprehension that she would break her word. Then the cane tapped my bum, rose, and whistled down to land back across my cheeks and set me howling in pain and dancing on my toes one more time. I began to cry again, soon blind with tears.

'Five, Miss Sophie,' I managed, my words broken by choking sobs.

'It'll soon be over . . . you big baby,' she said, and once more the cane tapped my bum.

She lifted, swung, and once again my bottom exploded in pain, sharp and harsh, to leave me whimpering and shaking my head, with one leg cocked up and shaking hard. I'd done it, though, taken all six, just so long as Sophie kept her word. She bent down, by my head, to kiss me, then whisper.

'By the way, we're only allowed six each, no counting games, or we get disqualified.'

I couldn't even find words to answer her, and her smile had grown to a manic grin as she stood up. I'd sucked a finger that had been up my own bum, for no reason, in front of a hundred or more strange men, and my own cousin. The only consolation was that it was less awful than having done the same on Monty's cock when I'd got carried away.

'Up you get,' she said happily, and slapped my bum, right on my fresh welts, to make me wince.

I climbed off the stool, feeling dizzy and not just with the drink I'd put back. Like it or not, I was fully aroused, and eager to be put through my paces once more. Sophie bowed, and I managed a curtsey to the audience, then stumbled down from the block.

There was Champagne on a little table, and I swallowed a glass in one. The girls had come down from the bathroom during my caning, AJ and Sam now in leather and denim, Jade nude, Zoe in just a pair of minuscule green panties and looking very resentful indeed. Annabelle had been taken onto the stage by one of the Germans, and as I swallowed my second glass of Champagne I heard the meaty thwack as she took her first cane stroke.

My bottom stung crazily, and I was shaking so hard I could barely hold my glass. I wanted to do something about my high, soon, and something rude. The girls had scared me, and I was very, very glad I'd been rescued, but they put the fantasy in my head too, and I was even wondering if I could trust them to slap my breasts into the same state as Jade's, but leave my face alone. A tiny part of my brain was still sober, and calm. I knew it was a fool idea, but it was so tempting. Maybe if I asked Morris to look after me, or Mel, or Amber . . .

On the block, Annabelle was taking her punishment stoically, just hissing between her teeth at each cut, but with her well-splayed sex so wet that the juice was running down the insides of her thighs. The German was hard, and not too accurate, landing most of the strokes from too close and too low, to mark her thighs. It made me look a complete baby, with my tears and screaming, especially as my own marks were all neatly grouped on the crest of my bum.

I was going to have to wait, but with just Jade and Zoe to go, it wouldn't be long. Naomi joined the others, decent again, with her jeans up, and she gave me a hard look. I blew her a kiss, hoping she'd make me lick her out as she watched the caning, but she had already turned to stand beside AJ. The last stroke whistled down across Annabelle's bum and a wave of clapping and cheers spread through the audience.

I watched, entranced, growing ever more horny, as first Jade, then Zoe, were caned. Jade took it well, holding back the tears until the last stroke. Sam did it, hard and accurate, making her count and kiss the cane afterwards. Zoe was less good, sulky, pouting, and crying even before the little green panties had been pulled down. AJ stripped her anyway, pulling them off and throwing them into the audience, then dishing out the six fast and furious, to send poor Zoe into a maddened frenzy so that she had to be held down by her hair. Despite it all, Zoe still managed a curtsey. That was it, and as soon as they'd left the stage Morris stepped up as Melody took the score sheets from the judges. A hush fell as he raised his hands.

'An excellent show, as I'm sure you'll all agree!' he announced. 'In a moment we will be able to announce the winners, but meanwhile, while my lovely wife adds up the scores, a little something to hold your attention. If one of our ladies . . . no, sorry, make that sluts, could step up to the stage? Penny, perhaps – yes, Penny, up you come. Nothing painful, my dear, just a little demonstration.'

I was a little surprised, but I went, really quite eager for whatever humiliation he had in mind for me. It couldn't be much, if Melody just had a few figures to add up, but it was sure to keep me on heat. He reach down for the chair he had been sitting on to judge, and put it at the front of the block as I climbed up.

'Take a seat,' he offered. 'If you can, that is?'

It was the oldest joke in the book, but it still got a laugh. Even I smiled, but I did wince as I sat my tender bum down on the chair. Morris was in casual clothes, as usual, including a polo-neck jumper. He began to pull it off, up over his head, and again he addressed the audience as he pulled his arms free.

'Observe, ladies and gentlemen, that I have no ropes, no tape, nothing, yet I can have little Penny in helpless bondage within seconds . . .'

Even as he spoke he had whipped the polo-neck down over my head and the chair too. I had no chance to react, and was engulfed, my arms trapped to my sides, and as my head popped out of the top he was already tying the arms together under the chair.

'. . . by a technique I recommend to all of you who may from time to time need to tie up your wives without giving the game away in advance,' he finished.

It was pretty weak, and I could get out anyway, with a bit of wriggling, but the audience gave him a drunken cheer and a few rude suggestions as to what to do with me. He was still behind me, and I only realised he had tape when I heard the distinctive rasp of the roll being pulled open. The next instant it was across my mouth, my face had set in shock and the audience had burst out laughing again. Rathwell went on.

'But, my friends, bondage is not always enough. Shutting them up is also important, and we can also manage it with a few simple household items.'

He had continued to work as he spoke, adding a second strip across my mouth. I gave him a puzzled look as sudden concern penetrated my alcohol-dazed brain. He grinned, and applied a third strip across my mouth. I began to struggle, cursing myself for falling for such a simple trick. It was too late. Morris quickly wrapped the thick tape around my body and under the chair, up and around again, to make a clumsy but highly effective spider's web of tape. In seconds I was genuinely helpless, and beginning to panic. Melody looked up from her clipboard, smiled, and I knew for certain. I was for it, and in public.

I wriggled, squirming on my chair to make it move, and tried to plead with my eyes. Her smile simply grew broader as she stood up. Morris gave way to her as she jumped to the stage, taking a firm hold on the back of the chair to keep me still.

'Don't be silly,' she said. 'You'll fall off the edge and hurt yourself.'

I twisted my head around, to look up into her eyes, begging.

'Relax, girl,' she said. 'I promised, didn't I? Didn't I?'

I nodded reluctantly.

'Then what's the problem? I said I wouldn't shave you, and I'm not going to. Where's the razor, foam, water, anything? I'm just going to have a bit of fun with you. You're staying like that while you suck the winners' cocks, that's all. Silly girl.'

She tousled my hair and I relaxed, a little, far happier to have to suck three men off in front of an audience than to have my head shaved, better still if it was pussy licking. Yet I knew, and she knew, that all she'd have had to do was order me to get on my knees and suck, or lick the girls. Now I couldn't, and I wasn't even showing any flesh. She soon solved that, pulling up the bottom of the jumper to put my tummy and legs on show, then taping my ankles to the chair to force me to spread my pussy to the crowd before she spoke again.

'Okay, boys and girls, here she is, ready to suck cock and lick cunt to order, for each and every one of our three lucky winners. So, without further delay, and in reverse order. Third, we have . . . Gavin and Sophie.'

So I had to suck Gavin Bulmer's cock for him. At least I knew him.

'In second place,' Melody went on, 'we have . . . Andy and Emmeline, for one well-cute schoolgirl caning.'

Andy stood from the crowd, grinning in both embarrassment and delight as he stepped forward. That made two I knew, both male, neither too bad. I shut my eyes, praying Monty hadn't been the one to cane the brown-haired girl so he could do his awful trick of making me sick on his cock.

'And our winners,' Melody called out, 'for a caning of perfect accuracy and a piece of true sadism . . . Sophie and Penny.'

I was so relieved I sagged down in my bonds for a moment. Two cocks I could manage, I'd just have to. Licking Sophie was just nice. Again Melody spoke.

'So, if our three winning tops would care to step up, they can collect their prizes, and make free use of Penny – but, before we untape her mouth, there is one little detail to attend to. Her hair.'

The word hit me like an electric shock. I twisted around.

She was smiling, cool and relaxed. In her hand she held a large tube, pinched between finger and thumb so that I could see the words – depilating cream. She spoke.

'I always keep my word, Penny, so no shaving, but that doesn't mean you get to keep your hair. Now do stop struggling, you know this is fair, and it's going to happen anyway.'

I'd gone into a fit, wriggling in my bonds, shaking my head, fighting to get free, in blind panic for an instant before her words reached me. I was helpless, I could do nothing, and she was right. I did deserve it, it was fair, but that didn't mean I wanted to surrender to it.

Not that I could stop it. Morris and Harmony took hold of my chair, and I was left squirming and thrashing my head, all I could do, a pathetic effort that only made Melody laugh as she twisted the top from the tube. She was still laughing as she squeezed out a long, fat worm of cream onto her hand. Her eyes were shining, a mad glint, of pleasure and revenge and cruelty, and as she put her cream-laden hand right under my nose to make sure I got a good look at it, I knew she was really going to do it.

I went wild, thrashing in a desperate, futile effort to break free, kicking my legs against the unrelenting tape, wriggling my bottom, my shoulders, my whole body, and nodding like some sort of demented puppet. Melody caught me, by the chin, her fingers locking onto my cheeks, hard, and the instant my head stilled she had slapped the full load of depilating cream onto the top of my head.

For one final moment I was in a state of furious, agonising consternation, the knowledge that it was now too late, and that my hair was really coming off burning in my head, an unbearable anguish, worse even than that final, awful moment before Zoe had stuck my head down the lavatory, or Monty had forced me to be sick on his bloated penis.

Then I had given up completely as she began to work the cream into my scalp. My face set in misery and shame, my eyes screwed up as my tears came. It was more than I could take, with her fingers massaging the cream into my scalp, each movement destroying more of my precious hair. I was filled with self-pity, imagining what a clown I'd look bald, and knowing that even if she stopped now I would have a bare patch on top, and look more ridiculous still.

'Don't be a baby about it,' Melody warned, 'at least try and take it like a grown woman. You do deserve it, you know.'

Despite myself I nodded my head. It was true. I'd done it to her and now she was getting her own back, but it did nothing to dilute the agonising humiliation of having it done to me, in public, and with my legs taped apart to show off my bare pussy to the entire hall.

I tried to stem my tears, snivelling, but it was no good. Still they came, hot and strong, trickling down my cheeks, while my nose had begun to run as well, with the snot bubbling out as I struggled for breath. That wasn't all either, when I was done I was going to have to suck cock, with my bald head glistening in the light. They'd probably spunk on my dome for a joke, I was sure they would.

Melody began to whistle as she rubbed, the stupid song the dwarves sing in *Snow White*. Immediately my condition came to seem more pathetic still, my guilty, self-inflicted misery made the subject of a silly joke. My tears came harder, and I began to sob, blowing snot from my nose as I lost all control of my breathing, until I was gasping behind my gag and shivering all over.

'Sh,' Melody chided, 'it'll soon be over.'

I shook my head, spraying tears and detaching a long streamer of snot which had been hanging from among the bubbles under my nose. She had done almost my entire head, and I could feel my hair starting to come out when her thumbs brushed the parts she had done first. Fresh panic hit me and I was struggling again, jerking my head away even though I knew it was too late, and utterly futile. Melody gripped my head, hard, and bent to whisper in my ear.

'Sh . . . be calm, girl. Don't fight it, just let it happen.'

I knew what she meant, and I was cursing her in my head and calling her a bitch over and over and over, because I knew it was true. She understood, she'd been there, but to give in was a surrender so deep, so absolute, that for all my knowledge, and drunkenness, and the sensations of my body, I still fought it.

She stopped, my head now fully lathered with the cream, my hair a tangle of black strands in foamy white muck, some already pulled free. New self-pity welled up at the realisation that this was the last anyone was going to see of me with hair until it had grown back properly, in maybe a year, or more. A new burst of crying overwhelmed me, great, racking sobs that once more left me trembling and more snotty than ever, with the whole area under my nose a mass of bubbles and several long streamers hanging from my chin. My tears were strong too, blinding me, to leave the rapt audience a blur of figures, none distinct. Melody spoke.

'There, a minute or two to let it soak in, and we'll be done, won't we, Penny? Now, just a little for the cunt.'

I shook my head, but it was a feeble, broken gesture. Inevitably she would want my pussy denuded too, and I knew that protests or wriggling would only get me laughed at. I could just about see through my tears as new cream was squirted out, and then her hand had been slapped to my pussy and she was rubbing it in. Fresh misery hit me, but not so strong, my capacity for self-pity already at the limit. I felt my pussy coated, my mound, my lips, and lower, two fingers slipping down, under me, to circle my bumhole and rub the cream well into the little nest of fur around her.

Melody chuckled as she slipped a finger up into my anus. I gasped, my will coming within an ace of snapping at the touch, and then my eyes had come wide as my ring began to burn. She laughed to see me react, and traced her finger up the groove of my sex, to linger on my clitoris before she stood back. I looked at her as the burning sensation spread up from my bumhole to my pussy. I was on fire, my skin crawling to the furious heat, my bumhole pulsing.

I clamped furiously, biting down the pain at the realisation of what was going to happen if I gave in to my body's demands. I could feel the weight of what was in my rectum, the bulk of dung from more chocolate cake than any normal person would willingly eat in a week. In no time I was shaking my head in frantic resistance to the pain in my sex and anus, determined not to give in, not sitting splay-legged in front of a hundred or more staring, leering people.

Everybody would see, my friends and playmates, people to whom I was just a sex toy, people who didn't know me at all. They'd laugh, they'd clap, they'd call out encouragement, filthy suggestions, exclamations of disgust, as my mess squeezed out from under my bum and between my pussy lips. It couldn't happen, it just couldn't . . .

I held it, by an effort of will that left me weak and panting through my nose, but I held it, the burning pain of the cream dying slowly as my skin accommodated it. Not that I had escaped, new endorphins flooding my system to add to those from my spanking, my buggering and my caning. Disgracing myself wasn't the only thing I was fighting against, with the urge to force my arms down between my thighs and rub myself to ecstasy growing stronger by the second. Melody knew, and she laughed, a sound so cruel, so triumphant, that it forced new tears from my eyes.

'Here goes,' she said. I heard the splash of water, and once more her hands settled on my scalp.

For one brief moment I fought, then gave in, hanging my head in surrender as she began to tease my ruined hair from my scalp. I felt it come in clumps, some bits sticking, some already free. All I could do was sit there, limp and snivelling, with the tears and the snot running slowly down my face and my pussy juice pooling slowly underneath me. My senses were thick with the horrible odour of the cream, but I could still smell my own sex, and I knew those near me would be able to as well. Not that they needed to, with my pussy soppy and puffed up and my nipples straining up through the wool of Morris' jumper.

Water foamy with depilation cream had began to run down my forehead, and I was forced to shut my eyes tight. Mel took no notice, concentrating on working my hair free from the top of my head. Soon I could feel the cool air on the naked skin of my crown, and once more had to bite down the rising panic of frustration and shame at my fate. It hurt too, but I was barely aware of the pain, floating in my sea of endorphins and alcohol as I was slowly, purposefully denuded.

She slapped on more cream, doing my eyebrows as an afterthought, and went back to pulling out my hair. It had started to come faster, in big clumps, and handfuls, with the foam running freely over my face and down the back of my neck. The back of my head came nude, the longest part gone. She started to work on the front, my fringe and the neatly cut wings of the bob I had worn since college. A memory came back, of how pleased I'd been to see myself in the mirror after that cut. Melody's fingers twisted into my fringe and off it came, wings and all, in one mass of ruined hair, and I was bald. Once more I burst into tears.

'Oh, sh!' she chided. 'Did I cry?'

I nodded my head. She had cried, and it had made me feel so guilty, because she wasn't a cry-baby and I was. She said nothing, but pulled out a few bits of hair she'd missed. A moment later a wet flannel had been slapped onto my naked dome and she was cleaning the foam off. That was it, I was done – only I wasn't, not quite.

She gave my head a quick polish, then slipped the flannel down between my legs. I moved a little forward, helping her to denude my pussy in hopeless resignation. She began to pluck, pinching my hair off and rubbing with the flannel. It came quickly, my mound, my sex lips, my anal area, and all the time with her touching my clit, over and over, each time sending a jolt of pleasure through me. She even poked the flannel up my bum and pussy for an instant, at the same time, making my skin sting again, so that once more I came within an ace of losing my self control.

I was squirming in my seat as she wiped my pussy, struggling to hold in the bulging mass inside me. It had started to hurt, and my bumhole felt loose and sore. One more finger up me and it was going to happen, and that was that, but Mel gave my clitty a last little rub and stood up. Two brief, painful wipes and my eyebrows were gone too, leaving me as bald as an egg.

Melody stepped back and gave a little bow. The audience began to clap. I looked up, through the haze of my tears, my vision swimming, dizzy with drink and arousal and a burning, mind-numbing humiliation. I felt exhausted, broken, or not quite, because my hot bumhole was still clamped tight shut.

The words barely registered as Melody announced that I was now going to pleasure the winning caners. I recognised Sophie though, by her blonde bob, so pretty, so feminine, and in the same style I had worn myself. Again my tears started, even as she took a gentle hold on the back of my head.

'Hey, cheer up, Penny,' she said, 'that was dead cute.'

She had bent down, and held my head as she peeled the tape from my mouth. I was still running snot, and was left gasping for a moment before she wiped my face. I managed a smile, sheer, pathetic gratitude.

'Here, this'll cheer you up, slut,' she said, and stood, to pull my face into her sex.

I got a mouthful of plump, furry pussy mound, and then I had found her crease and was licking, full on her clitty. She sighed and began to stroke me, her hand moving on my denuded skin, keeping my condition right in the front of my mind as I licked her. I could taste her pussy, excited, strongly feminine. She had already begun to moan, and I knew it would take only moments. Sure enough, she gave a little, choking cry and she was coming, full in my face, the girl who'd caned me, who'd tricked me into sucking her dirty finger, who'd made me kiss her bumhole . . .

If I'd been masturbating I'd have come too, but I didn't dare, for all that I knew I could get my hands to my sex. The audience didn't matter, I could come in front of them, but I couldn't soil myself. Yet I knew that if I was to frig I might lose all control, both physical and mental.

Sophie released me and bent to kiss me, first on my lips, then on top of my bald dome, which drew a laugh from the crowd. My eyes had cleared a little, and even as she stepped aside I saw Andy, his cock in his hand, half-erect, just a step away. The next instant my mouth had been stuffed full of penis and I was sucking.

He left nothing to chance, wanking into my mouth as I fellated him, eager to show off for the crowd. I tried to suck deep, trying to control him so I could take it in my mouth and spit rather than swallow or let him soil my face. It didn't work. As he began to grunt I sucked hard on his helmet, a sure trick. It worked, but he was already pulling his erection from my mouth and I caught the full load in my face, over my dome, blinding one eye and smeared across my cheek as he finished off by rubbing himself on me.

The crowd cheered, calling for more. Gavin had stepped up, his cock stiff in his hand, and he was wanking fast even as she pushed it deep down my throat. I began to gag immediately and that was it, his load delivered down my gullet, to leave me choking, with spunk bubbles foaming from my nose and around my lips as he held himself tight in.

Someone in the crowd gave a cat-call. Another yelled out, demanding to know why Gavin hadn't done it in my face. He shrugged as he moved away, but another man was already climbing onto the block, the big German who fancied me. I gave a weak protest, which was ignored as his huge, red erection was thrust in my face. I took it, resigned to sucking off whoever wanted to use my mouth.

There were plenty. His friends were pushing forward, and others, men I'd never seen before that night, each keen to add to my spunk face bath. Soon they were jostling to get onto the block, and those already there were wanking furiously, determined to come on me before they were pulled back. Only the big German was unhurried, and nobody dared dispute his right to the full use of my mouth.

Someone behind me spunked across the top of my head, another over my ear and down my neck, a third in my open eye. Suddenly I could see almost nothing, blinking the sperm away before my eyes could sting. More spattered over my bald head, another load hit my face, and a third, right in my ear.

They were laughing, and joking to each other as they used me. At last the big German came, full in my mouth, and it became a free-for-all, cocks pushed at me from all around, two in my mouth at once, just the helmets in, others rubbing over my bare scalp, my ears and cheeks, down the back of my neck. They were groping too, hands snatching at my boobs, feeling my bum through the jumper, rubbing my sex and forcing the mouth of my vagina.

I could do nothing, gagging on cock, blind, deaf, with spunk in both my eyes and both my ears, unable to speak, unable to move, barely able to breathe. There was a curtain of sperm running down around my head, thick and sticky as it moved slowly over my skin. More was plastered onto my bald dome, rubbed in by eager cocks, while so much had been done in my mouth that it was running from the sides even as I sucked and continuously frothing from my nose.

It was only when a fat, hairy belly squashed up hard to my spunk-smeared face and a particularly large cock was jammed down my throat that I realised Monty was taking his turn, or maybe Jeff, but he tasted like Monty. He'd put it right in, blocking my throat, and forcing me to blow out through my nose, covering his cock in spunk and snot which an instant later had been fed back into my mouth. He took a grip on my neck, and moved, making me turn my head. Somebody complained as his own cock slipped down my slimy scalp. Monty answered and I knew it was him.

'She needs her cunt frigged, you selfish git!'

I tried to shake my head, in utter desperation, but I was stuck hard on his erection and held tight. If he noticed he gave no sign, but reached down, to take me firmly by my cunt, cupping me with his thick, soft fingers. One touched my bumhole, another slid up my pussy, his palm spread my lips and I was being rubbed, frigged off as I sucked his penis.

It was going to happen, there was no question, and I could do nothing. He was fucking my head, deep in with each push, to make my sperm-laden stomach jerk and twitch in rebellion. My pussy was twitching too, close to orgasm, and my tender, aching bumhole pulsing to his tickling finger. He had my clitty squashed hard under the ridges of his palm, rubbing me, and I was there.

My muscles started to lock, my control went, and suddenly I wanted it, all of it. I wanted a bald head, a bald cunt, and worse, my belly tattooed, my bum branded, anything to show what a dirty little fuck slut I was. I want to be spunked over, in my face and over my boobs, up both holes and everywhere else, rolled in it, bathed in it. I want to piss myself, and foul myself, and for everyone to see, and laugh at me as I masturbated in it.

Monty gave, in abundance. His fingertip popped my bumhole and I was penetrated behind. His cock jammed deep into my gullet and my stomach tightened in a single, hard spasm. His hand mushed out my cunt flesh as I came, applying merciless friction to my clitoris. Every muscle in my body seemed to contract at once and I was coming, in an agonising, totally unbearable climax as my mouth filled with his rock-hard penis.

He called out in ecstasy and caught me hard by the jaw, forcing me to swallow my sick and the spunk he was spurting down my throat. My head shot back, off his cock, a huge quantity of spunk spewed out over my tits as his second shot caught me in the face, and I was screaming in pure, blind ecstasy, my whole body in spasm, every muscle, including my bumhole. My ring gave up the unequal struggle and let the contents of my rectum out, hot and thick and squashy, a good kilo of it, squashing out onto the chair beneath me. Monty snatched his hand back, and my last sensation, at the very peak of my climax was of the whole filthy mess squashing out between the lips of my well-splayed cunt. On final image came to me, as perfect ecstasy, of myself, ruined, soiled, a filthy, bedraggled mess, and I had passed out.

Twelve

The first person I heard as I regained my senses was Morris Rathwell.

'What the fuck have you done to my jumper?'

A freezing sponge was pressed to my face, wiping off the clotted sperm and my eyes came open, to find myself looking into a ring of faces, one of them green, and hairless. It spoke.

'You are one cool bitch!'

Another face replaced it, Susan, holding the sponge and looking concerned as she began to dab at my face once more.

'Are you all right, Penny?' she asked. 'Talk to me! Get some more ice, Fungus . . .'

'Fine . . . thank you,' I managed, tried to rise and collapsed.

I blew my breath out, my head still swimming. Nothing seemed to matter, and for some reason I just wanted to giggle at Susan's boyfriend, and point out that although I might be bald, at least my head wasn't green.

Melody had me propped in her arms, and she lifted me, my head clearing slowly as I was carried. Susan was with me, and Amber, and Jade, other girls too, with Morris, Monty and Fungus trailing behind. There was nobody else there, which seemed weird, and I found myself where they were. Susan hushed me with a gesture and I went limp in Melody's arms.

It was so soothing, being held, and lowered gently into a warm bath, and bathed by Mel and Amber, with their fingers probing into every crevice until I had begun to wriggle with pleasure. I was told to behave and I stopped, immediately obedient, with no real self-will at all.

I only came back to my senses slowly, as I sat wrapped in a warm towel in the downstairs bathroom. The men had been hustled out, and beyond the door I could hear the noises of the party breaking up. All my closest girlfriends were around me, and everything seemed rather nice, including the sting of my cane cuts and the dull ache of the rest of my body. I wasn't even bothered by my baldness, until they started to discuss where I should sleep.

Susan offered to take me back to her flat, on the grounds that then she could give me a lift the next morning. Memory hit me like a sledgehammer. I had to be home by the morning, to organise the hall for the family lunch. I was bald. I was stark, staring bald, and I had to be at a lunch for my entire family within less than twelve hours.

I begun to panic, totally irrational, struggling to get up, so that, who'd had her arm around my shoulders, had to hold me down. It stopped, after a moment, and I just sank my face into my hands. Susan spoke.

'Don't worry, Penny. It won't be you who gets bitched at, not when they see Fungus.'

'But what am I supposed to say?' I demanded. 'Look at me!'

'You look fine,' Jade said.

I could see myself in the bathroom mirror. I didn't look fine. I looked ridiculous.

'Yes, in a dyke bar!' I snapped, and immediately regretted it. 'Sorry, Jade.'

'Tell them you lost a bet,' Kay suggested.

'Gavin Bulmer already suggested that,' I answered. 'I'll have to, I suppose, unless . . . a wig maybe? No, Mum'll notice, for sure.'

'You really are . . .' Susan began, addressing Melody, but I raised my hand to stop her.

'No, she was right,' I admitted. 'It was only fair and, believe me, that was some climax.'

Susan made a wry face, Mel moved close to kiss me.

'We'd better go,' Susan said.

They had my clothes, and I dressed, adding a pair of Annabelle's lacy black panties to the clothes I'd taken off what seemed like weeks before, also a hat. I still felt weak, and Amber supported me out to the cab they'd called. Half-an-hour later I was back at Susan's, stretched out on the couch, and I was asleep in moments.

I woke cold, stiff and sore. It took a moment for everything to sink in, relating each ache, pain and weird sensation to an experience; my sore bumhole and being sodomised, my aching bottom and the caning, the truly bizarre sensation of having no hair with the climax.

The thought of facing my mother was ghastly, but I couldn't find it in myself to blame Melody, or Monty and Jeff, or anyone but myself. Then there was the lingering memory of the sheer power of my orgasm, perhaps the best of my life. I still felt bad-tempered, nervous and insecure. A call to Gabrielle and Poppy to assure them that I was all right just made it worse, as I went over the details. It grew worse still as we got ourselves together and drove out on the M4 in Fungus' car. By the time we arrived at my flat my emotions were at boiling point.

I went straight to the church, my hat clamped firmly to my head against a cold wind blowing in from the north. I was on time, the congregation still coming out of the church, which meant David and the elderly couple who looked after the hall wouldn't have begun to worry what was going on. He was at the door, talking to the people as they came out, and as I drew near I saw that among them, standing on the steps as if waiting for somebody, was Marjorie Burgess.

She had barely crossed my mind since Monty and Jeff had bagged me up, and I simply didn't have time for her now, or patience. She had seen me, though, and was walking down the church steps with a look of angry determination on her face. I walked past, to where my cousin Kate, Jeremy and the two girls were getting out of a car. A second drew up, my mother's, and I hurried forward to the door of the church hall, determined to at least look efficient.

It was only as I pushed inside that I realised Marjorie had followed me. I had to hold the door, or let it swing shut in her face. She stormed in, all righteous indignation as she rounded on me.

'Kindly explain this,' she snapped.

'What?' I demanded.

'This, your recidivism.'

She had a piece of paper, and handed it to me. I scanned down the list on it, which were website addresses, the ones I'd visited over the last few days. There, at the bottom, the last one I'd been on before collapsing into bed on the Friday night, was Melody's femdom group 'Black Goddess'. I had forgotten about the virus.

There was no denying it. One look at Melody in her leather cat suit would have confirmed her worst suspicions. I just didn't have the time for her anyway.

'Yes,' I answered her. 'I visited the site. She's a friend of mine, all right?'

'Another addict, I suppose, or a common prostitute?'

I rounded on her as we reached the cluster of tables and chairs set out in the middle of the hall.

'How dare you! Melody is my friend. She is worth ten of you, you patronising, condescending, stuck-up, self-righteous, Christian bitch!'

I should have remembered her dinner party. I didn't. I was too angry, too emotional. She was still a lot bigger than me.

Even as her mouth came open in an O of affronted dignity she was snatching for my arm. I jerked back as she caught it, but she hung on, wrenching me forward. I went, off balance, too weak to really fight after the night before, screaming in horrified consternation as she tipped me down across her knee.

'No . . . not that!' I screamed, at the top of my voice as my hat fell to the floor.

It was too late. One hard jerk and my coat was up, a second and my skirt had joined it, a third and my tights were down. Behind me I heard the door of the hall bang and a gasp of surprise.

I caught one brief glimpse, my mother closest, staring wide-eyed; Elaine, Kate and the others, almost as shocked, and Jemima and Pippa, mouths round as they took me in, from my bald head to the seat of my fancy black lace knickers. I got in one last scream of consternation and despair, and then my panties had come down, to show off my cane-striped bum, my well-buggered anus and my equally bald cunt, in front of my entire family.

NEXUS BACKLIST

This information is correct at time of printing. For up-to-date information, please visit our website at www.nexus-books.co.uk

All books are priced at £5.99 unless another price is given.

Nexus books with a contemporary setting

ACCIDENTS WILL HAPPEN	Lucy Golden ISBN 0 352 33596 3	☐
ANGEL	Lindsay Gordon ISBN 0 352 33590 4	☐
BARE BEHIND £6.99	Penny Birch ISBN 0 352 33721 4	☐
BEAST	Wendy Swanscombe ISBN 0 352 33649 8	☐
THE BLACK FLAME	Lisette Ashton ISBN 0 352 33668 4	☐
BROUGHT TO HEEL	Arabella Knight ISBN 0 352 33508 4	☐
CAGED!	Yolanda Celbridge ISBN 0 352 33650 1	☐
CANDY IN CAPTIVITY	Arabella Knight ISBN 0 352 33495 9	☐
CAPTIVES OF THE PRIVATE HOUSE	Esme Ombreux ISBN 0 352 33619 6	☐
CHERI CHASTISED £6.99	Yolanda Celbridge ISBN 0 352 33707 9	☐
DANCE OF SUBMISSION	Lisette Ashton ISBN 0 352 33450 9	☐
DIRTY LAUNDRY £6.99	Penny Birch ISBN 0 352 33680 3	☐
DISCIPLINED SKIN	Wendy Swanscombe ISBN 0 352 33541 6	☐

DISPLAYS OF EXPERIENCE	Lucy Golden ISBN 0 352 33505 X	☐
DISPLAYS OF PENITENTS £6.99	Lucy Golden ISBN 0 352 33646 3	☐
DRAWN TO DISCIPLINE	Tara Black ISBN 0 352 33626 9	☐
EDEN UNVEILED	Maria del Rey ISBN 0 352 32542 4	☐
AN EDUCATION IN THE PRIVATE HOUSE	Esme Ombreux ISBN 0 352 33525 4	☐
EMMA'S SECRET DOMINATION	Hilary James ISBN 0 352 33226 3	☐
GISELLE	Jean Aveline ISBN 0 352 33440 1	☐
GROOMING LUCY	Yvonne Marshall ISBN 0 352 33529 7	☐
HEART OF DESIRE	Maria del Rey ISBN 0 352 32900 9	☐
HIS MISTRESS'S VOICE	G. C. Scott ISBN 0 352 33425 8	☐
IN FOR A PENNY	Penny Birch ISBN 0 352 33449 5	☐
INTIMATE INSTRUCTION	Arabella Knight ISBN 0 352 33618 8	☐
THE LAST STRAW	Christina Shelly ISBN 0 352 33643 9	☐
NURSES ENSLAVED	Yolanda Celbridge ISBN 0 352 33601 3	☐
THE ORDER	Nadine Somers ISBN 0 352 33460 6	☐
THE PALACE OF EROS £4.99	Delver Maddingley ISBN 0 352 32921 1	☐
PALE PLEASURES £6.99	Wendy Swanscombe ISBN 0 352 33702 8	☐
PEACHES AND CREAM £6.99	Aishling Morgan ISBN 0 352 33672 2	☐
PEEPING AT PAMELA	Yolanda Celbridge ISBN 0 352 33538 6	☐

PENNY PIECES		Penny Birch	ISBN 0 352 33631 5	☐
PET TRAINING IN THE PRIVATE HOUSE		Esme Ombreux	ISBN 0 352 33655 2	☐
REGIME	£6.99	Penny Birch	ISBN 0 352 33666 8	☐
RITUAL STRIPES	£6.99	Tara Black	ISBN 0 352 33701 X	☐
SEE-THROUGH		Lindsay Gordon	ISBN 0 352 33656 0	☐
SILKEN SLAVERY		Christina Shelly	ISBN 0 352 33708 7	☐
SKIN SLAVE		Yolanda Celbridge	ISBN 0 352 33507 6	☐
SLAVE ACTS	£6.99	Jennifer Jane Pope	ISBN 0 352 33665 X	☐
THE SLAVE AUCTION		Lisette Ashton	ISBN 0 352 33481 9	☐
SLAVE GENESIS		Jennifer Jane Pope	ISBN 0 352 33503 3	☐
SLAVE REVELATIONS		Jennifer Jane Pope	ISBN 0 352 33627 7	☐
SLAVE SENTENCE		Lisette Ashton	ISBN 0 352 33494 0	☐
SOLDIER GIRLS		Yolanda Celbridge	ISBN 0 352 33586 6	☐
THE SUBMISSION GALLERY		Lindsay Gordon	ISBN 0 352 33370 7	☐
SURRENDER		Laura Bowen	ISBN 0 352 33524 6	☐
THE TAMING OF TRUDI	£6.99	Yolanda Celbridge	ISBN 0 352 33673 0	☐
TEASING CHARLOTTE	£6.99	Yvonne Marshall	ISBN 0 352 33681 1	☐
TEMPER TANTRUMS		Penny Birch	ISBN 0 352 33647 1	☐

THE TORTURE CHAMBER	Lisette Ashton ISBN 0 352 33530 0	☐
UNIFORM DOLL £6.99	Penny Birch ISBN 0 352 33698 6	☐
WHIP HAND £6.99	G. C. Scott ISBN 0 352 33694 3	☐
THE YOUNG WIFE	Stephanie Calvin ISBN 0 352 33502 5	☐

Nexus books with Ancient and Fantasy settings

CAPTIVE	Aishling Morgan ISBN 0 352 33585 8	☐
DEEP BLUE	Aishling Morgan ISBN 0 352 33600 5	☐
DUNGEONS OF LIDIR	Aran Ashe ISBN 0 352 33506 8	☐
INNOCENT £6.99	Aishling Morgan ISBN 0 352 33699 4	☐
MAIDEN	Aishling Morgan ISBN 0 352 33466 5	☐
NYMPHS OF DIONYSUS £4.99	Susan Tinoff ISBN 0 352 33150 X	☐
PLEASURE TOY	Aishling Morgan ISBN 0 352 33634 X	☐
SLAVE MINES OF TORMUNIL £6.99	Aran Ashe ISBN 0 352 33695 1	☐
THE SLAVE OF LIDIR	Aran Ashe ISBN 0 352 33504 1	☐
TIGER, TIGER	Aishling Morgan ISBN 0 352 33455 X	☐

Period

CONFESSION OF AN ENGLISH SLAVE	Yolanda Celbridge ISBN 0 352 33433 9	☐
THE MASTER OF CASTLELEIGH	Jacqueline Bellevois ISBN 0 352 32644 7	☐
PURITY	Aishling Morgan ISBN 0 352 33510 6	☐
VELVET SKIN	Aishling Morgan ISBN 0 352 33660 9	☐

Samplers and collections

NEW EROTICA 5	Various ISBN 0 352 33540 8	☐
EROTICON 1	Various ISBN 0 352 33593 9	☐
EROTICON 2	Various ISBN 0 352 33594 7	☐
EROTICON 3	Various ISBN 0 352 33597 1	☐
EROTICON 4	Various ISBN 0 352 33602 1	☐
THE NEXUS LETTERS	Various ISBN 0 352 33621 8	☐
SATURNALIA £7.99	ed. Paul Scott ISBN 0 352 33717 6	☐
MY SECRET GARDEN SHED £7.99	ed. Paul Scott ISBN 0 352 33725 7	☐

Nexus Classics

A new imprint dedicated to putting the finest works of erotic fiction back in print.

AMANDA IN THE PRIVATE HOUSE £6.99	Esme Ombreux ISBN 0 352 33705 2	☐
BAD PENNY	Penny Birch ISBN 0 352 33661 7	☐
BRAT £6.99	Penny Birch ISBN 0 352 33674 9	☐
DARK DELIGHTS £6.99	Maria del Rey ISBN 0 352 33667 6	☐
DARK DESIRES	Maria del Rey ISBN 0 352 33648 X	☐
DISPLAYS OF INNOCENTS £6.99	Lucy Golden ISBN 0 352 33679 X	☐
DISCIPLINE OF THE PRIVATE HOUSE £6.99	Esme Ombreux ISBN 0 352 33459 2	☐
EDEN UNVEILED	Maria del Rey ISBN 0 352 33542 4	☐

------ ✂ ----------------------------

Please send me the books I have ticked above.

Name ....

Address ....

....

....

.... Post code.....................

Send to: **Cash Sales, Nexus Books, Thames Wharf Studios, Rainville Road, London W6 9HA**

US customers: for prices and details of how to order books for delivery by mail, call 1-800-343-4499.

Please enclose a cheque or postal order, made payable to **Nexus Books Ltd**, to the value of the books you have ordered plus postage and packing costs as follows:

UK and BFPO – £1.00 for the first book, 50p for each subsequent book.

Overseas (including Republic of Ireland) – £2.00 for the first book, £1.00 for each subsequent book.

If you would prefer to pay by VISA, ACCESS/MASTERCARD, AMEX, DINERS CLUB or SWITCH, please write your card number and expiry date here:

....

Please allow up to 28 days for delivery.

Signature ....

Our privacy policy

We will not disclose information you supply us to any other parties. We will not disclose any information which identifies you personally to any person without your express consent.

From time to time we may send out information about Nexus books and special offers. Please tick here if you do *not* wish to receive Nexus information. ☐

------ ✂ ----------------------------